All The Broken Places

THE HEALING EDGE - BOOK ONE

ANISE EDEN

DIVERSIONBOOKS

Diversion Books
A Division of Diversion Publishing Corp.
443 Park Avenue South, Suite 1008
New York, New York 10016
www.DiversionBooks.com

For more information, email info@diversionbooks.com

First Diversion Books edition February 2016.
Print ISBN: 978-1-62681-930-6
eBook ISBN: 978-1-62681-929-0

CHAPTER ONE

In my dream, there was no thought of suicide. We were simply potting begonias on the back porch, getting our hands dirty and inhaling the dueling scents of spicy flowers and sweet earth.

My mother tried—and failed—to sound light and casual. "So, Catie, have you met anyone interesting lately?"

A man, she meant. Without looking up to meet her probing gaze, I said, "Come on, you already know the answer to that question."

"Okay, okay. I can't help it, though. I have to keep asking." She smiled as though she knew something I didn't. "Maybe soon."

In one of my typical clumsy moves, I dropped a large clump of potting soil on the floor.

"You don't have to get it absolutely *everywhere*, you know," she teased.

I slid my hand down her forearm, leaving behind a dark streak. "Like that, you mean?"

"No, like this," she replied, dabbing a glob of wet dirt onto my nose. At once, the dirt-smearing competition was on.

In the midst of our squeals and contortions, I noticed a black pen mark peeking out from beneath the neck of her t-shirt. "What's that?"

"What's what?"

"That mark." I pointed.

She looked down, puzzled, and stretched her collar out until we could both read the words that had been written across her collarbones: "Do Not Resuscitate."

My dirt-streaked palms flew up to cover my mouth. Mom gazed at me, her eyes heavy with unshed tears. "You'd better go now."

"No," I begged. But in an instant, I was levitating. I floated up above the clouds and flew southwest toward the city.

The next thing I knew, I was back in my bed, cotton sheets damp with perspiration. The thunder outside was so loud that it shook the windows. Grey light filtering through the storm clouds told me that morning had arrived. I pulled the bedspread over my head. Inside of my mind waged the usual battle: should I wake up and admit that the day had started, or go back to sleep in the hopes of finding my mother again, even for a few more moments?

You can't find her again, the realistic part of my brain chimed in. *She's gone, remember? And she's not coming back. It was just a dream. Get a grip.*

I dried my cheeks on the pillow, threw off the bedspread, and groped around on the bedside table for my cell phone. The screen read nine-thirty a.m. and showed a calendar reminder of my eleven a.m. appointment. I reproached myself for having fallen out of the habit of setting an alarm. If I hurried, I'd have just enough time to check in on my clients, call the office, and get ready for my doctor's appointment—and I couldn't be late to see Dr. MacGregor. While I had never been to a psychiatrist before, I was fairly certain that lateness would be interpreted as some sort of Freudian pathology, or at least make a bad impression—and I *needed* to make a good impression. My job—the only real thing I had left—depended on it.

It was time to get started. I put down the phone and lay flat on my back, closing my eyes and stretching my arms out to the sides. Slowly, steadily, I inhaled and exhaled, concentrating on my breath. I visualized the filaments in my heart: tiny strands of light rooted in my chest and branching outward in all directions, connecting me to the people I cared about. I narrowed the focus to my psychotherapy clients. One by one, I visited each of them, probing their emotions.

First, I checked in on Mack, a longshoreman who had become depressed after an injury put him out of work. A few days before, I had sensed that he was in crisis, so I had called Simone, my supervisor and best friend. She found out that Mack's disability check was late and he was facing eviction. But as I reconnected with him that morning, I felt that he was calm, stable. Simone must have found a way to help him. As a Baltimore native who had been working at the clinic for years, she always seemed to know the right people to call and strings to pull to make things happen.

After Mack, I moved on to the next person. Then the next. Fortunately, everyone seemed to be doing all right—until I reached my last client, Elana. When I focused on her, a river of anger and bitterness flowed into my chest.

With her limpid blue eyes and tiny, sparrow-like frame, Elana had always reminded me of a fairytale nymph mistakenly dropped into a harsh urban landscape. I sensed that she had suffered some kind of betrayal—probably something to do with Don. Her on-again, off-again boyfriend worked as a drug dealer and was one of a series of men to whom she had attached herself, mistaking their aggression for strength.

In spite of the intense feelings I was sensing from her, I could tell Elana's crisis was not acute, nor was she having any dangerous impulses. Still, anger was such a volatile and energizing emotion that anything could happen. I pulled out of my meditative state and reached for the phone.

Simone was the only person I'd ever told about my "intuitions." Over time, she had come to trust them as I did, so I knew I could count on her to check in on Elana. I dialed her office number and said a silent prayer of gratitude: as pathetic as my life had become, at least Simone hadn't given up on me yet.

• • •

The Clash roared, "Should I Stay or Should I Go?" over the radio as I drove through the sheeting rain and pulled up to the gate. I rolled down the window, getting half-drenched as I punched the code I'd been given into the security panel. The gate swung open, and I pulled my beat-up red hatchback into the fenced-in parking lot.

I dug my fingernails into the steering wheel. What kind of psychiatrist worked out of a boarded-up church on a block of abandoned row houses? What exactly was I getting myself into?

The old granite church looked as though it had once been majestic. It took up a quarter of a city block and rose several stories high. The windows were almost entirely covered with plywood, but sections of ornate stained glass were still visible near the top of the building, high enough to be safe from robbers or stray bullets.

Baltimore was a city of extremes. Every day on the way to the Waverly clinic where I worked, I drove north past the aspirational, cutting-edge buildings of the prestigious Washington Hill Hospital. But where the hospital campus ended, a very different neighborhood began—block after block of long-empty homes, skeletons waiting for a wrecking ball to crush their bones into dust. My clients had told me plenty of horror stories about what went on inside some of those shells. I usually drove through the blighted areas of town as quickly as possible while trying to ignore the chill running down my spine. Not this morning, however.

There were three other cars in the lot: a silver SUV with tinted windows, an enormous black Land Rover, and what appeared to be a convertible beneath a canvas cover. Clearly, Dr. MacGregor's practice was doing well.

So I'd made it there. But I hadn't gone inside yet. I could still turn around and go home.

One thought of my boss, however, killed the idea of turning tail and running. Dr. Nelson was the medical director of our clinic. With his shock of white hair and black-rimmed glasses, he looked like Colonel Sanders and had the grandfatherly charm to match. But I knew after working closely with him for over two years that his suggestions were actually orders, and that his charm disappeared quickly when they weren't taken seriously.

In my case, his suggestion had been that I go see Dr. Angeline MacGregor, his fellow psychiatrist and colleague from medical school. Dr. Nelson was certain she could cure whatever ailed me. I'd been off of work for ten weeks, using up almost all of my sick and vacation days, and I could still barely leave my house, let alone return to the office. Therefore, it had been more of an ultimatum than a suggestion—keep this appointment, or my job would be in jeopardy.

Although a shamefully large part of me would have been happy to remain a recluse, there was no way I could risk losing my job, because that would mean losing my clients—and they were my reasons for getting up every morning. Well, that settled that. I shut off the radio and turned to gather my purse and half-broken umbrella from the passenger seat.

I gasped as three sharp raps on the driver's side window sent my body into a panicked leap. I twisted around, but all I could make out through the dripping, fogged-up window was a dark suit with a man in it.

"Cathryn Duncan?" a deep, no-nonsense voice demanded.

My heart pounded so loudly that it drowned out the rain. Cautiously, I rolled the window down halfway. "Yes?"

"I'm Ben, the clinic manager. Is everything okay?"

The clinic manager? What was he doing knocking on my car window? "Yes, everything's okay. Why?"

He leaned down and looked inside. As our eyes met, we froze, like two stunned animals stumbling across one another in the forest. Neither of us moved or spoke, just stared. There was something familiar…had we met before? I figured he must have been wondering the same thing because he looked as surprised as I felt.

After several moments, Ben broke the silence. "You," he began, but there was a catch in his voice. He cleared his throat. "You arrived late, and you've been sitting out here with your car running for ten minutes. I wanted to make sure you were all right."

My stomach clenched. He had been *watching* me? Even more embarrassing, had I really spent ten minutes vacillating? "How do you know how long I've been out here?"

"Security cameras," he said matter-of-factly, as though I should have expected as much. Then he added a bit more softly, "I'm sorry if I startled you."

A flash fever heated my face—whether due to shock or irritation, I wasn't sure. I hoped that the grey day would hide my blush. "I'm fine," I bit out the words. "Everything's fine."

"Glad to hear it."

I tried to compose myself by closing my eyes and taking a slow, deep breath—but that just provoked another question from Ben. "Are you coming in?"

"Yes, yes," I snapped, once again flustered. "I'll be right there."

He took two steps back as I rolled the window up. I turned off the engine, grabbed my things, and stepped out of the car.

Ben immediately moved in to cover me with his enormous black umbrella. Up close, I could see that if I'd met him before, I would have remembered. He appeared to be about my age, maybe a bit older, and was tall enough that I had to look up to meet his eyes. Everything about him was squared off—the shape of his face, his hairline, the way he held his shoulders. Although his collar was unbuttoned and he wasn't wearing a tie, he still gave an impression of formality. Even the seams and folds of his suit seemed to stand at attention.

Ben pointed to a door at the top of a short staircase. "This way," he said, then waited for me to go first.

As I headed toward the stairs, Ben shadowed me, holding his umbrella over us both. I couldn't help breathing in his scent; it was a pleasant mixture of old leather, crisp cotton, and fine wool. I was certain that I, on the other hand, smelled like a wet dog. My broken umbrella had offered me little protection as I'd darted from my house to the car earlier.

When we reached the top stair, Ben opened the door and followed me inside. He shook out his umbrella and leaned it against the wall. "May I take your jacket?"

I blinked, then blinked again. Was he actually offering to touch my manky windbreaker? But his expression was perfectly serious. He held his hands out expectantly.

"Um, okay. It's kind of wet." Unsure what else to do, I allowed him to peel it off of me.

He hung my jacket on the coat rack as carefully as if it had been a fine fur. "Don't worry," he said, "it'll dry in no time."

With my outer layer of clothing gone, I became acutely aware that I wasn't exactly dressed to impress in my pair of well-worn yoga pants and decidedly wrinkled, decade-old t-shirt from art camp. I'd grabbed the first clean clothes I could find after my call to Simone had taken longer than expected. She had told me all about the great caseworker she'd found to help Mack, and we'd discussed Elana... My hands flew up to check on the state of my hair. My French braid was crooked and I could feel wavy bits of my dark brown hair sticking out. Just perfect.

But Ben had shifted his facial expression into neutral. If he had any reaction to my appearance, he wasn't showing it. "This way," he said, turning on his heel. I followed him down the hallway, unable to shake the impression that I was being taken to the principal's office.

He led me into a small, slightly dusty office with arched ceilings and high windows, the bottom two-thirds of which were covered with plywood. What light there was outside entered near the ceiling, bathing the room in a soft fog. The walls were lined floor-to-ceiling with shelves overflowing with books. The antique desk was heavily burdened with papers, creating an atmosphere of academic disorganization.

Behind the desk sat a woman I presumed to be Dr. MacGregor. She was a petite white woman in her sixties, but wiry-looking. Her eyes were inquisitive as she peered at me over the rims of her red-framed glasses. She wore a fitted Jackie O-style suit and had gathered her silver hair in a bun at the nape of her neck.

"Cathryn Duncan, I presume." Dr. MacGregor gave me a once-over that made me feel as though I was being evaluated for admission to school. "You're late."

Good God, I thought, *these two don't miss a thing.* "I'm sorry. And please, it's Cate."

"Have a seat, Cate. I'm Dr. MacGregor."

Her voice was crisp with the echo of an accent—Scottish or English maybe, I couldn't be sure. As I sat down across from her, Ben leaned back against a bookshelf. Now they were both scrutinizing me. I felt like an ant under a magnifying glass.

Fortunately, my auto-manners kicked in. "It's a pleasure to meet you, Dr. MacGregor. And Ben." I wondered if he was going to stick around for my appointment.

Dr. MacGregor seemed to read my mind. "Benjamin manages our clinic and its various programs," she explained. "I trust you don't mind if he sits in on this meeting."

I *did* mind, but it was clear that she wasn't really asking my permission. I just bit my lip and nodded.

"Let's get right to it," Dr. MacGregor began. "Dr. Nelson tells me you're a very promising therapist with special talents, but that he's been worried about you for some time. He also said you haven't been back to work since your mother's death. Is this correct?"

"Yes, that's right," I said, although I hadn't known that Dr. Nelson had been worried about me "for some time." It had only been a couple of days since he'd not so gently suggested that I get professional help. I tugged on the collar of my T-shirt to create more breathing room.

"I see." She cocked her head to one side. "Why don't you start by telling us what's been going on with you?"

What had been going on with me? That left it a bit wide open. I had no idea where to begin. Should I start with the fact that I desperately wanted to get back to work, but it felt as though a huge, leaden hand was pressing me into my house, the only place where I truly felt safe? Since my mother's funeral, I'd become a virtual shut-in. Sid had dropped in to pay his respects, but then he'd left town on an extended business trip. If Simone hadn't come over for lunch once or twice a week, I would have turned into a complete hermit.

Ben leaned down and whispered something in Dr. MacGregor's ear. She nodded. "Perhaps we should start with the loss of your mother—three months ago, was it?"

"Ten weeks." I hated the phrase "loss of your mother." It made it sound like I had misplaced her out of carelessness. Of course, that might not have been so far from the truth. An emotion tried to work its way into my throat, but I swallowed it down.

"I'm sorry," Dr. MacGregor said, her tone softer. "Would you like to talk about it?"

The lump in my throat returned. I'd have to change the subject or risk losing control. "No, not really. I'm dealing with it. I'm not here for that."

"All right, what are you here for, then?"

"Well..." My face began to burn again. I was a therapist, for God's sake. I was supposed to treat these kinds of problems, not have them. "The reason I can't go to work or do anything else, really, is that lately I'm afraid to be around people. Not people I'm close to, I mean. I'm fine around them for some reason. But with other people, including clients...I'm afraid this is going to sound weird."

"Go ahead." She waved her hand.

Apparently "weird" was fine with her. "It just feels like I've become hyper-sensitized to people's emotions, almost like I'm allergic to them. Whenever I'm around someone who is in emotional distress, I can feel it slamming into me like a wave. It throws me completely off-balance. I don't leave the house most of the time because of it."

To be more precise, the only time I left the house at all was to go to the twenty-four-hour grocery store between three and four in the morning when I was likely to be the only customer. I even used the self-checkout line to avoid the cashiers. I opted not to share that information with Dr. MacGregor, however—and especially not with Ben—for fear of sounding even more pitiful.

She tapped her pen against the desk. "You left the house today, and here you sit with two strangers, but you don't appear to be overwhelmed. How do you account for that?"

My cheeks heated up again. I had always despised the fact that I blushed so readily. "I just kind of assumed you'd be safe to be around—you know, emotionally stable. Plus, I took some pills."

Her eyebrows lifted slightly. "I beg your pardon?"

"Dr. Nelson gave me these pills to take when I have to leave the house."

"Oh." She held out her hand. "May I see them?"

Feeling like a child who had been caught shoplifting from the corner store, I fished the samples out of my purse and handed them to her. "They're for anxiety," I explained. "They don't stop me from getting emotionally slammed, but they help me worry less about the possibility that it might happen."

She examined the pills. "Ah. Well, you won't need these after a few days here," she said, handing them back to me. "So, can't be around people, unable to leave the house. Any other symptoms?"

"Those are the major ones." I decided that I might garner more respect from her if I used some professional jargon. "I've also been having insomnia, along with some other depressive symptoms—low mood, no energy, anhedonia...and social isolation, I guess you could say, but that kind of goes along with not leaving the house."

"I see." She absently jotted some notes down on a pad. "Anything else?"

Either I was imagining things or she looked positively bored. Was this the brilliant Dr. MacGregor who had come so highly recommended? Well, if *she* thought that she had obtained a complete clinical picture in less than five minutes, *I* thought it was about time she said something useful. "No, that's pretty much it," I said. "So what do you think?"

Dr. MacGregor slowly removed her glasses, folded them, and placed them on the desk. "Miss Duncan, so far, you haven't told me anything about yourself that can't be fixed by those pills Dr. Nelson gave you, perhaps alongside an antidepressant. In order for this meeting to be anything other than a waste of time for all of us, you're going to have to tell me *everything* that's going on with you. No leaving things out, no holding things back because you're afraid they'll sound strange. What's that you always say, Benjamin?" She gestured over her shoulder at him with her pen.

"Embrace your inner freak." I thought I saw Ben flash me a droll smile, but it happened so quickly I couldn't be sure.

"Yes, that," Dr. MacGregor said. "So tell me then. What *else* is going on with you?"

My stomach churned uneasily. My inner freak? Surely she couldn't be talking about...no. Simone was the only person who knew I had "intuitions" about my clients, but even she didn't know how I got them. And I'd never told anyone about the other strange things I did. Was it possible that Dr. MacGregor had sensed it somehow?

Once again, she showed her keen sense of perception. "Don't worry, dear, this meeting is confidential. I won't be sharing any details with Zeke."

My leg began to bounce up and down. As long as it wasn't going to get back to Dr. Ezekiel Nelson, maybe I could reveal my inner freak—just a little. "Well," I ventured, "there *are* some things I've never told anyone, but they're kind of bizarre. And I'm not even sure they're real."

"Yes. Those kinds of things." She held her arms open wide, as though to encompass the room. "The 'bizarre.' That's what I want to hear about. Go ahead."

A tight fist formed in my chest. I had never tried to explain my unusual experiences to anyone before. "Well, I do have this technique I use with clients that's sort of unconventional. No one else knows about it, though."

"Yes, good," Dr. MacGregor said. "Tell me about that."

They already knew I was crazy. I sighed in resignation. "All right, well, if I look into someone's eyes and concentrate, I can sort of…go inside of them. I get a general sense of the person and I can feel what they're feeling. Sometimes I get flashes of images, too—from their memories, I think. And sometimes I can even hear them talking to me, but they're not really talking. Out loud, that is." I half-smiled to indicate that I was aware of how insane that sounded.

"Interesting." She pursed her lips and examined me. "And why do you do that, instead of just asking your clients what they're feeling?"

"I *do* ask them what they're feeling, and a lot of other things." I slouched down in my chair a little. "But when I mind-meld with a client, I can see what's going on in their subconscious—things they may not even be aware of, but that are keeping them stuck where they are and preventing healing. Once I see those things,

I have a better idea of how to guide the session for the client's greatest benefit."

One of Ben's eyebrows arched. "Mind-meld?"

Just when I thought I was finished blushing for the day. "I grew up on *Star Trek* reruns, okay? What would *you* call it?"

"Empathic submergence," Ben said matter-of-factly.

I couldn't tell if he was serious or just had a really dry sense of humor. "You mean it's actually a thing? There's a term for it?"

"Yes," Dr. MacGregor said, "and people who have certain natural talents can be trained in this skill. You seem to have learned it all on your own, however." She gave an appreciative nod. "I can see why Zeke thinks you're so talented. Tell me, when you submerge into someone else, does it have any side effects?"

"Oh, no," I shook my head vigorously. "My clients don't even know I'm doing it. And I don't tell them what I see. Since the conscious mind blocks things for a reason—usually to protect us—I respect its wisdom. I just use the information I've gathered while inside to figure out where the client's pain is and how best to approach it."

She leaned forward and pointed her pen at me. "That's very wise. But what I meant was, are there any side effects for *you*?"

"Oh." I looked down at my hands as my fingers twisted around each other. The truth was that each time I returned from mind-melding with a client, I brought some of their pain back with me. I'd never thought of it as a side effect, though. I figured it was just part of being a healer; you alleviate others' suffering by taking it on yourself. But over time, the accumulated pain had grown heavier. I worried that at some point, I'd reach capacity and wouldn't be able to take on any more.

I didn't know how to explain that to Dr. MacGregor, though, so I just told her what Simone always said about me. "I tend to take my work home with me more than the other therapists do."

"I see," she said with a note of skepticism. Ben pulled out a pad and started taking notes while Dr. MacGregor asked, "Is that all, or is there more?"

What was he writing? I pressed my hand down on my knee to stop my leg from bouncing. "More what?"

"More weird."

"Oh. Well…" I couldn't tell whether she was really curious, or whether she was convinced that I was nuts and was humoring me to get more information.

It was Ben who spoke next. "There's no need to feel self-conscious. Believe me, you can't tell us anything we haven't heard before."

I fought to keep from rolling my eyes. Fine. If he was so sure that nothing I could say would surprise them… "Then maybe you can explain why I can tell what my clients are feeling, even when I'm not with them."

"Meaning?" Ben asked.

"I don't know," I lobbed back. "I wish I did. All I know is that in some sense, my clients are with me all of the time. After a couple of sessions with someone, it's as though a filament forms between us. It's not visible, of course—I can only see it in my mind's eye—but it connects us. Then, whenever I wonder how they're feeling, I can focus my mind on that filament, and just…know."

Dr. MacGregor asked, "And what use do you make of these filaments?"

She actually appeared to be taking me seriously. I slid forward in my chair. "When I was still at work, I used them to check on clients I was worried about. For example, if someone missed a therapy session and I couldn't reach them by phone, I'd use their filament to connect with them and make sure they weren't in crisis." In spite of Dr. MacGregor's promise of confidentiality, I decided not to confess that I was still doing those daily check-ins. I was pretty sure that Dr. Nelson wouldn't approve, and I didn't want to say anything that might get Simone in trouble.

"And how did you know the information you received from the filaments was accurate?"

"That's a good question." It was a question that I'd never been able to answer to my full satisfaction. Years of good, solid Western education had left me constitutionally uncomfortable with anything for which there was no scientific explanation—and that included filaments and mind-melding. I was relieved to discover that Dr. MacGregor was appropriately skeptical and appreciated the need for evidence. "There's no way of knowing for sure, I guess, but I have been keeping documentation—writing down what I was feeling about which client and when. As far as I know, all of the information I've gathered so far has corresponded with my clients' objective experiences."

"Very interesting." Dr. MacGregor gave me a collegial smile. "I can tell you that the filaments you describe are related to empathic submergence. *How* is a subject that will be covered in good time."

"Oh, wow. Okay." They didn't seem to think I was crazy after all. *There must be something wrong with them,* I thought, but allowed myself to feel slightly encouraged.

"In the meantime, I'm pleased to hear that you have an instinct for research—something we have in common." Then she turned and said something to Ben. He left the office, closing the door behind him.

I barely had a chance to wonder where Ben was going before Dr. MacGregor said, "You've said you're not here to work on your grief issues, and that's fine. We won't force you. But I still need to obtain a family history, starting with your mother."

A bit thrown off by the abrupt change of subject, I slid back in my chair. Family history was a fair topic of discussion, though. "Okay."

The mask of Dr. MacGregor's professional composure slipped, replaced for a few moments by a pained expression. "Dr. Nelson said your mother overdosed on pain pills. Did she have a pain condition?"

"Fibromyalgia."

"That can be very difficult. Do they know if the overdose was accidental, or…?"

Or suicide, she meant. I supposed she was trying to be sensitive by not asking outright.

One of my mother's coworkers at the hospice had stopped in to check on her after she didn't show up for her morning appointments and wouldn't answer her phone. Mom had still been alive, but barely. An ambulance had taken her to the hospital, where I'd arrived just in time to spend a few minutes with her before…

Tears slithered into my eyes. I blinked them back. "She was found in bed with a copy of her 'Do Not Resuscitate' order tucked under her arm." That was my mom—meticulous, detail-oriented. Never leaving anything to chance.

"I see." There was a long, aching pause. Finally, Dr. MacGregor cleared her throat. "Did she have a history of mental illness?"

"Not that anyone knew of." In other words, not that her own daughter, a trained psychotherapist, had observed. I clasped my hands together in my lap, squeezing until my fingernails dug painfully into my skin.

"What about the 'weird' experiences you've been telling me about? Did your mother have those, too?"

"What? No." At least not that she'd ever told me about. Mom had an uncanny ability to sense how I was feeling, but she'd always chalked it up to "mother's intuition." If she'd had the types of strange experiences I was having, there was no reason why she would have kept it from me.

Dr. MacGregor jotted something down on her notepad. "And on your father's side? Any history of mental illness?"

First my mother, then my father. I turned to look out the window, but all I could see was boarded-up glass. "I don't know. He left us before I turned one. My mother never told me much about him, not even who he was. Or is."

"All right, then," she said, returning to her usual businesslike demeanor. This time I welcomed her coolness. Over the years, any pain I had felt about not knowing my father had dulled to almost nothing. I certainly didn't need any comforting about it.

She paused for a moment, then leaned forward. "And you? Do you ever have suicidal thoughts?"

She gave me an incisive look, like a bird of prey that had just spotted a rabbit on open ground. I suspected that if I gave the wrong answer to her question, I'd end up in the back of an ambulance on my way to the psych ward.

Suicide had always been an evil force that I fought against, a dangerous enemy that I tried to keep as far away as possible, both from others and myself. But in the wake of my mother's death, I'd felt compelled to better understand my nemesis by drawing closer to it. I tried to imagine what it would take to make me suicidal, and was alarmed to discover that it wouldn't take much. After all, what use was my life anymore? I'd failed my mother in the worst way possible. By definition, I was failing my clients since I couldn't even make it in to work. And although they'd never admit it, I knew I was starting to become a burden to my friends.

As I thought more about suicide, I started to develop a strange relationship with it. At my lowest points, it appeared dangerously seductive, beckoning to me with a long, dark finger. But most of the time the thought of it was somehow soothing. Just knowing that death was a possibility—that there was a way out, should I ever need one—made it somehow easier to tolerate the pain.

I found myself spending hours online reading about various methods, searching for the most painless and idiot-proof. I had also developed a new obsession: practice-writing suicide notes. It turned out to be harder than I thought to compose something that explained my hypothetical act of self-destruction while also saving the reader from feelings of guilt, outrage, or sadness. Discarded drafts lay scattered around my house.

But Dr. MacGregor could rest easy. I had no intention of actually *acting* on any of those thoughts. I reasoned that I was simply appeasing my shadow self, entertaining its morbid fantasies so that it wouldn't take me to even darker places. Besides, I was a therapist; I knew better. However, I had no way of knowing whether Dr. MacGregor would take my word on that.

So instead of the truth, I told her what I thought she expected to hear. "Look, I don't have very many people in my life, but the ones that I do have—I would never put them through what I've been through lately."

She tapped her pen against the desk like a metronome. I could tell she was trying to decide whether or not she believed me. "I understand," she said. My shoulders dropped with relief. "The good news is that we can help you."

"What?" Another quick change of direction. "No more questions?"

"I know everything I need to know."

"So you know what's wrong with me?"

"Nothing is wrong with you, dear. You're grieving, but as you requested, we'll leave that alone for now. The problem is that you have some special abilities that you don't know how to handle properly. You're like a toddler playing with a pocketknife; naturally, you keep hurting yourself. In order to treat your symptoms, we have to teach you how to manage your gifts."

"Hurting myself? Gifts?" I shook my head. "I'm sorry, what are you talking about?"

Ben walked back into the office carrying some papers and a clipboard.

"I'll leave that to Benjamin to explain," she said. "I'm afraid I have to run. He'll take care of you from here." Dr. MacGregor put on her coat. "It was nice to meet you, Cate. I'll let Zeke know that you'll be joining us."

I stood as she headed for the door. "Joining you for what? I don't—"

She waved me aside. "Don't worry, just follow Benjamin's instructions. I'll see you sometime next week."

The door closed, and all at once, she was gone.

Chapter Two

I could have caught flies in my wide-open mouth. I turned around to find Ben sitting at the desk, arranging papers on a clipboard. While Dr. MacGregor had been with us, Ben had faded into the background. Now that she was gone, his presence seemed to expand into the room, pressurizing the air around me.

My self-consciousness crept back. I figured that the peculiar interview I'd just been through had thrown me off-balance. I tossed my hands into the air. "What just happened?"

Ben glanced up. "What? Oh yeah, Dr. MacGregor can be a little abrupt. Don't take it personally." He returned to the papers.

"I…what…" I hated being at a loss for words. Finally, I landed on, "What are you doing?"

"Preparing your admission forms," he said without bothering to look up.

"Admission to *what*?"

"Our program."

"What program?"

"She didn't tell you?"

"No, she didn't tell me anything."

"All right, I'll tell you." He folded his hands together on the desk and looked over at me. "Dr. MacGregor has developed a program to help people with special abilities like yours. Today's interview confirmed that you're appropriate for the program, which is why I am now preparing your admission paperwork." He wore an expression of relaxed confidence, as though he had explained everything.

My head began to spin. "But what program, and what special abilities?"

"The special abilities you described to us: the filaments, empathic submergence." Then, in response to what must have been an uncomprehending look on my face, he added, "The anxiety and depression you've been experiencing are not uncommon among people with gifts like yours. These problems occur when someone doesn't know how to handle what could be described as an excess of empathy."

"Oh." At least "excess of empathy" sounded like a fair, non-pathological description. "So, what? You're going to help me reduce my empathy?"

"No. We probably couldn't, even if we tried. But our program is designed to help you to manage your empathy so that it doesn't cause you so much difficulty. My mother created it to help people like you develop a specific set of coping skills."

"Your *mother*?" I exclaimed, realizing too late that I sounded more shocked than was probably polite.

He chuckled—an unexpectedly stirring sound. "Yes, sorry, I should have mentioned that earlier. I'm Ben *MacGregor*. I manage the program. My mother is the clinical director."

Ah-hah. That explained some things at least. Ben and Dr. MacGregor did seem a lot alike. They had the same pale skin and unusual light-brown eyes, and they shared a few facial expressions. But Ben's broad, straight nose, his square jaw, and his dark ridge of eyebrows must have come from his father.

"And those are the admissions forms?"

"Yes, if you could start filling out the highlighted portions." He handed me the clipboard and a pen.

"But I still don't know what the program entails."

"Of course," he said casually, as though he weren't about to say something completely outrageous. "You'll be here eight hours a day for three weeks, including weekends."

"Eight hours a day? For *three weeks*?" I had never heard anything so ridiculous. What had they been thinking, that I was going to drop everything and turn my entire life over to them? "Look, there must have been some kind of misunderstanding. I can probably come in once or twice a week for an hour or so, but no more than that."

"I'm sorry, I must have missed something." He tilted his head to one side. "Are you telling me that you have conflicting engagements?"

I revised my first impression that Ben was somewhat handsome as I realized what a piece of work he was turning out to be. Maybe I didn't have "conflicting engagements" per se, but I had staring-into-space to do, lunches with Simone to eat, online poker games to play—not to mention that Sid would be back from his business trip soon, if he wasn't already.

I slammed the clipboard onto the desk and reached for my purse. "I'm sorry," I snapped, "but it appears this has been a waste of time for all of us. Please thank Dr. MacGregor for me, but this isn't what I'm looking for."

Ben considered for a moment, apparently trying to decide whether I was serious. Then he nodded. "I'm truly sorry to hear that. I'll let them know." He picked up the phone handset from the desk and began to dial.

I leaned toward him, eyes narrowed. "Who's 'them?'"

He looked at me as though he were wondering why I was still there. Then he resumed dialing. "Dr. MacGregor and Dr. Nelson."

"Dr. Nelson? You're not calling *him*, are you?"

Ben's non-answer told me that yes, in fact, he was. He leaned back in his chair and put the handset up to his ear. I heard a ringing sound.

I bolted to my feet. "You do not have my permission to talk to my boss! Do you hear me? Hang up that phone right now!"

His eyes locked onto mine as he spoke into the receiver. "Zeke? It's Ben," he said with infuriating familiarity. I could hear Dr. Nelson's muffled voice coming through the earpiece. Ben answered, "Yes, my mother thinks she's perfect for the program, but Miss Duncan doesn't think it's for her." More muffled Dr. Nelson. "As a matter of fact, yes, she is." Ben held the phone out to me.

I imagined a freak lightning bolt cutting in through the top of the window and striking Ben where he sat, leaving his charred remains on the chair in a neat pile of ash. With no other option, I took the phone. "Hi, Dr. Nelson."

"Hi, Cate. What seems to be the problem?"

Still fuming, I sat down, doing my best to sound calm and rational as I explained to Dr. Nelson how ridiculous the program requirements were. But his delight that Dr. MacGregor had accepted me seemed to render him temporarily deaf.

Just as I was about to begin pleading, Dr. Nelson asked, "Are you saying that you don't need their help because you're ready to come back to work?"

Oh, hell. He was calling my bluff. "No. I mean, nothing's changed," I mumbled, feeling about the size of a dried pea.

Dr. Nelson's voice took on a hard edge. "Cate, it's up to you. I can't force you to attend their program as a condition of your employment. However, if you can't come back to work *and* you refuse do what's necessary to help get yourself back to work, then you and I will have to have a serious conversation about your future at the clinic."

My future at the clinic—or lack thereof. I watched my options fly away like a cloud of starlings. There was no escaping it: I had been snookered. "Okay, Dr. Nelson."

"Great. Don't worry about a thing. We'll keep taking good care of your clients as usual. When does Ben want you to start?"

I stared at a random spot on the desk and covered the receiver with my hand. "He wants to know when you want me to start."

"Sunday," Ben said.

"*What*?" Two days away, and on a weekend? Was he serious? But the look on his face told me that he was, in fact, serious. I uncovered the receiver. "Sunday."

"Fine, fine. Cate, don't worry about a thing. The MacGregors are great people. They'll take good care of you. I'll check in every so often to see how you're doing."

I could not believe what was happening. I barely managed another "Okay, Dr. Nelson."

"Work hard and good luck!" *Click*.

I stared at the phone because it seemed a better option than looking at Ben. Eventually, however, I had to look up again. I could tell he was trying not to look smug, but he wasn't trying quite hard enough.

"So we're good, then?" he asked.

"We are in no way good." I glared at him. "You had no right to do that."

"But you're going to do the program."

"That is beside the point. You had no right to call Dr. Nelson without my consent."

"I thought the point was that you're going to do the program—or did I misunderstand your half of the phone conversation?"

It took a moment for me to identify the hot, heavy feeling in my stomach as hatred. Reluctantly, I met his gaze. "Yes, I am, but under duress and against my better judgment, in order to save my job—"

"Great!" He cut me off, again handing me the clipboard and pen.

I hated being snookered almost as much as I hated needing help. Well, there was no reason I had to be the only one to suffer. In an effort to perturb Ben, I took my time with the paperwork, pretending to painstakingly review each page. The truth was that I was too exasperated to concentrate on anything I was reading. I told myself that it didn't really matter since they all looked like boilerplate forms anyway.

That was, until something jumped out at me on the last page, the program contract. It read, "Participants must commit to completing the entire twenty one-day program, during which the following are prohibited: smoking, drugs, alcohol, meat, and sexual activity."

I held up the clipboard and turned it to face Ben. "What is this?"

Ben leaned forward. "Oh yeah, the contract. Those are just the program rules."

No sexual activity? No *Sid*? My heart knocked against my ribcage like a fist pounding on a door. "But this is outrageous! I don't understand how what I eat or any of my other…activities are any of your business, or how they could possibly have an impact—"

Ben interrupted me. "I know more than you might realize how strange all of this must sound to you," he reassured. "If it helps you to know this, I have a Ph.D. in psychology."

"You…huh?"

"I'm Dr. MacGregor too, which is why I don't usually mention it. It would cause too much confusion. Besides, I studied organizational psychology, not clinical, so I'm not qualified to treat clients. My role here is strictly managerial. Still, I have some understanding of how strange this may seem to you."

My head began to ache. I held my hand over my eyes. "Then would you mind please explaining all of this to me, starting with these insane rules?"

"I will explain in time. But everything you'll be learning here will be new to you. If I jump too far ahead, it won't make any sense and will only confuse you more. Cate, please look at me."

I removed my hand and looked at him. His eyes focused on mine like two warm, chocolatey tractor beams. "We're here to help you," he said gently. "All we're asking for is your trust, and some patience."

I wondered if he had any idea how ironic that sounded, coming from someone who had just called my boss without my consent and was now trying to rush me into signing a ridiculous contract. "Trust, patience—and that I spend the next twenty-one days living as a vegetarian nun."

He gave me his mother's tight-lipped smile. "Not entirely vegetarian. You can still have eggs, fish, and dairy products."

A wave of exhaustion washed over me. My fighting energy was tapped. Besides, if Ben did have a Ph.D. in psychology, maybe I should give him the benefit of the doubt. It wasn't like I had a choice.

As I reached over to the desk and picked up the contract again, a hopeful thought dawned on me. "And when exactly do I have to start following these rules?"

"Sunday, when you start the program." He gave me a sly glance. "Maybe you should plan a steak dinner between now and then."

After everything that had just happened, was he actually trying to make a joke? "Maybe I will!" I scrawled my signature on the contract and thrust the clipboard at Ben. I felt compelled to remind him, "You know that I'm not at all happy about this."

"Yes, I got that." He moved onto the next topic as though my happiness or lack thereof were of absolutely no consequence. "Since you've been having trouble getting out of the house, Pete, my assistant manager, will pick you up on Sunday morning at eight forty-five."

My jaw dropped. They were going to chauffeur me? I didn't know whether to be impressed by their thoughtfulness or outraged by their presumptiveness.

Before I had a chance to decide, Ben said, "Here's my card. Call me with any questions."

The urge to get the heck out of there overcame any desire to argue. I stood up, took his card, and picked up my purse.

Ben stood as well. "Would you like me to walk you out to your car? It's still raining, and I noticed your umbrella…"

"No, thank you."

"All right. See you Sunday."

I bolted out of the office and down the hallway, grabbed my windbreaker, and escaped into the parking lot. Not even bothering with my umbrella, I held my jacket over my head as I struggled to unlock the car door.

Once inside, I slammed the door behind me, fished my cell phone out of my purse, and speed-dialed. Voicemail. "Hi, this is Sid. Leave a message."

Merely hearing Sid's voice helped me start to breathe normally again. I hoped I wouldn't sound too desperate on the recording. "Hi, it's me. I hope you're back, because I really need to see you, the sooner the better. Okay. Hope you had a good trip."

I knew the last sentence sounded like the afterthought that it was, but I also knew that Sid wouldn't take it personally. We didn't call each other to chat.

I raced out of the parking lot and sped down the abandoned streets toward home.

Chapter Three

I was lucky enough to find a parking spot right in front of my house. I lived in one of the tiny row homes that lined the side streets of Highlandtown. It was small, but just the right size for a person who lived alone and didn't like to do a lot of housekeeping. The front door opened into my living room, and beyond that was a small kitchen. A narrow staircase led up to my bedroom and bath.

Community mental health, while rewarding in other ways, was not a generously paying gig. My one big splurge had been a soft, brown leather couch and matching armchair that I had purchased at a second-hand store in Fells Point. I sank onto the couch just as my cell phone rang. Expecting Sid, I quickly picked up the phone and slid my finger across the screen without looking to see who was calling. "Hello?"

"Hi, Cate," chirped a female voice.

"Oh. Hi, Simone." I tried not to sound as disappointed as I felt.

"Good to know you're so glad to hear from me!"

I glanced at the clock. Seven p.m. If Sid hadn't called by then, he probably wasn't going to. "Of course I am. I'm sorry. I'm just a little tired. How was your day?"

"No way. You first. How did things go with Dr. Nelson's friend?"

I suppressed a groan. "Not as well as expected, let's put it that way."

"Here we go. Tell me what happened."

I propped my feet up on the long coffee table. "Well, Dr. MacGregor was okay, I guess. But they've roped me into this totally unreasonable treatment program. I have to go every day for three whole weeks, eight hours a day—including weekends!"

Simone gave a low whistle. "Wow, that does sound unreasonable. Especially for someone who isn't working…and who never leaves her house…and whose only hobby is online poker…"

I would have smiled if her words hadn't brought to mind Ben's sarcastic remark about conflicting engagements. "Very funny. And I'm fully aware of how messed up I am, thank you."

"I'm sorry. You're right, that does sound pretty intense. But think about it. Dr. Nelson has his flaws, but clinical judgment isn't one of them. If he's recommending this program, it must be top notch. Plus, he told me he's paying for it from the clinic's continuing education fund, so he must have a lot of faith in whatever they're doing."

"Why are you taking his side? Are you getting a kickback or something?"

"If only," she said dryly. "Look, you know I love you, and it hurts me to see you like you've been lately. I know your house is your comfort zone, but you can't hide out there forever. I want the old Cate back, and so does everyone else. I know it's not what you had in mind, but maybe this program is the kind of thing you need."

"I don't know," I said, but I suspected that she might be right. Since returning home from my mother's funeral, I'd been expecting the natural emotional healing process to kick in. When it didn't, I used every therapeutic intervention I could think of on myself to push through the stages of grief, lift my mood, challenge my anxious thoughts—whatever might help me feel better. But nothing had worked. If anything, I'd become more firmly entrenched in my depressive state—something Simone had no doubt noticed on her visits. I had to admit that if I could have figured out how to fix my problems on my own, I would have done so already. "You might be right," I acquiesced.

"I'm always right."

"I know, I know," I said, smiling because she was, usually. "But the other problem is that the clinic manager is Dr. MacGregor's son, and he's a grade-A jerk."

"Oh no. Please don't tell me he hit on you."

I wish. The thought came unbidden, but my mind quickly beat it back. "No, worse. He's one of those people who expects you to do what he says without asking any questions, just because it's *him* saying it."

I heard an explosive "Hah!" followed by exuberant laughter. I could picture Simone's long dreadlocks flying as she tossed her head back. "Oh wow," she finally said. "He's definitely tangling with the wrong girl then. Come on, you can handle this guy. Think of it as entertainment. At least you won't be bored while you're there."

I smiled in spite of myself. "Okay, all right. You win. It's a done deal anyway. I've already signed the admission papers."

"Good. Now that we've got that settled, let me tell you about Elana."

According to Simone, I was right: Don had been the source of Elana's woes. She had caught him *in flagrante* with another woman. Overwhelmed by emotion and afraid that she might lose control, Elana had checked herself into Washington Hill's psychiatric ward. "I'm not sure if she went in because she was really feeling that badly or because she wanted to get away from Don," Simone said. "Either reason would be a good one, if you ask me. He sounds like a real asshole."

I closed my eyes and tried to focus on the filament that connected me to Elana. "That's the impression I got, too, but I think Don is really the only person she's close to here in town. Her family's in North Carolina, and Don has done his best to drive her friends away." I could feel Elana's hurt and disappointment flowing into me, but she also seemed steadier, more peaceful. "Is she doing okay now?"

"Yeah. Better since she got to Washington Hill. She's still undecided about whether to forgive Don or kick him to the curb. I told her I'd be her temporary therapist when she gets out."

"Thank you so much," I said as tears began to blur my vision. "Thank you for taking care of her, and everyone else. I feel terrible that I'm not there."

"Good. *Feel* terrible. Maybe that will motivate you to finish this program and get better so you can come back. I miss you like a limb."

The telltale "beep" of call-waiting interrupted us. "I'm sorry, can you hold on? It's another call."

"No, it's all right. Go ahead and get it. But call me at some point and let me know how it's going, okay?"

"Okay, I will. And you'll fill me in if anything happens with Elana?"

"Deal. Now go. Talk to you later!"

"Bye!" I clicked over. "Hello?"

"I got your message. Hard day at the office?"

The sound of Sid's voice vibrating into my ear sent a warm flush through my body. "A hard day, yes—which would improve considerably if you came over."

"Your wish is my command, as always. I just got home from the airport, though, and I have some work to finish up. How about tomorrow night at six? I'll bring Chinese."

Relief washed over me. It wouldn't be immediately, but at least he was coming. "That sounds perfect." I forced myself into normal conversation mode. "How was your trip?"

"Successful. I'll bore you with the details tomorrow if you like."

"I can think of some other things I'd rather do tomorrow."

His chuckle heated up the phone line. "Oh, so it's like that, is it?" But then his tone became somber. "Look, we can hang out and talk. I just want to see you. I feel terrible that I had to take off so soon after…last time."

"Please don't feel bad." Following his visit after the funeral, he'd had to go abroad for two months to help his father with their import/export business. "There was nothing else you could have done. As for tomorrow, I appreciate your offer to hang out and talk, but what I really need is a good distraction."

"Hmm." There was a pause. "You're sure?"

"Never been surer."

"Well, I *am* good at distracting you."

"That's what I'm counting on."

"Then I will not disappoint you in your hour of need, my dear. Tomorrow at six, okay?"

"Perfect. I'll see you then."

"In the flesh," he murmured before hanging up. He knew I would be thinking about *that* for the next twenty-four hours.

Click. I fell backward onto the sofa and let everything drift out of my mind, save one thought: Sid was coming over. Everything was going to be all right.

• • •

Sid and I had met at a mutual friend's party in graduate school. Sid was short for Siddhartha, I learned. Although his parents were Zoroastrians from Iran, they had named him after the Buddha. The name seemed to fit; his build was uncommonly tall and broad, and he had a bit of a belly that he carried sensuously.

It was clear from the start that we weren't going to fall in love; we just didn't click in that way. Despite that, though, his body and mine were like two magnets of opposite charges being pulled together. It was a new experience for me, being attracted to someone who didn't interest me romantically. I had no idea how to handle it.

The truth was that my history of handling physical attraction in general was abysmal. I'd had a few romantic attachments in the past, and a couple of those relationships had even seemed promising. But they had never progressed to the point of physical intimacy. For some reason, whenever things started to get serious—either emotionally, or we moved beyond a chaste kiss or handholding—a panicky feeling would overcome me. I would start to hyperventilate and feel convinced that if I didn't get away from the person immediately, I would suffocate to death.

While I knew intellectually that my survival was not in jeopardy, the urgent need to escape had always proven too strong. I'd broken off several relationships just as they had begun to blossom. Eventually, my grief over losing those men and my guilt over having hurt them became too much to bear. I gave up dating altogether, much to Simone's consternation, and comforted myself with the thought that there were far worse things than dying a virgin.

But being with Sid at the party felt safe, comfortable—different. By the end of the night, he'd convinced me to see him again, "to figure out what this thing is between us." While we never did fall in love, there was definitely a mutual attraction, and intimacy with him was calming, not panic-inducing—maybe *because* there were no romantic feelings between us. Before I knew it, we had fallen into a semi-regular friends-with-benefits arrangement.

While I was still in school, Sid came over every month or two. Waking up next to him gave me the delicious illusion of companionship, but when he left—always with no promise of when he would return—my true loneliness stood out in stark relief. I pushed that feeling aside with great force, though. I couldn't seem to manage a normal relationship; if what I had with Sid was as good as it was ever going to get for me, I was determined not to ruin it by being maudlin. Instead, I tried to focus on the positive aspects of our dalliance.

Once I started working as a therapist, however, an element of need began to enter the equation. Over time, I discovered that a night with Sid seemed to take the edge off of the pain I'd accumulated while mind-melding. Before long, whenever the pain grew too heavy, an internal pressure would start building inside of me, and I would feel compelled to see Sid as soon as possible. I became agitated and restless, unable to think of anything else until I finally saw him.

With each passing month, the problem worsened. If my need for Sid went unmet for too long, waves of nausea would start to hit. Then flash fevers would burn through me. Eventually my skin would become so sensitized that even the slightest touch from Sid would sear painfully—but only temporarily. After the first lovemaking event of the night, the sickness disappeared and I was able once again to experience pleasure.

I wasn't sure why, but I hadn't felt that compulsion to see Sid since my mother's death—luckily, since he had been out of town. But something about my interview with the MacGregors had triggered my need. I tried to distract myself by cleaning the house, including gathering my practice suicide notes into an envelope and hiding them in the closet. Fortunately, by the time Sid rang the doorbell the next evening, the flash fevers were only in their early stages, so I was able to act relatively normal. I ran my fingers through my hair one last time and opened the door.

There he stood, smiling out from underneath the hood of a dark green rain poncho. His overnight duffle was slung over his shoulder, and he was carrying a bag of Chinese takeout. He looked me up and down and smiled. "You look delicious."

I took the food from him and smiled back. "And you look like someone who's been away for too long."

Sid left his soaked poncho on the stoop outside, then came in and shook off the remaining moisture like a wet bear. His presence sent surges of anticipation through my body. I put the food in the kitchen and joined him in the living room. "Welcome back."

He put his arms around my waist and pulled me to him, his pupils blackening. "Am I to understand that you missed me?"

"Well, you were gone for two whole months," I replied, only half-teasing.

Wrinkles of concern gathered at the corners of his eyes. "You're sure this is how you want to spend the evening? I brought some cards in case you changed your mind." He pulled a pack of playing cards out of his pocket and tossed it onto the coffee table.

I tried hard to sound casual as I suggested, "Strip poker?"

Sid's lips stretched into a grin. "Oh, so that's how it is, is it?" He put his hands on my hips and pulled me closer. "Well, since we both know how *that* game would go, why don't we just skip to the end?"

In spite of the urgent need clawing at me, my good-hostess manners kicked in. "Unless you want to eat first. The food might get cold."

"Tonight, I think you need an appetizer." He slid his fingers under the bottom edge of my blouse and rested his hands on my bare waist.

I gasped as the fever inside of me rushed to meet Sid's caresses like metal filings rushing to a magnet. Flames licked my skin everywhere he touched me. At the same time, Sid's hands seemed to act as poultices, drawing the fever out of my body—a process that made me dizzy with a mixture of agony and relief. Fortunately, the arousal he triggered in me overwhelmed the pain—if barely.

As he gently kneaded my waist, my heart pounded in my ears. He guided me over to the couch and laid me down. A scalding heat followed his touch as his hands slid up my sides, then seared through me to meet his lips as his mouth found my bottom rib. The rush of sensation was so excruciating that I cried out.

"Patience, my dear," he murmured. "I know what you need."

"I know," I said, the words half-moan. As desperate as I felt, Sid was right. The more he took his time, the more the sickness seemed to abate and the better I felt afterwards. Not that I'd ever explained that to *him*, but Sid had his own ways of measuring my levels of satisfaction. I tried to stay calm and keep breathing as he diligently went about his work.

Meanwhile, I kept my physical torments to myself, letting him believe that my gasps and cries were purely due to arousal. While I'd heard that pain and pleasure could be an erotic mixture, some unsettling Internet research had led me to the conclusion that *my* experience was definitely not normal. If I told Sid what was really happening, I might risk losing him—and that, I couldn't stand.

Coated in a light sweat, my body began to writhe involuntarily, longing for Sid to give me my final release. Eventually, I reached the cusp of my tolerance. I was on the verge of begging when Sid sat back and unbuckled his belt, looking me over in careful appraisal. Then he leaned forward again, put his hands on my shoulders, and whispered in my ear, "Now let me take care of you." Tears of gratitude swelled in my eyes. Soon, the torture would be over.

Chapter Four

Ah, sweet oblivion. I lay in the tangle of sheets on the bed next to Sid. His presence next to me was silent and infinite, like an endless desert stretching out under the sun.

Everything from my intense need to the burning heat had disappeared after our initial encounter on the couch. I felt quiet, peaceful, and empty of painful emotions. It was exactly what I'd needed, and Sid had made it happen. Eyes still closed, I leaned over and gave a grateful kiss to the nearest part of him that my lips could reach, which turned out to be his thigh.

Sid placed his hand heavily on my forehead. "Oh no, don't start that again," he said in not-entirely-mock exasperation.

I wondered how long he had been awake, sitting there and watching me sleep. "I wasn't trying to start anything," I said. "I just wanted—"

"To thank me for being such an amazing lover. I know. You're welcome."

"You're so full of yourself." I gave his thigh another kiss.

Sid sat with his back against the headboard. I was glad I had invested in a king-sized bed that could easily accommodate my outsized guest. A wingback chair held Sid's neatly folded clothes, while a richly colored Persian rug he had gifted me covered the floor.

Sid began to stroke my hair. He knew how that made me melt. "You know, Cate, there's something I've been meaning to talk to you about."

"Mm-hmm?"

"Don't take this the wrong way, but I'm a little worried about you."

I usually enjoyed our pillow talk. It had allowed our friendship to deepen over time. But it sounded like Sid wanted to have a *serious* conversation—something for which I was not in the mood. "Sid, please, I don't want to talk about my mom, okay?"

"Okay." He took me by the shoulders and shifted me into a half-seated position against the pillows. "But that's not all that's worrying me. I realize this might sound like an unusual concern for a lover to express, but for some time now, I've felt as though you need almost more than I can give." He winked. "Almost."

"What do you mean?" I asked, trying to sound innocent. I twisted the edge of the sheet around my finger.

"I'm talking about our unspoken agreement—if one of us calls, the other makes themselves available as soon as possible. I'm just starting to worry that one day, you might need me like you did tonight, and I won't be able to be there for you." He frowned. "I worried about you while I was away, you know. Were you…okay?"

"Yeah, I was fine. I guess I was too busy grieving to think about anything else."

"Of course." Sid kissed the top of my head. "How insensitive of me."

I felt a stab of shame as it occurred to me that Sid might have been inconveniencing himself to satisfy me. "No, I'm the insensitive one. I know how demanding your job is, and I've been calling on you way too much."

"Don't be ridiculous; that's impossible. And I don't want you to feel bad. Haven't you been listening? I'm actually *worried* about you." He placed his hand on my cheek and tilted my face toward his. "Don't get me wrong; you know I live for our rendezvous. But it's not just my availability that I'm concerned about. Take tonight, for example. The first time, you went almost limp in my arms, and—well, I know this sounds strange, but it seemed as though you might be in pain."

Oh, no—he had figured me out! I rubbed my eyes in an effort to disguise my expression of alarm. .

But Sid was determined to get an answer. He leaned in so close that the tips of our noses nearly touched. "Is there something going on with you that you haven't told me about?"

Like the fact that I was so messed up in the head that I'd been practically homebound for ten weeks? Unable to meet his eyes, I turned away, leaning my face into his shoulder. "Kind of."

"Do you want to talk about it? We can *talk*, too, remember?"

I was grateful to him for trying to lighten the moment, and I had no reason not to trust Sid. But I also didn't want to scare him off by giving him too many sordid details. "Work has been really overwhelming me, I guess. And it's been much worse since my mother…you know."

"Yes, I know." He placed a soft kiss on the top of my head. "So, my dear, what are you doing about this problem?"

I sighed in resignation. "Funny you should ask. My boss is sending me to a three week-long program, starting tomorrow."

"Really?" Sid sounded impressed. "I'm glad that he appreciates you enough to invest in you. What type of program is it?"

I tried to think of the least alarming way to describe it. "I'm not exactly sure. It's like a program for people with excess empathy or something, to teach us how to manage it so we don't get overwhelmed."

"Hmm. Too much empathy does sound like it could apply to you."

"I guess," I muttered. "I don't know *what's* wrong with me, but I know I have to do something."

"I for one am glad to hear you say that." He tossed the sheet over me, the nonverbal gesture we had developed to indicate to one another that it was time to go to sleep. "I couldn't stand it if anything bad were to happen to my favorite concubine. Besides, you've told me that you respect your boss. If he thinks this will help, then who knows? Maybe you'll manage to squeeze something useful out of it—if you go into it with a positive attitude, that is, instead of with the sour look you currently have on your face."

I smirked. "That might be harder than you think." I explained about the program's absurd requirements and rules—including "no sexual activity."

"Well, that is a bit odd—and a bitter pill to swallow, I'll admit." Sid resumed stroking my hair. "On the other hand, we've survived longer than three weeks before, and if this program is going to help you, who am I to object? I just thank the heavens we had tonight. Otherwise I might've had to kidnap you."

"You mean rescue me." Fishing for more sympathy, I added, "I tried to get out of going, but my boss basically trapped me into it."

"Oh?" Sid asked with a glint in his eye. "And what's wrong with that?"

I scowled. "Isn't it obvious?"

"Not to me." Suddenly, Sid was on top of me, pinning me to the bed. "Keep in mind, my dear, you are speaking to the one person on earth who knows how much you love being trapped."

And it turned out that it wasn't quite time to go to sleep after all.

Chapter Five

I was dragged out of a sound sleep by loud bangs on the front door. I opened my eyes to find Sid dressed, packed, and tying his shoes.

"Shall I get that?" he asked.

Oh no—I had forgotten to set my alarm again. It was Sunday, and Ben hadn't been bluffing: he *had* sent someone to pick me up! I glanced at the clock by the side of the bed. Eight forty-five a.m. Right on time.

Fortunately, Sid liked to get an early start to the day, even on weekends. He preferred to leave before I lured him into breakfast and the whole day got "shot to hell," as he put it. I rolled out of bed and pulled on my fuzzy white bathrobe. "It's probably someone from that program coming to get me."

Sid nodded sagely. I skittered down the stairs and stumbled over to the front door. "Who is it?"

A muffled voice said, "I'm Pete. Ben MacGregor sent me to pick up Cate Duncan."

I opened up to find a man standing on the stoop who could only be described as…a cowboy. A real, honest-to-God cowboy in well-worn boots and a Stetson.

I rubbed my eyes, but when I looked again, he was still standing there tall and lean, with tanned, leathery skin that told of overexposure to the elements. Apparently, I was going to be chauffeured by Wyatt Earp. At least he'd brought the sun with him. The rain had finally given way to dry, crisp autumn weather.

I heard Sid's footsteps on the stairs. He joined me at the door as my half-asleep mind tried to formulate an introduction. "I'm Cate," I finally said. It was way too early, and I had gone to bed way too late.

Pete's eyelids were hooded, forming triangular slits through which his pale blue eyes examined me. From the movement of Pete's hat, I saw that he was taking in Sid. They were both over six feet tall. I suddenly felt insignificant.

Sid walked around beside me, duffle bag slung over his shoulder, and addressed Pete directly. "Sorry I didn't have her ready in time. I didn't know to expect you." He winked down at me.

Pete appeared unruffled. He hooked his thumbs into an enormous brass belt buckle featuring a bronco, then looked me over as though I were a rodeo bull and he was considering how difficult I would be in the ring. "No problem," he said in a gravelly voice.

I felt my face start to redden. "Sid, isn't it time for you to go?"

Sid nodded. "Right you are. See you soon. And don't keep this gentleman waiting too long." Pete stepped to one side. Sid paused on the stoop and said just loudly enough for me to hear, "Be careful, she's a live one."

Pete nodded, eyeing me as though he were expecting me to make a sudden move.

Sid headed down the walk, looking back to flash me a grin. "See you in twenty-one days, and not a day more!" Then he was gone, leaving me alone with the cowboy.

A ball of nervousness slammed into my stomach. I let my auto-manners take over. "Um, I'm sorry, Pete. As you can see, I'm not quite ready. Care to come in and have a seat?"

Pete followed me inside, his boots clomping on the hardwood. With relief, I noticed that the night before, Sid had picked my clothes up off of the living room floor. Pete leaned gingerly against the back of the armchair.

Well, fine, I thought. *If he doesn't want to make himself comfortable, there's nothing I can do about it.* I trundled upstairs and tried to mentally calculate which outfit I could put on the fastest. Sid had draped my jeans and slinky silk blouse from the night before across the arm of the chair. I made the blouse decent by throwing a tweed blazer on over it. Not knowing what to expect from the day, I opted for comfort over style and slipped on a pair of casual loafers, then threw my hair into my go-to braid.

Thankfully, I'd showered the night before. A brief onceover with my toothbrush and I was reasonably presentable. I swallowed three of Dr. Nelson's little white pills and hoped they would kick in quickly. Sid and I were close enough that I never felt overwhelmed by his emotions, but God only knew how many new people I'd have to deal with over the course of the day—starting with Mr. Cowboy Congeniality. Grabbing my purse, I headed back down the stairs.

"Okay, ready," I said. "Sorry to keep you waiting."

Pete was sitting on the couch, fingering the pack of cards that Sid had brought over. I noticed for the first time that the deck was decorated with nude pin-up girls from the 1950s. I felt myself blushing again.

"No problem." It appeared that Pete had a limited vocabulary. He tossed the cards back onto the coffee table. As he did, I glimpsed a piece of folded-up, marbled blue stationery peeking out from between the cushions on my couch—a practice suicide note I'd missed while cleaning up the day before. Well, it wouldn't do to have anyone find *that* lying around. When Pete's back was turned, I pulled it out of the couch and slid it into the back pocket of my jeans.

He opened the front door for me. As usually happened when I tried to leave the house, my heart fluttered in an irregular beat, and I felt like an invisible hand was holding me back. This time, though, the weight of Pete's presence beside me and a strong desire not to humiliate myself proved to be sufficient motivation to propel me forward.

Pete's vehicle turned out to be a beat-up, white Ford pickup with actual steer horns mounted on top of the cab. We climbed in and he pulled away from the curb. My embarrassment over the fact that a perfect stranger had met my lover, seen me in my bathrobe, and discovered pictures of nude women on a deck of cards in my living room—all within the space of ten minutes—grew as we drove. I felt compelled to break the silence. "That was Sid. He's—"

"None of my business," Pete cut in, and his tone made it clear that he was truly uninterested in hearing another word about it.

Terrific, I thought. *Next, I'm going to find out that this guy is my new therapist or something.* "So," I asked, "what's your job at the program?"

"Whatever needs doing," he said, staring straight ahead.

That was promising. "Whatever needs doing" sounded more like operations or administration than anything clinical. I probably wouldn't be expected to confide in him.

The thought of having to confide in anyone reignited my irritation at having to attend the program in the first place. Since I didn't like being rousted out of bed early on a Sunday morning, Pete would just have to work through his apparent dislike of talking to me. I became determined to wring a conversation out of him. "You're not from here, are you?"

"Wyoming."

"Let me guess," I said, drawing on my memories of *Gunsmoke*. "Some kind of ranch?"

Pete nodded. "Cattle."

I made an effort to sound annoyingly sunny. "So what brought you to Baltimore?"

He sighed a long drawn-out sigh, and I could tell that he was hoping I would stop talking and let him drive in peace. "Ben asked me to come out and help him after we got out of the Corps."

"The *Marine* Corps?" I was so surprised that I didn't even have time to hide the shock in my voice. Ben and the cowboy? Elite soldiers?

"That's the one." The corners of Pete's mouth twitched upward.

I had no words. Ben was a Marine, *and* he had Ph.D. in psychology? As I tried to absorb that new information, Pete's voice cut through the cab of the truck like an icy wind. "So with the two of us around, you better not try any funny stuff. We'll take you down in a second."

A chill went down my back. Funny stuff? Take me down? Who *was* this nut job? I didn't know what I had gotten myself into, but whatever it was, I was getting right back out. "You stop and let me out of this truck right now!" Marine or no Marine, I wasn't giving in without a fight.

Pete glanced over at me, and for a moment, I thought he might kill me right there. Then he let out an enormous whooping laugh. "I gotcha. I gotcha with that one! 'We'll take you down.' Hah!"

I took a deep breath. "Very funny."

"Yeah, yeah, it was. You should have seen the look on your face." He imitated me in a high falsetto, "You stop this truck right now!" That started him laughing again.

I looked at him through narrowed eyes. "Very professional. I'm glad to see that I'm entering such a high-class treatment program."

"Treatment program? Oh yeah, right. Man, but you remind me of my little sister, Lydia. She'll believe anything, too." His face settled into a permanent grin. "And she's a pain in the butt."

Impressed as I was by the sudden torrent of personal information coming from previously taciturn Pete, I was completely uninterested in having any further conversation with him. Apparently my mood showed on my face because Pete looked over at me again and chuckled. "All right, sulk if you want to. I was just playin' with ya'."

I was *not* sulking. "I am not sulking."

He nodded. "Sure you're not."

Something about this Pete character was really getting under my skin. I glared at him. "If you really want to know, I want to get to the church and get started so I can get this so-called program over with as soon as possible and get back to work. Is that okay with you?"

He whistled appreciatively—at what, I wasn't sure. "Okay with me, ma'am, but it's not up to me." We had arrived at the church. Ben was standing on the sidewalk pointing at his watch. "You're going to have to talk to the boss about that." Pete pulled up to the curb, reached over me, and opened my door from the inside. "Have a nice day." He was grinning again.

"Thanks for the ride," I shot back as I climbed out of the truck. I could hear Pete chuckling as he drove away. I turned to face Ben with the intention of telling him exactly what I thought of his assistant, but he beat me to the punch.

"You're late again, and I know it's not Pete's fault."

Ben looked at me the same way my middle-school gym teacher had when he found out that I was ducking into the equipment shed every day instead of running laps. I could see the "military" in Ben; he seemed like he'd be very comfortable in the role of a drill instructor.

I decided to ignore his comment about my lateness. "You know, your assistant could use some training in how to deal with people."

"You'll get used to him." He folded his arms across his chest. "But that doesn't explain why you're late."

Good grief, he really *was* like a drill instructor. "My alarm didn't go off," I lied.

"You mean you either forgot to set it, or you hit 'snooze' one too many times. Don't let it happen again."

If Ben was expecting me to follow orders, I hoped he was accustomed to disappointment. "I can't make any promises," I said dryly.

His hardened expression eased into one of amusement. "Come on in," he said. Resigned to my fate for the moment, I fell in behind him as we walked toward the front doors of the church.

Chapter Six

The chapel was impressive with its vaulted ceilings, marble columns lining the aisle, old wooden pews, and an intricately carved altar on a raised platform. As we walked, I was surprised to see rows of candles burning along the walls.

"Is this church in use?" I asked.

"No, it isn't," he said, "but we use this space for some of our activities."

Another vague answer, I thought with a sigh. I followed Ben through an opening behind the altar and into a hallway with closed doors along both sides. We stepped through an archway into a lounge. Dark leather sofas and armchairs were arranged in a square, set off by coffee tables of different shapes and sizes. There were vending machines and a small table holding coffee and tea supplies.

A door led off the back of the lounge into Ben's office, where a high-backed chair loomed behind a large mahogany desk. Several photos hung on the walls featuring either classic cars or men wearing camouflage.

Ben gestured toward two leather club chairs in front of his desk, then sat in the taller chair behind it. I got the impression that the furniture had been carefully arranged to give Ben a superior position. "Welcome," he said with a tight-lipped smile. He folded his hands together on the desk and looked down at me. "I'm glad you're here and I know you have a lot of questions. Unfortunately, since you were late, we'll have to wait until after tai chi to begin orientation."

"Tai chi?" I asked with mild alarm.

"Yes. We do it every morning."

Ben and martial arts: that made sense. Whenever he moved,

Ben appeared simultaneously relaxed and ready for action. However, as someone who had always been at war with her own sense of coordination, I had no confidence at all in my ability to pick up a new physical skill—especially while wearing such an unyielding outfit. I looked down at my blazer and jeans.

"Don't worry, you'll be fine. I can loan you some gear." Ben fished around in a duffle bag next to the desk and handed me a pair of sweats. "Just laundered. You can change in the studio bathroom."

I followed behind Ben, unable to shake the unsettling feeling that I was about to have my sense of balance thrown off again. I hoped it wasn't going to be like that for the whole three weeks.

• • •

I examined myself in the bathroom mirror. Even after fixing my braid so that it was somewhat straight, I still had that "just rolled out of bed" look. Tired circles ringed my eyes, and the navy-blue sweats Ben had loaned me weren't livening up my pale complexion.

The other problem was that the sweats didn't fit. They stretched tightly across my chest and backside. Evidently what Sid referred to as my "bountiful figure" wasn't meant to be squeezed into men's sportswear. Also, the arms and legs were too long, so I'd had to roll up the wrists and ankles. To top it off, I didn't have suitable footwear, so I had to go barefoot. I shook my head at my reflection.

I stepped out of the bathroom into an exercise studio located in the church's basement. Multicolored Indian tapestries with elaborate geometric designs hung on the walls. There was no furniture in the room, and the floor was lined with large, gray gymnasium pads. Four new faces—two men and two women—had joined Ben in the small, windowless room. They, too, wore navy-blue sweats and all appeared to know one another. After a moment of brief panic at finding myself in a group of strangers, I noticed with relief that I wasn't getting slammed by anyone's feelings. *None of them must be in emotional distress*, I concluded.

Ben waved me over to a back corner of the room. He switched

on a stereo that began to play ambient music. The others spaced themselves out and stood up straight, facing the front of the room with their hands at their sides. Ben said, "Watch me and do your best to follow along. I'll come help if you're getting into trouble."

I leaned toward him and whispered, "Are these the other clients?"

Ben gave me a brief look of surprise. "No, we're all staff members. You're the only participant in our program right now."

The only participant? I'd never heard of a treatment program that could survive on one client. While I tried to figure out what that might mean, I did my best to blend in. I stood up straight and faced the front of the room with the others. Ben went to the front and assumed the same position, standing with his back to the room. Then all at once, the group started to move in unison, slowly and gracefully, as though performing a carefully choreographed dance.

I did my best to follow along, managing a poor imitation of the others' movements. After several minutes, though, my self-consciousness got the better of me. I gave up and slumped against the back wall.

Ben gestured to the others to continue as he came to the back of the room. "Don't stop now," he murmured. "You're doing great. Come on." Reluctantly, I followed him out onto the floor and held my arms up like the others were doing.

"Try dropping your shoulders," he whispered.

"What do you mean?"

He positioned himself behind me and rested his hands on my shoulder blades, pressing gently downwards. As I allowed my shoulders to fall, a layer of tension I hadn't known was there melted away.

"That's it." Ben reached out and supported my hands lightly with his. "Form is the most important thing. Relax for a minute and let me guide you. We'll focus on the arms for now."

I let my arms go limp. Ben stepped in closer. My breath quickened. Was I that out of shape?

Ben noticed as well. "There's no need to be nervous. Just try to breathe normally."

Where Ben's hands touched mine, my skin tingled. Like a water faucet being turned on, a tickling warmth began to flow down my arms. *What is this?* I wondered. *Some sort of tai chi thing?*

As he guided my movements, his breath fell on the back of my neck and I shivered. The warmth from my arms spilled into my chest, and a heavy heat began to move through my body like a lava flow. Lulled by the sensation, my eyes closed and my head tipped backwards…

"Cate?" Ben asked. "Are you all right?"

"Oh! God." I whirled around, snapping myself away from him.

Ben took a quick step back. "What is it?"

"Nothing." I looked everywhere but into his eyes. "I just—give me a second." I rushed into the bathroom and shut the door behind me. Leaning against the sink, I tried to catch my breath.

I looked at my flushed face in the mirror as I tried to process what had just happened. The tingling feeling, that heavy heat… It had taken a second for me to identify them, but I knew without a doubt what those sensations meant. The only other time I felt that way was when I was with Sid.

I leaned my cheek against the cool wall. "Not good," I said into the mirror. I turned on the sink and splashed icy water on my face, then let it run over my hands until they ached with cold.

As I hurriedly tore off Ben's sweats and put on my own clothes, I tried to tell myself that I had misinterpreted my body's signals. I was just anxious about being in a new place and a strange situation. That was all there was to it. I wasn't very convincing, however.

I heard a soft knock on the door, followed by Ben's voice. "Is everything okay?"

"Yes, fine." I did my best to sound normal. "I'll be out in a sec."

I could sense him waiting on the other side of the door. I would have to pull myself together before I went out there. Closing my eyes, I visualized myself as a futuristic spacecraft putting up maximum shields. I concentrated until I could imagine an impenetrable barrier around myself. Once I felt ready, I grabbed Ben's sweats and opened the door.

There was mild surprise on his face when he saw that I had changed clothes. The tai chi session had ended, and the others were stretching and drinking bottles of water. "Everyone," Ben said to the group, "when you get yourselves together, let's meet in the lounge so we can do introductions."

Ben gestured for me to follow him. "I know this is more people than you're used to being around lately," he said as we climbed the stairs. "Just tell me if you start to feel uncomfortable."

With his back to me, I rolled my eyes. *Now* he had to start being nice to me.

In the lounge, a generous spread of fruit, bread, and cheeses had been laid out on a coffee table, and I could smell hot tea brewing. I sat in an armchair in the corner. I felt more secure with my back to the wall, where nothing and no one could take me by surprise. After taking back the sweats he had loaned me, Ben sat on the end of the sofa nearest to me and gave me a searching look. "What happened back there?"

There was no way in *hell* I was going to tell him what happened back there. I racked my brain for a cover story. "I don't know," I lied. "I felt lightheaded all of a sudden."

I immediately felt guilty as concern shot through his expression. "How are you feeling now? Have you eaten yet today?"

"No, actually I haven't." As though on cue, my stomach growled.

Ben hopped up and walked over to the food. "That's not good, Cate. What can I get you? Do you want some pineapple? Banana bread?"

I knew I was going straight to hell, but my alibi was too good. I had to keep playing along. "Whatever you think," I said in a theatrically weakened voice, "and maybe some tea."

"You got it." Before I knew what had happened, I had a plate heavy with food in one hand and a mug of hot tea in the other. "Milk? Sugar?"

"Oh no, I'm fine," I said, smiling up at him. "This is great, thank you. I'm sure I'll be back to normal in no time."

"Good." He sat down again and raked his fingers through his

hair. "I'm sorry. I didn't realize Pete rushed you over here before you had breakfast."

"Oh no, he didn't rush me." I already felt bad enough for lying; I couldn't cause a rift between them as well. "I rushed myself. He was perfectly patient."

Ben nodded. "Be sure to eat before you come in from now on. We usually don't serve anything here until lunchtime, and I don't want you passing out on me."

"Okay, got it."

He gave me a curious look. "Your eyes changed color, by the way."

I squeezed them shut. "What?"

"Down in the basement," he observed casually, as though he weren't uncovering one of my most embarrassing secrets. "They were green before, but when you came out of the bathroom, they were dark grey. Do you wear contacts?"

Sid had observed on more than one occasion that my eyes turned from green to grey when I was…in a certain state. I swallowed hard. "No, no contacts. They just do that sometimes."

Ben nodded. He looked like he was about to say something else. Fortunately, the others began to arrive. I had been so self-conscious in the tai chi room that I hadn't even taken a good look at them.

One of the women appeared to be of East Asian ancestry. She was a few inches shorter than I was with a solid athletic build and multiple facial piercings. Her black hair was worn in gravity-defying spikes tipped with purple. The other woman in the group looked as though she had stepped out of a Bollywood film. Doe-like brown eyes dominated her pretty, refined features. She had a perfect hourglass figure and a wall of shining hair, and her makeup was miraculously still in place after the exercise session.

Of the two men, one was a young-looking black man about Ben's height and of slight build. His head was shaved and he wore silver wire-framed glasses. The other man was taller and thin and wore his dark, shoulder-length hair in expertly cut layers. When I caught a glimpse of his face, I saw that he had the oversized, striking features of an androgynous fashion model. He was also wearing more makeup than Miss Bollywood.

As everyone filtered into the room, the spread of food was met with murmurs of approval. They filled their plates and settled into various seats, talking easily and teasing one another. I made out a clipped English accent coming from Miss Bollywood. The group's energy was bright, warm, and inviting. However, I reminded myself that they were the "staff" and I was the "client." I felt a longing to be back in my office sharing a morning coffee with Simone, looking over our schedules and going through our cases for the day.

Ben clapped a few times to get everyone's attention. "Good morning, everybody. As you all know, Cate is starting with us today. I want to begin with introductions. Since most of you are chewing, I'll do the talking."

He turned to me. "All of the staff members have been here for somewhere between two and four years. With the exception of Pete and me, they all work here part-time while engaging in other pursuits. And all of them—again, with the exception of Pete and me—have special abilities like yours, but we'll go into those later. For now, I'll give you the rundown on what everyone's role will be in your program."

Ben stepped behind the Bollywood star and put his hands on her shoulders. "This is Vani." Vani flashed me a glamorous smile and waved a hand holding an apple slice. "She works in advertising, but her real passion is history. She is also sort of our resident diagnostician. Is that a fair title, Vani?"

She nodded but remained silent, her mouth full of apple. Ben continued. "She will be involved in your orientation and will help us to learn more about your abilities."

I smiled and nodded at Vani, wondering what someone in advertising could have in the area of diagnostic skills. *Keep an open mind*, I admonished myself. *You'd better, if you're going to be here for three weeks.*

Ben walked over to the guy with the glasses and rubbed his bald head. As the young man good-naturedly smacked Ben's hand away, I recognized in him the familiar physical awkwardness of someone who lived mainly inside of his own thoughts, and felt an instant kinship.

"This is Asa," Ben said. "He's working on a graduate degree in computer science in his free time. He'll be teaching you Reiki. It's a Japanese healing technique geared toward relaxation and stress reduction, among other things."

"I'm trying to get everybody to call me Ace," Asa said, clipping his name down to its first syllable, "but it's not catching on yet." He gave a self-deprecating smile. "Welcome to the asylum!"

"Thanks!" I smiled back, appreciating that he made me feel less like a client and more like a colleague. I'd heard of Reiki before, but I didn't know much about it. However, I could use some stress reduction; it couldn't hurt to try.

Ben pointed across the room to the girl with the spiky hair. "Eve is our acupuncturist. She tries to keep us all running in peak condition." I examined her facial piercings, counting at least five rings in her eyebrows and one each in her nose and lower lip. It made sense to me that she would be comfortable with needles.

"Eve is also the baby of the group," Ben said, "a mere college senior!"

Eve stuck her tongue out at him. That, too, was pierced. Then she smiled at me and all of her piercings seemed to rearrange themselves. "Welcome!"

"Thanks!" I tried to conceal a sudden pang of anxiety. A college senior was going to be sticking needles into me? How much experience could she have?

Finally, Ben sat down next to the tall man with the expertly applied makeup. "This is Kai." Kai gave me a graceful fingers-only wave. "He is our resident artisan and expert in ancient religions and rituals. He will be teaching you some techniques to help you access and channel your abilities."

"Kai is a name in many languages, but in my case it's Greek," he said in answer to my unspoken question. He had a honeyed tenor voice with a Southern lilt. Kai's eyebrows had been shaped into high, thin arches, and an elaborate palette of purple eye shadows set off his light green eyes. "And Cate, if you have any questions or problems, or if Ben here is giving you a hard time," he said while poking Ben in the ribs, "you come tell me and I will be more than happy to help."

The sound of Pete's boots resonated as he entered the back of the room. Everyone called out greetings to Pete, their affection for the cowboy evident. Apparently I was the only one whom he rubbed the wrong way.

"Cate, you already know Pete," Ben said as he stood up and offered Pete his seat.

Pete sat down and gave Kai a discreet kiss on the cheek. Then he tipped his apparently ever-present ten-gallon hat at me. "Ma'am."

Kai and Pete? Although I hadn't seen that one coming, I managed to keep my expression neutral. I was already positively disposed toward Kai; after all, he'd offered to help me deal with Ben. The fact that he was with Pete made the cowboy seem a little more tolerable. I managed a half-smile. "Hello again."

"Pete's second in command here at the clinic, and he's in charge of security," Ben explained. Then he turned to the group. "You will all have an opportunity to get to know Cate better over the next few days, and Cate, of course, will get to know you. For now, let's get back to work. Cate and Vani, in my office."

The group slowly broke up and moved out of the lounge, carrying plates of food with them and calling out, "See ya', Cate" and "Nice to meet you." At least the rest of the staff seemed friendly enough. With their support, I could probably handle the Marines.

CHAPTER SEVEN

As Vani and I settled into the chairs in front of Ben's desk, he pulled a computer tablet and stylus out of a briefcase. Vani closed her eyes.

"This meeting is a sort of second diagnostic session," Ben explained. The casual warmth he had displayed in the lounge gave way to a more businesslike demeanor. "Vani is what we call an aura reader, which is to say that she can see and read the energy fields around people and objects."

An aura reader? Was he serious? "I'm sorry, I thought we were going to be doing orientation next."

"This is part of orientation," Ben replied.

"Oh, I see." I forced a smile. "Go ahead."

"Vani will be doing some research into your special abilities to let us know more precisely what they are and whether there might be any problems we need to know about."

As he spoke, I had to bite my lip to keep from smirking.

"Cate," Ben murmured, "you could at least *pretend* that you're trying to keep an open mind."

With her eyes still closed, Vani frowned. I didn't want to insult her, but aura reading was a bit more "woo-woo" than I had bargained for. "I'm sorry, I'm trying, but—and please don't take this personally, Vani—I don't believe in all of that New Age stuff, like auras and whatnot."

Vani's eyes flipped open. "Well, I can't speak to the 'whatnot,' but is there anything I can tell you about aura reading that might put you more at ease?"

Absolutely not, I thought immediately, but I didn't want to snub her. "Okay, sure. How exactly does it work?"

"It's different for each aura reader, but I can tell you about my process," she said. "I close my eyes and look at the subject using my spiritual sight. That enables me to see the subject's aura, which appears mainly in the form of colors and images."

"Colors and images?" Vani seemed so sincere that I began to feel guilty for pretending to be interested.

"That's right. Naturally, the difficult part is interpreting what you're seeing. To perfect that skill, I studied with a spiritual teacher in Gujarat, as well as at the School of Advanced Psychic Studies in London." She cocked her head to the side, as though inquiring whether those qualifications were good enough for me.

"I see. Very interesting." I was at a loss as to how else I could possibly respond.

"Okay then," Ben said, "are we ready to get started?"

Vani closed her eyes again and appeared to concentrate.

I figured I might as well play along. If nothing else, it might be amusing. "What do I have to do?"

"Not a thing," Ben said. "Vani and I will talk. She'll tell me what she sees and answer any questions that I ask her."

I nodded. "And this is going to tell us what exactly?"

Vani said in a perfectly smooth voice, "That you got laid last night, for one thing."

What the *hell?* I stared at her, slack-jawed.

Vani was the picture of calm with her eyes still closed and her hands pressed together in front of her heart. "Several times actually," she added.

She was guessing; she *must* have been guessing. And she was trying to embarrass me—probably to get back at me for not believing in her mumbo-jumbo. Well, it had worked. I felt my face flush with heat.

"Vani," Ben warned, "remember that conversation we had? The one about using more discretion when sharing information about people's auras? Nothing too personal, nothing that might not be relevant to the issue at hand?"

"Oh right. Sorry, Boss," Vani chirped. I glared at her.

"Let's stick to answering my questions for a while," Ben suggested. "All right if we continue, Cate?"

I nodded, wondering what she would come up with next.

"Vani," he said, "tell me what you see in terms of Cate's special abilities."

Vani's eyes fluttered beneath her eyelids. "She's an emotional empath, and a strong one. She's from the Caledonian tribe."

What kind of diagnosis was *that*? "I'm sorry, what's an emotional empath?"

Vani opened her eyes again. "Most people are able to imagine how others are feeling to a greater or lesser extent—what we refer to as empathy. But an emotional empath doesn't have to imagine, because they're able to have a direct emotional experience of what it's like to be the other person."

The filaments. Empathic submergence. Is that what she was talking about? "What about that other thing, the tribe?"

"Caledonian," Ben said. "We'll discuss that after lunch. For now, let's let Vani do her reading."

Bewildered, I didn't know what else to do but nod.

Vani closed her eyes and resumed. "She primarily experiences her emotions somatically, as physical sensations in her body."

Ben took notes on his tablet as she continued. "And there are some psychic connections there, too."

Psychic connections? I immediately thought of those psychic hotline scams that advertised on late-night television and cheated vulnerable people out of their money.

Vani continued, "Oh, and she can do it on demand—think of someone and connect with them immediately, even over long distances. Like tuning into a radio frequency."

I remembered my conversation with Dr. MacGregor about the filaments that connected me to my clients. I figured Dr. MacGregor must have told her to say that.

"Interesting," Ben said. "Where do you see blockages?"

"There aren't any that I can see."

"Really?" Ben looked surprised as he turned to me. "Usually

someone with special abilities who hasn't had any training has a lot of energetic blockages to work through." He turned back to Vani. "How do you account for that?"

She appeared to be concentrating hard. "She's been using a catalyst."

"Ah, okay," Ben said as though something he'd suspected had been confirmed.

I coughed to suppress a snort of laughter. "What's a catalyst—I mean, in your definition?"

Vani answered matter-of-factly, "It's a quick fix for dealing with excess negative energy. Kind of like using cocaine to lose weight instead of diet and exercise."

In response to my dubious expression, Ben elaborated. "Empaths are like sponges, absorbing emotions from those around them. If you don't find ways to discharge the negative emotions, they can accumulate to toxic levels. Prior to training, most empaths do this by using a catalyst. Different types of catalysts work for different empaths, depending upon the individual's physical and energetic makeup, but the most common ones are drugs, alcohol, and bingeing on heavy foods. Do any of those sound familiar?"

Apparently, Ben's ramrod-straight eyebrows had hinges. When he raised them both at the same time, they formed an "M," giving him the appearance of an interrogator.

"Well, I don't use drugs, and I only drink one or two ciders once in a blue moon," I said in my defense. "And yes, I do like to eat, but not any more than most people." My attention was drawn uncomfortably to the fact that my body was more jiggly than taut.

"Interesting. Vani, can you dig a little deeper and tell us what she's been using as a catalyst?"

She wrinkled her nose. "You really want to know?"

"Of course," Ben said.

"It's *personal,*" she said, her voice lightly dusted with sarcasm. "Are you sure?"

I rolled my eyes. "Yes!" Ben and I said in unison.

"All right. She's using her boyfriend."

Ah-hah! At last, the charlatan would be unmasked. "I don't *have* a boyfriend," I declared.

Vani frowned. "Oh, I'm sorry, that's right. He's just a hookup."

My jaw dropped like a hinge had snapped.

"A what?" Ben asked, trying—and failing—not to sound surprised.

"A friend she sleeps with, to be more precise," Vani said. "A big, dishy Persian chap. Mesopotamian tribe. Looks like he can handle quite a bit of toxic emotion. A very effective catalyst, I'd guess."

"I see," Ben said. I didn't have to understand everything that was happening to know that Ben *did* see—the one thing that for some reason I'd not wanted him to see.

I covered my face with my hands as I searched my mind for some rational explanation as to how Vani could have known about Sid. Surely the MacGregors couldn't have been spying on me; that would be crazy. And there hadn't been any opportunities since my arrival for Vani to talk to Pete about Sid. Even if they had somehow managed to have a conversation, he could have told her that Sid was big and "dishy"—but Persian? There was no way Pete could have possibly deduced such a specific detail from his brief interaction with Sid that morning. Panic clutched at my chest as I struggled to hold my mind back from reaching the only possible non-paranoid conclusion that fit the evidence: aura reading was real, after all.

I could feel Ben's gaze boring through my hands, willing me to remove them from my face. But there was no way that was going to happen. I knew that I had likely turned bright red by that point. I silently begged the universe to let me disappear.

Ben apparently took pity on me. "Thank you, Vani. That will be all for now."

Vani must have felt some sympathy for me as well once she saw the state I was in because she patted me on the shoulder as she walked past. "See you later," she said lightly. I heard the door click shut behind her.

I remained perfectly still. I saw absolutely no reason to ever move again, in fact. I thought it would be fine to sit right there, hands over my face, for the rest of my born days. I nursed a tiny hope that if I didn't move, Ben might eventually leave, allowing me to slip out the door unnoticed.

No such luck. I heard him walk around the desk, pull the chair Vani had vacated closer to mine and sit down. His presence thrummed directly in front of me. "Cate?"

I thought about lying outright and saying that I didn't have a "friend I slept with" and had never met anyone from Persia. However, years of ending up naked during card games while Sid remained fully clothed had taught me that I had absolutely no poker face. Given that, and the fact that Ben wasn't an idiot, I suspected that any attempt at denial would only cause me further embarrassment. "Please leave me alone," I said, my voice muffled by my palms.

"Look, I know that must have been more information than you wanted shared," Ben said carefully, "but it's all important to your progress."

Important to my progress? That sounded suspiciously like bullshit. I dropped my hands from my face. "How exactly is getting some rude, passive-aggressive aura reader to drag my private life out into the open important to my progress?"

Ben was calm but insistent. "It's important because we have to know where your problem areas are before we can help you. A toxic build-up of negative emotions can be dangerous, even deadly," he explained. "Since you're sitting here talking to me right now, whatever you've been doing has obviously been working. If you're looking for someone to pass judgment on you, you're going to have to look elsewhere."

Even when he was trying to be helpful, condescension apparently came effortlessly to Ben. "His name is Sid," I snapped, "and he's a normal flesh-and-blood person, not some sort of New Age release valve!"

"Catalyst."

"Whatever."

"I'm sure he *is* a perfectly normal person. Most human catalysts are. But they also happen to have a unique energetic composition that enables them to collect and disperse negative energy without absorbing any of it themselves. It makes them ideal tools for empaths."

"Well, I am not using him as…as that! You know nothing about Sid and practically nothing about me, so I would appreciate it if you would refrain from speculating about the nature of my personal relationships."

Even as I objected, though, I wondered if there might be some truth in what Ben was saying. My compulsive need to see Sid, the physical pain I went through when I was with him…could those things be related to this catalyst business?

"My apologies." Ben brushed some imaginary dust from his sleeve. "Of course, none of this relates to you. Nothing about you is out of the ordinary, right?"

I clenched my fists so hard that my nails dug into my palms. "Look, I know I'm a freak, okay? And I know that I need help—which in case you haven't noticed isn't easy for me to admit. I'm usually the one doing the helping. But here I am, admitting it, and all you have to offer me is tai chi, acupuncture, and aura reading—courtesy of a couple of college students, a Bollywood star, and a Greek supermodel?" I threw my hands up. "Is this really your entire program?"

As Ben's eyebrows rose, I felt a pang of guilt. I shouldn't have been so flippant in my descriptions of the staff. After all, with the exception of Vani, they had been nothing but kind to me so far. "I'm sorry, I shouldn't have…" I stammered. "I didn't mean…"

"No need to apologize," Ben insisted. "Your skepticism is understandable, although I'm certain it will subside over the next couple of days. In the meantime, though, please don't censor yourself with me. I want to know how you really feel about things."

I met his gaze, which transmitted sincerity. Since I also preferred openness and honesty, that was reassuring. Then my attention was caught by flecks of gold shimmering in the light brown irises of Ben's eyes. When I realized that I was staring, I forced myself to look down at the desk.

Ben noisily cleared his throat. "As to your question, my plan was to spend the rest of the time before lunch going over some aspects of the program that may be of greater interest you."

Finally! "Yes, please," I said with a little too much zeal.

He dropped his chin, and I could tell he was trying to suppress a smile. "Well, for starters, in addition to teaching you how to protect yourself from the potentially harmful aspects of your gifts, we'll also teach you how to use them more effectively for enhanced healing."

"Oh." I hadn't been expecting that. My curiosity was slightly piqued.

"From what Dr. Nelson told us, it sounds like you're a natural healer. He says you're an excellent therapist with good instincts, and that you facilitate rapid recovery in your clients. But there's a tool called empath healing that can help you work with better efficiency and focus. We can teach you how to use that tool, while at the same time protecting yourself from becoming emotionally overwhelmed."

"That would be nice." The dark cloud over my head lifted slightly. If the MacGregors could help me become a more effective therapist, the program might not turn out to be a *total* waste of time.

"Second, if you consent, we'd like to include you in an ongoing research project we're running. My mother is trying to uncover scientifically sound explanations for special abilities like yours, explanations that fit within the paradigm of Western science and medicine. She's also seeking to shed some light on their nature and origins."

"That sounds interesting," I said with guarded enthusiasm. It would be nice if someone could finally make sense out of how the filaments worked, not to mention how I could enter someone else's mind. If there were genuine scientific explanations, I might start to feel like less of a misfit. "I'll think about it."

"Good." Ben stood up and clapped his hands together. "It's time for lunch. Oh, and just so you know, there are no secrets here. So while we *do* rely on self-enforcement, if you choose to break the program rules—to use your catalyst, for example—Vani will see it in your aura, and she'll pass that information along to me."

The bastard. I willed the earth to open up and swallow me whole.

Chapter Eight

Ben went off to check on lunch, but I couldn't wait. After *that* morning, I needed chocolate.

Vani caught up with me in the lounge where I was fighting to get a candy bar out of the vending machine. I had paid for it, but it was hanging on the ledge, taunting me by refusing to fall into the bin.

"Hey, sorry about earlier," she said.

I sincerely doubted it. "Whatever."

"Look, I've been dealing with skeptics my whole life, people calling me a fake and a fraud," she said, flipping her shining mane of hair from left to right. "When I actually get an opportunity to show one up, it's hard to resist."

While I could understand that impulse to a degree, she couldn't undo what had been done. "I see." I kicked the vending machine. The candy bar didn't budge.

"But I should have been more judicious. I mean, I wouldn't have said that about you getting laid last night if I'd known you were hot for Ben."

I spun around to face her. "What?"

"Yeah, I'm sorry. I didn't see that part of your aura until I was getting ready to leave the office."

I determined that I was going to be very careful how much time I spent around Vani. "I am *not* hot for Ben."

"Then I guess I misread something." She shrugged. "It's just as well, anyway. Ben's married to his work."

"Oh," I said, trying to sound disinterested.

With the uncommon combination of strength and grace I

normally associated with ballet dancers, Vani banged her hand on a spot on the side of the vending machine. My candy bar fell. "Yeah," she said, retrieving it from the machine and handing it to me. "I think he's gone on three dates in the four years I've known him."

I suspected that by letting me know that Ben was single, Vani thought she was doing me some kind of favor. "Thanks." I took the candy bar and considered accepting her olive branch.

"My pleasure." Vani waved over her shoulder as she walked away.

Single or not, Ben had shown no signs that he thought of me as anything more than a client. And even if he *did* like me, he would probably never act on it. Since he wasn't my treating clinician, there wouldn't be any doctor/patient ethical issues with us getting together. But the program probably still had rules against that kind of thing. Plus, Ben struck me as the type who liked to maintain professional boundaries—which was just fine with me. My aberrant physical reaction to him notwithstanding, I wasn't interested, either. And even if I had been, there was a reason I'd given up on romance. For me, it always ended in disaster.

I fished my candy bar out of the bin, tore off the wrapper, and bit into the chocolate with undue violence.

• • •

Lunch was sushi, catered for the whole staff. I concluded that the MacGregors must be independently wealthy if they could afford to feed everyone while treating only one client at a time. I had been looking forward to hanging out with the staff and getting to know them better, but as soon as they had their plates of sushi, they all scattered, saying they had work to do.

Ben was the only one who didn't take any sushi. I began to wonder when he ate. He had changed back into business attire and was wearing charcoal-grey suit pants, shiny black leather shoes and a light-blue dress shirt, once again with the collar open and no tie. Ben appeared to not be a fan of ties.

He pointed to the empty chair next to me. "Mind if I join you?"

My mouth was full of tuna roll, so I nodded.

"I just wanted to fill you in on the program structure." With a broad smile, he announced, "The first week, we call Hell Week."

I tensed at visions of mandatory push-ups. "Is that some kind of Marine Corps thing?"

"Pete told you about that?"

"Yes—Pete, and all of the military photos in your office."

"Oh, yeah. I guess that's a give-away, all right. Well, no, it's not a Marine Corps thing. I borrowed 'Hell Week' from the Navy Seals," he said, appearing pleased with himself. "It'll go like this. We'll spend this week doing various exercises to open you up more to your abilities. The last two weeks will be an internship. We'll have you treating clients—with other staff members, of course, and under their supervision—to give you some hands-on training."

That was intriguing. "A real internship?"

"Yes. We find that people learn best by practicing their skills. All right with you?"

I nodded. Doing an internship sounded a lot better than being in a treatment program. I wondered if I could put it on my resume—and how exactly I would describe it if I did.

"During your last few days, we'll be closing you up, teaching you how to protect yourself from negative emotions and other sources of energy that could be harmful to you. That way, you'll be in complete control of your gifts."

"That sounds good." I started to feel tentatively optimistic.

"Right. That's why it is so important for you commit to staying until the end. If we open you up and you leave before we close you up again, you'll be more vulnerable and unprotected than you have ever been." He tapped his finger on the desk to drive this point home. "Also, next week, Kai will teach you how to release any pent-up negative emotions without using a catalyst."

I winced. "Do we really have to talk about that right now?"

"No," he said, sounding as relieved as I felt. "But Kai will meet with you after lunch, if that's all right. He needs to get some background information."

"Fine." As much as I really did not want to talk to anyone about catalysts, at least Kai had seemed friendly enough when we were introduced. Anything was better than discussing the subject with Ben.

• • •

With only fifteen minutes of the lunch hour spent, I'd finished my sushi. Ben said that he had something to take care of and asked me to wait for Kai in the lounge. He gave me an issue of *Scientific American* that had an article on acupuncture—"so you don't get bored," he said.

After about four paragraphs, the article began to delve into neurochemistry and I realized that I was in way over my head. I decided to take myself on a tour of the church. As I walked down the hallway, I noticed that the door to the parking lot was ajar. Seeing movement outside, I stepped out to investigate.

It was a glorious October day—bright and cool with the few nearby trees at the height of their colors. I breathed in the crisp air and looked down to find Ben in the parking lot. He was removing the canvas cover from the car I had guessed was a convertible. I stood at the top of the stairs and watched.

Ben had removed his suit jacket and draped it across the hood of the Land Rover, and his sleeves were rolled up to the elbows. He seemed to be treating Operation Canvas Removal with surgical precision, moving with the confidence of someone who had performed this task many times before. Sunlight glinted off of a bright, reflective surface. Ben's dress shirt tightened across his back and shoulders as he bent down and to the side, tugging at the canvas and carefully folding it as he went.

Suddenly, my mouth went dry. I coughed, drawing Ben's attention.

"Cate, what are you doing out here?"

I shrugged and tried to appear nonchalant, instead of like someone who just got caught gawking. "Just exploring. The acupuncture article was a bit above my level."

"Oh, okay." Ben straightened up and stretched, arching his back. I forced myself to look at some random point in the distance. "Don't worry, Eve will explain it to you later. Can I get you something else to read?"

But I couldn't work up any enthusiasm whatsoever for reading esoteric academic articles. "I'd rather see what's under there," I admitted, pointing at the canvas.

"Really?" Ben held a hand up to shield his eyes from the sun. "All right, come on down."

Ben had already removed the canvas from the front of the car, revealing dark green paint and a sparkling pair of old-fashioned headlights wreathed in chrome. I joined him, impressed by the auto's apparently mint condition. "What is it?"

Ben rested his fingertips on the hood. "A 1936 Jaguar SS 100. Do you like classic cars?"

Memories tugged at my heart like lead weights on a fishing line. "My mother did. We used to go to car shows in the summer." My grandfather had been a mechanic. I didn't remember him very well, but Mom always said that being around the kinds of cars he used to work on made her feel closer to him. I looked down at the Jaguar and thought about how much Mom had loved convertibles. The weight on my heart lifted slightly.

As though he'd heard my thoughts, Ben said, "These old cars hold memories for a lot of people." He pulled a cloth out of his pocket and wiped an invisible smudge off of the hood. "Hey, would you mind helping me take the cover off? It's quicker with two people."

I had been longing to touch the Jaguar, but knew better than to do so without being invited. "Sure, of course."

"Okay, so just start at the bottom..." Ben showed me how to unfasten the canvas cover and fold it back bit by bit. I felt relieved to be having a normal conversation with him, and to be engaged for a few moments in something totally unrelated to either my problems or his clinic.

As we worked our way from front to back, the two-seater revealed itself to be a masterpiece of restoration. The sweeping curves, the gleaming wire wheels…simply stunning. When we finished, Ben put the folded canvas in the back of the Land Rover. "I normally keep the Jag in the garage at home when it rains," he explained, "but that storm the other day caught me by surprise."

I didn't even try to hide my admiration. Ben beamed. "Would you like to sit inside?"

I must not have heard him correctly. "What?"

"Sit. In the car." He pointed at the right-hand seat where the steering wheel was located, British-style. "Driver's side, of course."

"Really?" As many car shows as I'd been to, no one had ever offered to let me get inside.

"Really." He walked around and opened the door for me. "Go ahead."

"Okay." Tentatively, I slid onto the seat. Ben shut the door behind me, then walked around and got into the passenger seat. All at once, I recognized the combination of scents that I'd noticed the first time I'd met Ben: old leather, cotton, and wool. Now the leather part made sense.

Ben seemed to be enjoying my reactions. I let myself relax a little. My hand hovered tentatively over the steering wheel. "May I…?"

"Of course."

I rested one hand on the wheel and ran the other along the side of my seat, which was tan and as soft as butter. I practically moaned, "My god, this *leather*…"

"Yeah, that took some work."

"What do you mean?"

Ben stroked the dashboard. "When I found this car, she was on blocks in a barn outside of Lancaster, covered with nothing but a tarp and a bunch of hay bales." He shook his head. "The body was in bad shape, but the chrome was savable."

My eyes widened. "You mean *you* restored it?"

He nodded. "Not by myself, of course. I put the word out online that I needed parts, and about fifty Marines sourced them for me from around the globe." He pointed to the speedometer. "That's from Melbourne. The wheels came from four different countries."

As Ben continued giving me the inventory of various car parts and their origins, his whole demeanor changed. His expression brightened and he relaxed, managerial stiffness giving way to boyish enthusiasm. I felt my own spirits lifting as I got caught up in his animated description of the invisible web of people who had worked to save the neglected Jaguar.

As he spoke, Ben rested his hand next to mine on the steering wheel, close enough that I could feel the heat of his skin. I inhaled deeply as the whispering warmth of attraction was once again ignited, tickling my hand and flowing up my arm… I cursed inwardly. So it hadn't been a tai chi anomaly after all. *It's okay*, I reassured myself, *you can handle this. Just back away slowly.* I slid my hand off of the steering wheel and sank back into my seat.

Fortunately, Ben didn't seem to notice my altered state. "This steering wheel came from Staffordshire in England," he said. "I guess you could say this car's a world traveler. I also have a buddy in Hampden who's a mechanic. He helped me with the work under the hood."

"How long did it take you?"

"A few years. She's still a work in progress."

A labor of love, then. I imagined Ben's hands massaging leather conditioner into the seats…then dug my fingernails into my palms and forced myself to focus. "It's gorgeous. A real work of art."

He gave a modest shrug. "It keeps me busy."

Ben seemed so at home in business suits; I never would have guessed that his hobby involved spending hours in a garage. I wondered if he would ever stop surprising me. "Where did you learn how to restore cars? In the Marines?"

Ben's jaw clenched. I sensed that I'd somehow stepped on a landmine. Within seconds, though, he reined in his reaction. "My father taught me the basics, but I learned the rest in the Corps."

I bit my lip, unsure where to go next. I decided that a compliment couldn't hurt. "Your dad must be really impressed by this beauty."

I was wrong about the compliment. Any hint of expression disappeared from Ben's face, leaving behind an inscrutable mask. "He died before I got this car."

"Oh." Grief tugged at me again—this time for *his* loss. "I'm so sorry, Ben."

"Don't be." His voice was as cool and hard as a pebble. "Don't trouble yourself."

I gasped softly as a small shard of his pain escaped the tight control Ben had over his emotions. It flew out of him and into me, bitter and rough with anger. My instinct was to reach out to him, but it was clear that he didn't want to talk about it.

As I sat there mentally searching for what to say next, a shout from behind made us both jump. "So *that's* where you are! What are you two doing out there?" Kai demanded from the top of the landing. He stood, hands on hips, wearing skinny jeans, a poppy-red tunic with kimono sleeves, and matching red platform heels. "Counting leaves? I thought Cate and I had a meeting!"

Kai's voice shook Ben out of his dark mood. He arched an amused eyebrow at me. Caught off-guard by his sudden show of levity, I pressed my lips together to keep from laughing. Ben turned toward the church and shouted, "We're coming!"

"Well, okay then!" Kai replied. I heard his high heels *clip-clip* off into the distance.

"We'd better go," Ben murmured. "You don't want to get in trouble with him, believe me. Wait there."

My reluctance to get out of the car must have been obvious as Ben stepped around and opened my door. "I'll take you for a ride sometime if you like."

"That would be great," I said, although I was sure he was just being polite. As he followed me back to the church, I wondered what had happened with Ben's father that had caused him so much anguish. It troubled me to think that I would never find out, that there was no way for me to help. *Once a therapist, always a therapist,* I thought with chagrin. *Just remember, you're the client now.*

• • •

Ben led me down the hallway to a small meeting room with a dark wood conference table and two chairs. On the table, Kai was arranging an assortment of rough-hewn crystals of various colors on a black velvet cloth.

As I walked in, Kai immediately embraced me. "Have a seat, you poor baby. Vani told me everything." He made a shooing hand motion at Ben. "Go away, leave us alone. We have things to talk about. And close the door on your way out."

Ben ignored my look of dismay and obeyed Kai's orders. "Bring her back to my office when you're done."

"Go! Shoo!" Kai said.

"Don't worry, Cate, you're in good hands," Ben reassured. "See you later."

"The best hands," Kai corrected. He sat down and gestured for me to do the same. "Here, hold this." Kai placed a cloudy white crystal in my palm, then closed my fingers around it and rested the back of my hand on the table.

I watched, mystified, as he closely examined the rest of the crystals. "What are those for?"

"Hmm? Oh." Kai looked up. "Well, you've had to use a catalyst, yes?"

So *that's* what Vani had told him. "I guess so..."

"But you didn't know that's what you were doing. I know." He patted me on the arm. "Well, as you tell me about this catalyst of yours, both of your energies will charge the crystals. Then I can read them to figure out what meditation technique you need to learn, what kind of totem you need...that sort of thing."

So Kai was a fruitcake. At least he was a kind fruitcake who for some reason appeared to want to help me. I figured there was no harm in going along. Besides, Ben had planted the idea in my head that I might have unwittingly been using Sid as an emotional toxic waste dump. If there were any truth to that at all, I wanted to know as soon as possible so I could put a stop to it. I took a chance that Kai might know something useful. "What do you want me to tell you?"

"Oh, anything. How you met, how things are between you—whatever comes to mind, really." With a sober expression, Kai gestured for me to begin.

I gave him the short version of my story with Sid. To my amazement, nothing I said seemed to surprise Kai. After I finished, he leaned forward and asked in a low, intimate tone, "And are you in love with this Sid?"

"No, no. It's not like that. We're just good friends."

"So he's not taking advantage of you or anything?"

"God, no. If anything, these days I'm usually the one calling him." I squinted at Kai. "Why would you ask that?"

He tapped my hands. "Open up." I opened my fingers. Kai removed the crystals and placed them carefully in a cloth bag. "A lot of empaths can't tolerate intimacy with non-catalysts, leaving them with only one option," he explained. "There are lowlife catalysts out there who take advantage of desperate empaths, trapping them in a cycle of dependency."

"Oh, no!" My face heated up as I realized what he was asking me. "It's not like that at all. Sid's a great person. He would never do anything like that. Besides, he's never even heard of this empath/catalyst stuff."

"Glad to hear it." Kai began studying the crystals again. "I was just checking to make sure Pete and Ben don't have to take him out behind the woodshed."

I smiled uneasily. I couldn't tell if he was joking and I didn't particularly want to find out. "You said a lot empaths can't…*be with* non-catalysts?"

"That's right. Hold this one for a minute." Kai folded an orange-yellow crystal into my hand. "When things get really intense in relationships, empaths tend to open themselves up and completely let down their defenses. That's not a problem when you're with a catalyst since they soak up all of the emotional energy. But with a regular person, you experience all of your own emotions *plus* theirs.

That's too much for any one person to handle. Usually it becomes overwhelming, even frightening."

"Oh." That explained a lot about my past romantic failures. I looked down at my hands.

"Don't worry, honey," he said, patting my arm again. "It's a problem that's easy to fix once you learn how. By the time you finish this program, you'll be able to be with anyone you like."

I wanted to believe him, but I'd already had too many failed attempts at "normal" relationships. I knew better than to let myself hope. I decided to change gears. "Absorbing all of that toxic stuff, does it harm the other person? The catalyst, I mean?"

"No, not at all. To a catalyst, toxic emotion is like water rolling off a duck's back."

"Thank goodness." Relief flooded me. At least I hadn't been hurting Sid.

Kai gave me a sympathetic look. "I hope you know that none of this is your fault. You're not alone, either. A lot of empaths have to use catalysts to survive until someone teaches them how to manage those toxic surges."

A cold feeling of dread settled in my stomach. "Toxic *surges*?"

"A surge of negative emotions," he explained, "the ones you absorb from other people. When they build up to toxic levels, it triggers a surge. That's what causes that sickness you get when you need to call Sid. What do *you* call it?"

"I don't have a name for it." I shrugged. "I just know that the pain inside of me gets too heavy sometimes. Being with Sid takes the edge off, makes it manageable again."

"For a while, you mean."

I nodded.

"Well, I'd put down money that this pain of yours reaches toxic levels pretty often with all of that empathic submergence you do at work—yes, Dr. MacGregor told me about that. And I guess she was right, too, that submerging into others costs you more than you let on. But don't worry." He covered my hands with his. "That's why you're here. I'll make you a totem—a pendant, I'm thinking—and create a customized meditation technique for you to learn. I should have the pendant in a day or two, and I'll have the meditation ready for you sometime next week. Then you can take care of your own toxic surges, catalyst or no catalyst. And eventually you'll learn how to submerge without bringing anything nasty back with you."

That sounded promising. It would certainly be nice never to feel that awful sickness again. And I was sure it would please Sid if in the future my phone calls came solely from a place of desire, not desperation. But still…I bit my lip. "What if I get a toxic surge before next week?"

"If you feel one coming on, just tell Ben and he'll get Vani and me." Kai smiled broadly. "Don't worry, we've got you covered. We have a lot of tricks up our sleeves."

"Okay." I did my best to feel reassured. Meanwhile, I couldn't get over how much effort Kai was willing to put into helping me, someone he'd just met. "Listen, I'm not sure why you're being so nice to me, but thank you. I really appreciate it."

Kai's face crinkled. "You don't have to thank me, baby." With an abrupt burst of concentration, he stared at my hair. "I'm a good judge of people, and I could tell right away you're a sweetheart." He reached over and began rearranging various strands of my braid, tucking some in and pushing some back. "That's better. Besides, I feel a little bit sorry for you."

He looked so concerned that it worried me. "Because of my hair?"

"No—well, a little, yes. We'll work on that. But mainly because of everything you've been through trying to help people. The point is, I like you, so why *wouldn't* I be nice to you?"

"Thanks." I smiled, his openness moving me to candor. "I like you, too, Kai."

"Of course you do." He gave a faux-modest head bow. "Everybody with a lick of sense does. I'll take that one now." I handed him the orange-yellow crystal, and he rolled it up in the velvet cloth with the others. "That was a citrine crystal, by the way, for cleansing. Never a bad idea." Then he stood up and walked around the table, draping his arm around my shoulders. "So, you ready for class?"

What I was ready for was a smoke break, although I hadn't had a cigarette since college. I fell back against my chair. "I didn't know there was a class."

"Oh, yes! Intro to Paranormality 101, or something like that." Kai gracefully offered me his hand. "Come on. It won't be boring, I promise. Let's go find Ben."

Chapter Nine

"How did it go?" Ben asked when we reached his office.

"Fine," Kai replied. "We covered everything we needed to cover, and I have what I need to put Cate's cure together. Isn't it time for class?"

"Yes. Let's go." Ben looked me up and down. "You look a little tired. Are you sure you're up for this?"

I tried to smile. "Kai promised it won't put me to sleep."

"He's right, there," Ben said enigmatically. He led us through the lounge and down the hallway to a small classroom where Vani appeared to be setting up some sort of presentation. She had placed a number of colored markers on the ledge of a large dry erase board in the front of the room. Kai joined Vani up front. He arranged some objects on a small desk, then draped a white linen cloth over them. In his bright red tunic, Kai stood in stark contrast to Vani who, while effortlessly glamorous, was businesslike in a dark suit, white cotton blouse, and tasteful black heels. Being in their presence make me feel like a prickly weed in a flower garden.

Ben retrieved two folding chairs from against the back wall and set them up behind a long table, facing the front. He gestured for me to sit in one, and he took the other. Vani announced that they were ready to begin. She had written "Parapsychology" across the top of the board and drawn the rough outline of a hand further down.

"Welcome, Cate! This is Parapsychology 101—or at least that's what we're calling it today, since Ben informs me that you're a fan of the scientific paradigm."

I gave Ben the side eye, but he pretended not to see. "Yes, I guess you could say that," I said to Vani, "but what other paradigm is there—I mean, for a subject that ends in 'ology?'"

"Oh, believe me, there are others," she said. "We just like to 'meet the client where she is.'" She put air quotes around the common social work maxim.

I couldn't help but smile. I was starting to appreciate Vani's sense of humor, even though it had teeth at times.

"First, my qualifications." She held up an imaginary piece of paper and pretended to read from it. "Dual bachelor's degrees in marketing and psychology with a parapsychology emphasis from the University of Northampton, first class honors; trained at the School of Advanced Psychic Studies in London, as I mentioned before; and I'm originally from India, where we believe that things do not have to be fully understood via the Western scientific paradigm before they can be considered real."

As that was not an insubstantial list, I gave a nod of acknowledgement.

"Just so I have a baseline," she asked, "what do you already know about parapsychology?"

I bit my thumbnail and considered whether to be honest or diplomatic.

"Go ahead," Ben quietly urged. "What you really think, remember?

I shot him a "don't push me" look. "Okay, well," I began, "all I know is that in grad school, they said it was a pseudoscience that kind of died out in the Eighties. They also said that a lot of scam artists were involved, and it had ties to the occult. And I've seen that reality TV show *Ghost Trappers;* they mention parapsychology on there sometimes."

"Not bad," Vani said. "*Ghost Trappers* is the extent of many people's exposure. Allow me to tell you what parapsychology *really* is." She turned to the board and wrote the definition as she spoke it. "It's the scientific study of psychological phenomena that cannot be explained by the known laws of nature."

So it was an actual field of study? I sat up straighter in my chair. "You mean things like aura reading and being an empath?"

"Exactly." Vani pointed to the hand she'd drawn. "There are five categories of these phenomena. The first is psychokinesis, in which the mind interacts with other people or objects from a distance. There are several sub-categories—the most well-known being telekinesis—but the only one we use here is psychic healing, which encompasses empathic submergence and empath healing."

"Empath healing is the technique I told you about earlier," Ben added.

"Right, I remember," I said, trying to look cool rather than incredulous. "But wait—telekinesis? Isn't that moving things with your mind?"

"Yes, although the jury's still out on whether that exists," Vani said. "Personally, I've never seen any evidence of it."

"That's because it's bogus," Ben grumbled.

Kai tsk-tsked. "Well, aren't *we* judgy this afternoon."

"As I was saying," Vani said crisply, "that's the first category." She wrote "psychokinesis" along one finger of the hand. "The second category is clairvoyance, or the ability to see and know things about people or objects that others can't. Aura reading fits in here, along with your other empathic gifts."

In answer to my questioning look, Ben said, "Your abilities to pick up on other people's emotions and to form the filaments you told us about."

I nodded, feigning comprehension.

Vani wrote "clairvoyance" on the second finger. "Third is mediumship, or the ability to communicate with the spirits of the dead. I know you must have heard of that, Cate."

"Yes." Those scam psychic hotlines—and any number of scary movies I'd watched in high school that featured psychics sitting in dark rooms, wearing turbans and hoop earrings and staring into crystal balls.

Kai held out his arm and pretended to examine his fingernails. "That's my area of expertise, in case you were wondering."

"Oh, wow." I forced myself to smile and nod. Kai, a medium; that seemed to fit. Anyone who believed they could talk to the dead must have an extremely fertile imagination, and Kai definitely had one if he believed in crystals and totems. Not that I doubted Kai's sincerity, just his sense of reality.

As Vani finished writing "mediumship" on another finger, she said, "Fourth is precognition, or the ability to see the future."

As the categories grew more bizarre, I shot Ben a "help me" look, but his attention remained focused on Vani.

"That's Eve's gift, although she's just starting to develop it. And finally we have telepathy, or the ability to read others' thoughts. Asa is a telepath, but don't worry." She gave me a wan smile. "He gets splitting headaches when he uses his gift, so he won't be eavesdropping on your thoughts. He only reads minds when absolutely necessary." Vani wrote the last two categories on the hand's remaining fingers. "Those are the five categories of parapsychological phenomena. Any questions so far?"

I looked down and rubbed my forehead, searching for something, anything that I could ask without trumpeting my skepticism. "Yes, okay," I said, "I have a question. That definition of parapsychology—what do you mean when you say 'phenomena that cannot be explained by the *known* laws of nature?'"

Vani looked impressed. "Good question. Ben, would you like to take that one?"

"Sure," he said, turning to face me. "As I'm sure you know, we're always learning more about the laws of nature. Quantum physicists have discovered some pretty mind-blowing things lately, like particles being in two places at once, popping in and out of existence, and appearing to be telepathically linked to one another. And they're probing dark matter at the CERN collider, even as many continue to deny its existence. There's much that remains unknown, and parapsychologists believe that once we provide evidence of paranormal abilities, science will simply incorporate that evidence by updating our current understanding of the natural laws."

"Oh," I said, surprised that he'd actually given me a reasonable-sounding answer.

"You don't believe a word of this, do you?" Kai asked,

visibly amused.

"Um…" I opened and closed my mouth a few times as I tried to craft a diplomatic response. "Well, this is all new to me, and I do tend to be a skeptic. But I don't have any other explanation for the empath stuff that happens to me. I've also seen what Vani can do, and I can't explain that, either. I don't have any experience with those other three categories, but I'm trying to keep an open mind." I plastered a smile on my face.

"Excellent! That's all we can ask." Kai grinned. "But just so you know, by the time you leave here, we'll make a true believer out of you."

I held my hands up in surrender. "I'm sure if anyone could convince me, it would be you and Vani."

Vani erased the definition of parapsychology and drew another hand in its place. "Shall we talk about the other paradigm?"

"Hang on." Ben turned to me, eyes downcast, and murmured, "If you'd rather wait, that's fine. I know this is a lot to take in, and I don't want to overload you."

Ben's reluctance to discuss this other paradigm only sharpened my curiosity. "I'm not overloaded," I said brightly. "I'd like to hear about it."

Vani held up her marker. "We could just do a quick summary."

Ben exchanged freighted glances with Vani and Kai as some unspoken communication passed between them. Then he looked at me, his brows forming a dark ridge. "You really want to hear this?"

"Oh, yes. More than ever."

"Okay," he grumbled. "A *quick* summary."

"Great! We'll start with some historical facts; I know Ben likes those." Vani beamed. "According to archeologists, the first known references to paranormal abilities came from the early Bronze Age—oh, wait, I keep forgetting you're an American, Cate." She and Kai exchanged wry smiles. "The Bronze Age began roughly five thousand years ago, and fell between the Stone Age and the Iron Age."

I smirked at the "American" barb, but couldn't raise an

objection, considering that she was right; I hadn't known when the Bronze Age was.

She continued, "Parapsychologists believe that during that historical period, the human brain took an evolutionary leap that gave us this new set of abilities."

Ben sat back in his chair and crossed his ankle over the opposite knee. A muscle in his jaw twitched with the effort of containing some unidentified emotion. Whatever was coming next, I figured it must be juicy.

"However, some believe that it's more appropriate to view all of this through a spiritual lens," Vani explained. "Do you identify with a spiritual or religious tradition?"

I shook my head. Spirituality was something of a mystery to me. My mother hadn't raised me in any particular religion. The only spiritual activity I ever saw her engage in was either thanking, cursing, or pleading with God, depending on the circumstances. It was a habit I had picked up from her, in fact. I didn't pretend to know whether or not God existed, but I figured that if he did, it couldn't hurt to keep the lines of communication open.

"Well, subscribers to the spiritual paradigm believe that during the Bronze Age, these gifts were bestowed upon humanity by the Divine Source—commonly referred to here as God—so that we could perform physical, emotional, and spiritual healing," Vani explained. "Five civilizations were chosen to receive the gifts, in theory because they had developed to the point where they were ready to take on these healing duties. For the sake of simplicity, even though the term isn't historically accurate, I'll refer to these civilizations as 'tribes.'" She picked up her marker and wrote the names of the tribes on the fingers of the second hand. "Kai was kind enough to bring replicas of Bronze Age artifacts as visual aids to represent each of the five tribes. First we have Egypt, Asa's tribe…"

Kai whisked the linen cloth off of the desk, revealing an assortment of strange, ancient-looking objects. His hands floated over them as though he were showing off a prize package in a game show. Then he picked up one of the objects from the table and held it reverently aloft. It was a short sword with what looked like an elaborately carved bone handle and a grey blade in the shape of an "S."

Vani paused for a few moments so we could take in the sight before she continued. "Then there is the Indus Valley, which is my tribe…"

Kai exchanged the sword for what appeared to be a small, finely sculpted bronze figurine of a voluptuous woman with one hand on her hip and an inscrutable expression her face.

"Mesopotamia, which is Kai's tribe of origin…"

After carefully putting down the figurine, Kai picked up a metal bowl decorated with a delicate, repetitive teardrop pattern and a geometric design around the rim.

"China, which gave us Eve…"

Kai held up to his face a bright copper mask wearing a stoic, angry expression beneath a helmet that came to a point. It was a bit jarring to see what looked like a mask depicting a warrior worn with a pair of red platform heels. I pressed my lips firmly together.

"And, last but not least, your tribe, Cate: Caledonia."

"Um, Vani?" I hoped the look on my face didn't resemble sheep-like ignorance. "Of course I'm familiar with the other civilizations you mentioned, but I've never heard the term 'Caledonian.'"

"Oh, sorry. It is a bit more obscure," she acknowledged. "Caledonia is what the ancient Romans called the land beyond the northwest frontier of their empire, or today's northern Scotland."

With a flourish, Kai put down the mask and picked up a gold collar necklace. It was hammered thin and shaped like a crescent, wide in the front and tapering back toward two points set into square clasps. It shone as though lit from within. My eyes must have been shining as well, because Kai said, "You can wear it sometime if you like."

"Really?" I asked in a tone of hushed reverence.

"Sure. I made it, so I decide who wears it," he said, holding it up to his neck.

I stared openly. "You *made* that?"

"He made all of these," Vani gushed. "He's an incredible artist. You should see his studio, Cate. It's fantastic."

"I would love that!"

"You two could come over this weekend," Kai suggested. "I could make my famous baklava and show you the rest of my jewelry collection…"

I was about to chime in with a "Yes, definitely!" when Ben interrupted. "All right, social calendars can wait. Let's finish up. Go ahead, Vani."

"Somebody's grumpy today," Kai muttered as, with some reluctance, he placed the necklace back on the desk.

Vani didn't miss a beat, however. "Ever since these gifts were given to the five tribes, they have been passed down through lineage. Of course, five thousand years of history has erased the genealogical records connecting us to our Bronze Age ancestors. Fortunately, that information is still stored in our auras, which is how I can tell to which tribes we're connected."

Bronze Age lineage. Spiritual gifts. Tribal origins that were visible in auras. I sat in stupefied silence. Never had I heard so much absurdity spouted from the front of a classroom in all my life. I began to understand Ben's reluctance to delve into the spiritual paradigm; it was comforting to know that I wasn't the only skeptic in the room. Not wanting to offend Kai and Vani, though, I worked to keep any emotion from showing on my face.

Vani smiled warmly at me. She must not have been reading my aura right at that moment. "Any more questions?"

"Uh…" I hardly knew where to begin. "Five categories of paranormal abilities." I held up one hand and spread my fingers out. "And five tribes." I held up the other hand. "So in other words, now that I'm here, you have a complete set?"

I wiggled all ten fingers and smiled, but no one joined me. Instead, a heavy silence blanketed the room. Kai and Vani froze and looked at Ben. Almost imperceptibly, he shook his head. Then he looked down, his lips pulled shut as though by a drawstring.

I kicked myself internally. Just as I was starting to establish decent relationships with Kai and Vani, I had to go and make a joke about something they took very seriously. I cleared my throat. "I'm sorry, I didn't mean—"

"No, it's okay." Ben waved a dismissive hand. "No need to apologize. But if you don't have any more questions, we should probably stop there for today."

Oh, hell. I must have really put my foot in it. My heart pounded like a horse kicking a barn door. I closed my eyes and tried to breathe.

Ben stood up. "Vani and Kai, thank you both for that excellent presentation."

I looked up to find Vani erasing the board and Kai carefully putting the tribal objects away into velvet bags. "It was our pleasure," Vani said softly.

Sick with guilt, I pushed myself to my feet. "Yes, thank you. I'm so sorry for making light of things. I really do appreciate your taking the time teach me all of this."

"No problem, baby." Kai smiled warmly and shook his finger at me. "And stop apologizing. Everything's fine."

"Of course it is," Vani added decisively. She turned to me with a smile, but it quickly turned into a frown. "You look exhausted, though—no offense. Ben's right; we should stop here for today."

As she spoke, I realized that I did feel worn out, mentally at least. She and Kai both gave me brief hugs on their way out the door, as though to reassure me that there were no hard feelings.

"My studio door is always open," Kai said with a wink.

"I can't wait!" I called after him as they disappeared down the hallway.

• • •

Back in Ben's office, I flopped into one of the club chairs and rubbed my forehead. Between my efforts to keep my expression neutral during class and my social faux pas toward the end, I was in the early stages of what promised to be a hefty headache.

Ben took his seat behind the desk and peered down at me.

"Are you okay?"

"No, I'm not okay! I feel terrible for offending them!"

His brow furrowed. "Offending them?"

I began to wonder if I was on the same plane of reality as everyone else, or if I existed in an alternate dimension. "Yes, remember? My bad joke about having a 'complete set?' The reason why you ended the class early? About three minutes ago?"

"Oh, that." He relaxed and ran a hand through his hair. "Don't worry. You didn't offend them. Believe me, it would take a lot more than that. And I ended class because they'd covered everything, and you didn't have any more questions—did you?"

I frowned. I was *certain* more had gone on at the end of class than Ben was acknowledging. Of course, it was also possible that I was starting to imagine things. It *had* been an incredibly weird day, and Dr. Nelson's pills might have been messing with me… I tried to clear my head by shaking it vigorously, but that just worsened my headache. I moaned.

Concern etched itself across Ben's face. "I'll tell you what. It's a little early, but we've done a lot today, and you look pretty beat. I think I should have Pete run you home."

"Thanks." Home. Suddenly, all I wanted to do was to be back in my house, lying on the couch with a cold washcloth over my eyes.

Ben went to the door and called for Pete, who soon appeared in the doorway. "Whatcha need?"

They spoke in low tones. Finally, I heard the tail end of the conversation: "Make sure she eats breakfast before she leaves."

"Hang on, wait a minute." Was Pete going to pick me up again the next morning? I hoped they weren't planning to chauffeur me in an ongoing fashion. What if I didn't feel like coming in? *Or what if you want to have Sid over again?* asked a petulant voice in my head, which I studiously ignored. Dr. Nelson's pills were working, and apparently, everyone at the MacGregor group was emotionally safe for me to be around. I was sure that I could get myself to the program without Pete's assistance. "That's very thoughtful of you, but I'm much better now. I can drive myself."

Pete looked at me, then at Ben, and then at the floor. Ben's voice hardened. "I'm glad to hear that you're feeling more confident," he said, sounding as though he didn't believe me for a second. "We're not taking any chances, though. Pete will drive you."

So they weren't transporting me out of courtesy; they just didn't trust me. Gone was the Ben who restored old cars; Manager Ben was back again. "Pete can drive back and forth to my house all he likes," I snapped, "but I'm not going to be in the truck with him."

Bright gold flecks shot through Ben's eyes again. With his gaze still fixed on me, he inclined his head toward Pete. "You'll follow her, then?"

Pete nodded as though that were a perfectly reasonable suggestion. "Sure thing."

Frustration burned through me. "Oh, for the love of God! Why is this such a big deal to you? What difference does it make?"

Pete looked at the ceiling. Ben walked over and stood closer to me than was, strictly speaking, necessary to carry on a normal conversation. "I want you to get here," he said, his voice low and insistent, "and I want you to get here in one piece. Baltimore can be a dangerous city. You shouldn't drive around in a vehicle that is anything less than one hundred percent reliable."

I felt a defensive surge of loyalty toward my car, even though Simone had nicknamed it Calamity Jane. True, it was old and a little beat up. And yes, I had felt lucky to escape unscathed several times when it had broken down on me. But that wasn't even the point. "What I drive is none of your goddamned—"

"Besides, you and I both know that left to your own devices, you might start inventing reasons not to come in."

The nerve! I wanted nothing more than to tell him off, but the fact that I'd actually had that same exact thought moments before made it difficult for me to find the right words.

"So, what'll it be? Chauffeur or caravan?"

I looked from Ben to Pete and back again. They appeared to have their heels firmly dug in. The image of Pete's steer-horned truck dogging my red hatchback through the city streets was too absurd to contemplate. Pain vibrated through my head like an enormous gong had been struck. Maybe it was time to pick my battles. After all, I could always resurrect the argument once I was in back in fighting form.

"I hope you two realize how ridiculous you're being." I folded my arms across my chest for emphasis. "Okay, fine. Pete can drive. But don't forget, I am *not* a Marine."

Pete guffawed. "You can say that again!"

"And I do *not* take orders," I declared, doing my best to stare Ben down.

Instead of looking chastened, Ben appeared heartily amused. "Of course not. I'm glad to hear it." He threw his arm out toward the doorway and pointed. "Now, go get in the truck."

Pete laughed again. "C'mon, let's go."

I shot Ben one last glare for emphasis and did my best to stroll gracefully out of the office.

Chapter Ten

Pete had the good sense not to try to strike up a conversation on the way home. As we neared my house, I managed to talk him into dropping me off at the curb instead of walking me to my door. I hadn't wanted to feel completely pathetic. I stood and watched as he turned the corner, then walked toward my stoop.

As I put my foot on the first step, a man emerged from the alley beside my house. I turned to look as he walked toward me and came to a halt about two feet away. The sun was behind him and shining in my eyes, making it hard for me to see him clearly. I stepped back off of the stoop and squinted at him.

"Cate Duncan," he said in a raspy voice. He was about six feet tall and looked to be around my age. His features were sharp, and his nose had the slightly crooked look of a bone that had been broken and never healed properly. Pallid and lanky with short brown hair, he wore a scraggly goatee and a hooded black shirt. Over that, he had on a baggy black tracksuit and flashy tennis shoes.

Either he was a drug dealer or he was trying to look like one. I wondered what he was doing, popping out of the shadows like that, and how he knew my name. Maybe he was a new neighbor I hadn't met yet. "Can I help you?"

"Yeah, I think you can." He scanned me with hawkish eyes.

"Who are you?" I asked in an effort to take charge of the situation.

"I'm somebody you know a lot about—more than you should."

Alarm bells rang loudly in my head. Should I scream for help? Run down the street to a neighbor's house? Try to push past him and into my house? Screaming seemed like the best immediate option, but as I opened my mouth to do so, he lifted his shirt to reveal the butt of a handgun sticking out of his waistband.

"Don't even think about it."

I froze. My brain was shouting at me to do something, but it couldn't cut through the paralysis of terror. I looked up at his face and saw that he was deadly serious. His eyes were cold and hard—the eyes of someone who had been the victim of a lot of suffering and then decided to inflict some himself. My breathing was suddenly fast and shallow. I tried again to move but my feet were stuck in place.

"I'm Elana's boyfriend," he growled. "You know Elana Bruter, right?"

After a moment, my brain clicked into gear. Don, Elana's boyfriend. Don, the drug dealer. Don, who according to Elana, was capable of violence toward anyone he perceived to be an enemy. I tried to form words but nothing came out.

"I just saw her in the hospital. She was thinkin' of leaving me, can you believe that? Maybe you *can* believe it. Maybe it was even your idea. I sure have a hard time believing it was hers. Well, don't worry, I talked her out of it."

Slowly, my brain started to move. If I couldn't escape, I had to de-escalate the situation. My first idea was to pretend that I wasn't Cate Duncan at all, and that I had no idea what he was talking about. But If I tried to deny it, it might anger him further.

"She told me you're a real good therapist, and she can talk to you about anything. Including me." He poked himself in the chest. "About what I do and where I go and the things I tell her. Private things. Things she shouldn't be telling nobody."

Oh, I got it: he was worried that I would tell somebody the things she'd told me about him—somebody like the police. Second idea: reassure him that everything Elana told me would be held in confidence. But due to confidentiality laws, I couldn't even confirm to Don that I knew Elana, let alone that she was a client of mine.

"So I wanted you to know that I'll be watching you. I know where you live." He pointed to my house. "I even know your shitty car. So keeping an eye on you will be easy."

The shallowness of my breathing was making me feel lightheaded. I began to notice odd details about my surroundings—my trash can needed to be taken inside; I would have to rake the leaves soon.

Third idea: express indifference. Tell him I didn't care anything about who he was or what he did. Therefore, even if I did know something, I would have no interest in telling anyone else. That might work. But as I opened my mouth and tried to speak, only a gasp of air came out.

Don stepped closer until I could feel his breath on my face.

"I told Elana she's not going to see you anymore. And I'm telling *you* to stay away from her. And if you ever breathe a word to anyone, anything about me," he pressed a finger hard into my rib cage, "you're going to wish you hadn't."

A tiny squeak escaped my throat. He stepped back again. "I'll be seeing you around, Cate Duncan." He slowly backed away from me, then turned and stepped into the alley. The echoes of his footsteps receded as I stood rigid with terror. Then I heard the sounds of a car with a loud exhaust starting up and speeding off.

Silence. Stillness. I could feel my heart beating, but I still couldn't move. Several minutes passed. Finally, I was able to take a few steps forward, far enough so that I could peer down the alley. It was empty. My hands began to tremble as I dug through my purse for my keys. I stumbled up the stairs to my house and opened the door.

Once inside, I quickly closed the door, locked and chained it. "Oh my god," I said, nearly choking on the words. I ran up to my bedroom and locked that door, too. I collapsed onto the bed, turning my bedspread into a cocoon as I wrapped myself up tightly. "Omigod omigod omigod." Hot tears flowed down my cheeks.

After a few minutes I began to think again. I considered doing what he said, and not telling anyone about what had happened. But I knew it was illogical to trust the word of someone who had just tracked me down and threatened me with deadly force. Besides, whatever happened to me, I had to make sure that somebody was looking out for Elana. That settled it. I reached out of my cocoon, picked up my phone, and called Dr. Nelson.

I gave him the blow-by-blow, and he asked me questions until he was sufficiently reassured that I was all right. He seemed genuinely alarmed. While our clinic staff had been attacked before, it had only happened at the clinic itself where there was a protocol for dealing with those types of situations—none of which had ever involved a gun.

Dr. Nelson promised to check on Elana at the hospital to ensure that she was safe and would have all the support she needed upon her release. He said that he would make a report to the police and send an officer over to my house so that I could do the same. However, we both knew that Don being who he was, it was unlikely the police would be able to find him if he didn't want to be found.

Panic started to tighten my throat. I lived alone. I didn't have an alarm system. I didn't have any way of defending myself. I had no family nearby. I lived paycheck to paycheck, so I couldn't even afford to stay in a motel. And even if I were to run away somewhere, Don had found me once; no doubt he could do it again.

Dr. Nelson was apparently thinking along the same lines. "I'm going to call Ben MacGregor and tell him what happened."

"Why?"

"Because you're in his program for the next few weeks, and I think it's important for him to know what's going on."

The incident with Don had made me temporarily forget about the day I'd had. All at once, it all started to come back to me. "Dr. Nelson—"

"Actually, now that I think about it," he interjected, "in light of what's happened, it's probably a good thing that you're going to be at the church every day instead of sitting at home."

"Please don't take this the wrong way," I ventured. "I know Dr. MacGregor is your friend, but the program is really weird so far."

This comment elicited a hearty laugh. "Yes, I suspected that you would find it challenging. I certainly hope you weren't thinking of giving up, though, especially after only one day. What would you say if you sent one of your clients to a program you believed was ideal for them and they wanted to leave after Day One?"

Damn him. "I guess I'd ask them to trust me enough to stick it out for a while."

"Well, that's what I'm asking you to do, especially after what happened with Don."

"Great," I mumbled.

He chuckled. "Come on, Cate, you work in mental health. You can handle a little weird, right?"

"I guess."

"All right, then. Keep an eye out for the police, and I'll call Ben." He paused to clear his throat, and I heard the emotion in his voice. "I hope I don't have to tell you how important your safety is to me. I'm so sorry this happened to you. We'll make sure it gets taken care of."

"Thanks."

I was alone with my thoughts again, and my anxiety grew. The fear that if I moved, Don might take a shot at me through the window kept me plastered to the bed. Fortunately, I had my purse with me. I fumbled through it until I found my bottle of little white pills and managed to swallow a couple.

I called Simone next. I wanted to warn her that Don had visited Elana in the hospital and that he, at least, was under the impression that they would still be a couple when she got out. After detailing the many unspeakable things she wanted to do to Don, Simone offered to get a babysitter for her kids so that she could come over. I was about to take her up on her offer when another call came through. Thinking it might be the police, I told her I'd call her back.

It was Ben, and his voice was tense. "I spoke to Zeke. Are you all right?"

"Yes, I'm fine. I'm just waiting for the police to get here."

"I'll be over in ten," he said, and then abruptly hung up.

Although I wasn't entirely comfortable with involving the MacGregors in my personal life, the knot that had formed inside of me when Don had appeared began to loosen. Whatever Ben had planned, it probably couldn't hurt. I called Simone to let her know that she didn't have to get a babysitter because the cavalry was on its way.

A wave of exhaustion swept over me. All I wanted to do was get the police report done and over with so I could get out of there—to go where, I still didn't know. My house had been the only place I'd felt safe for so long, but anywhere else seemed safer at that moment.

As I heard cars pulling up outside, I went to the bedroom window and peeked through the curtains. Ben arrived first in the Land Rover, which turned out to be the clinic's official vehicle, and Pete's truck was right behind. As they walked toward the house, I saw that Ben had changed into jeans, a dark T-shirt, and a black leather jacket. I cursed myself for noticing that he cut as striking a figure in casual clothes as he did in a suit.

As I let them into the living room, a new energy surrounded Ben and Pete. They were like two hound dogs that had been lounging at home all day and then were suddenly asked to hunt. It was strange to have Ben in my intimate space and embarrassing to have Pete back in my living room after the scene he'd witnessed that morning. They both seemed so focused on my safety, though, that I believed they weren't there to invade my privacy or pass judgment.

"Dr. Nelson explained your situation," Ben said, his eyes rife with concern. "He's asked us to keep you safe. Okay with you?"

My situation? My vulnerability, he meant. I didn't feel that I had much of a choice. It seemed as though forces beyond my control—Don, for starters—were determined to run my life for the time being. "Yes," I said reluctantly. "Thank you."

"Good." He pulled his tablet and a stylus from his jacket. "Pete and I have some experience in dealing with security threats. The first step is for you to tell us every detail you can remember about what happened."

Pete did a walk-through of my house, examining my doors and windows. Ben took notes as I gave him as much detail as I could without violating Elana's confidentiality. As we were finishing up, the police arrived.

Ben and Pete waited outside while I gave my report. The officers said they would put an APB out on Don and would let me know if there were any updates on the case. They also said that they saw things like this all of the time and doubted anything would come of it. "He's only trying to intimidate you," one of the officers explained. "I doubt he'll be back."

They offered to have a car drive by every so often to keep an eye on things. I appreciated the gesture, but I also knew that was all it was: a gesture. I was all the more grateful that Ben and Pete were involved.

"You look spent," Ben said after the police left.

I covered a yawn with my hand. "Yeah, it's been a long day. Look, I really appreciate you both coming over and being willing to help. I've never dealt with anything like this before. But you don't even know me really, so this is quite above and beyond the call of duty."

"Well, you're under our wing now, and we take our responsibilities seriously," Pete said with a smile. "Lucky for you, dealin' with some two-bit drug dealer is child's play as far as we're concerned."

"Until the situation is resolved," Ben said, "one of us will be with you at all times…within shouting distance, I mean. The church is secure, so you're safe when you're there." He looked to Pete, who nodded. "But one of us will stay parked outside when you're home, and we'll accompany you if you need to go anywhere." I must have looked as shocked as I felt because he added, "Only until this Don guy is dealt with, of course. I'll take the first shift. Pete, can you come and replace me at three?"

Pete nodded and headed toward the door.

"But…you really don't have to…I mean, when will you guys sleep?"

Ben and Pete exchanged sideways smiles. "Cate, we're doing this so you don't have to worry," Ben said. "You're going to make us feel inept if you start coming up with new things to worry about."

"That's right. You'd better cut it out before Ben starts cryin'." Pete ducked out the door as Ben tried to knock the hat off of his head.

"Bye," I called after him. I could feel myself softening considerably toward the cowboy. In spite of the first impression he'd made, Pete certainly was there in my time of need.

Ben took something from his pocket and handed it to me. "I brought an extra panic button from work." I recognized the small black cylinder with the red button on one end; we used similar devices at Dr. Nelson's clinic. "We connected this one to my cell phone and Pete's. Just push it and one of us will be here in a flash." I must have looked scared because he added, "Don't worry, we're not going to let anyone get in. It's just a safety precaution. And do you have an extra set of keys? If I do need to get in here for some reason, I don't want to have to break the door down."

I retrieved my extra set from a kitchen drawer. As I handed them over, I felt a pang of guilt. Here he was, offering to protect me, and I was going to let him sit outside in his car. "Wait a minute. Why don't you stay in here? In the living room, I mean. It would be a lot more comfortable, and you can watch TV and stuff." As I gestured toward the couch, I remembered that I hadn't seen him eat anything all day. "And I have some Chinese leftovers in the fridge. Help yourself." I thought it best not to mention that Sid had brought the take-out food.

Ben frowned. "Are you sure? I don't want you to feel crowded."

"Of course I'm sure. Listen, it's really nice of you to be doing this. I mean, it's totally not what I expected," I said, adding softly, "but I'm really grateful. I don't know what kind of state I'd be in right now if you hadn't come."

"It's no problem at all."

The next moment, I felt like I couldn't keep my eyes open for another minute.

"Go on up to bed. I'll be right down here. If you need anything, just holler." He gave me a reassuring smile. "And don't worry. Everything is going to be fine."

"Thanks," I said wearily, almost unable to form the word as I climbed the stairs. I was too tired to even think about undressing or brushing my teeth. I fell onto the bed and went straight to sleep.

CHAPTER ELEVEN

It was a typical summer afternoon in Delaware: hot, humid, and lazy. Mom and I were sharing a hammock in her cousin Ardis' backyard, swinging gently as one by one, I picked the white, ethereal seeds out of a dandelion and let the wind catch them.

"You know Ardis is going to kill you," Mom said. "Her yard is going to be littered with weeds."

I smiled. "Good thing her cousin is the Plant Whisperer."

Mom reached over and tugged on my braid. "You're a troublemaker."

"Ow!" I pushed her hand away, laughing. "You act like that's news!"

Her expression grew wistful. "Catie, you know I'm not really here, right?"

"Hmm?" I gave her a puzzled look.

"I'll visit soon, though," she said. "For now, I'm sorry to say you have to get back to reality."

"But Mom…" I whined.

"Go!" She threaded her hands and feet through the hammock so she wouldn't fall, then swung a few times and flipped it over, dropping me onto the ground.

The ground turned out to be my bed. Tears wet my temples. I picked up my phone and checked the time. Two a.m. I moaned and screwed my eyes shut again, willing myself to go back to sleep, back to my mother, away from reality. But sleep wouldn't come.

Then I remembered that Ben was downstairs in my living room. At least I thought he was. I didn't hear a sound.

I turned my attention inward and reached out with my senses.

Yes, he was there; I could feel his presence. A filament must have been forming between us. I could sense both his wide-awake watchfulness and his calm. Either he didn't think anything was going to happen that night or he was confident that he could handle it if something did.

Another thought occurred to me. As unpleasant as it would have been for me to submerge into Don, I should have at least made the effort during our encounter. Perhaps if I had, it would have created a filament that I could use to get some sort of read on him—to sense whether he was watching me, or asleep, or out getting drunk. Anything that would help me feel like I had some control over the situation. I kicked myself for missing the opportunity.

I would have to do something else to distract myself. I hadn't had a chance to check on my clients yet that day; that seemed like a good place to start.

I assumed my usual position, closing my eyes and folding my hands over my chest. Soon I could see the filaments, glowing brightly and reaching out into the night.

First, I went to Elana. She felt calm, stable. The stay at Washington Hill must be doing her some good. Then I moved on to the next person and the next, grateful to find no reasons for concern. I bid them all a peaceful night and moved on.

Filaments also connected me to Simone and Sid. I sensed that they were both sleeping, and I envied them. Finally, I came across the space where my mother's filament had been. It was an empty space, cold and painful like a bruise. *She's gone*, I thought, then shuddered as I realized: *You could have joined her today.*

Pushing away that thought, I tried to remember what it was like when she was alive. Growing up, I was her shadow. We lived in a small town northeast of Baltimore at the mouth of the Susquehanna River, spending holidays and weekends in Lewes, the town on the Delaware oceanfront where she grew up. From the safety of those bucolic nests, she had done her best to shelter me from most things harsh and ugly.

She may have been a bit too successful at that. When I left

home to attend college in Washington, D.C., I realized for the first time how profoundly naïve I was. I met students from all over the world and studied subjects I'd never heard of. I became painfully aware of how little I knew about the world outside of the bubble in which I was raised.

I had been working hard ever since to educate myself about all aspects of life. For some reason, I was particularly drawn to the dark, painful aspects of human existence. The more I learned about all the broken places, the more I wanted to heal them. Where that impulse came from, I didn't know, but going into the mental health field was an extension of that quest.

As long as I could remember, my mother had lived for two things: work and gardening. She never seemed to have many friends or much of a social life. Her explanation was that her job was stressful, so when she wasn't at work, she only wanted to spend time with her family and her plants.

But Ardis told me that growing up, Mom was always the life of the party—even more so after she met my father. It was only after I was nearly a year old and he left us that Mom started to withdraw into herself and away from the world.

Maybe I hadn't noticed how low her mood had become because it had happened so gradually. I'd always driven out to visit her at least a couple of times a month, but she'd never seemed particularly unhappy to me. I must have been too selfishly wrapped up in my own problems to see how stressed out and overwhelmed she was, how depressed she had become—and perhaps how exhausted. I wondered if she, too, had suffered from insomnia. I knew from experience that it could make the idea of sleeping forever seem very appealing.

The sad truth was that I had no idea why she'd taken her life. All of her colleagues from the hospice were shocked. They told me that Mom's two favorite topics had always been how proud she was of me and how much she loved her patients. They acknowledged that her most recent cases had been intense: a World War II combat veteran who was having traumatic flashbacks, and a twelve-year-old girl with leukemia. But they said Mom had handled them with her usual blend of compassion and patience.

We buried her in the family plot in Lewes. At the funeral, I'd talked to the few family members with whom Mom had stayed in contact. I'd also spoken to Ardis, her cousin and best friend. None of them had any idea why she had overdosed.

I couldn't let myself think about that, though. It would bring up emotions that I had worked too hard to push down and shut away. I needed to think about something other than Mom. And *definitely* something other than Don.

Given that he was right there in my living room, Ben seemed like a possible choice. But I hesitated. I'd learned early on to be okay with being alone, to be independent, and to rely on myself. After all, my mother's job had always required her to be on-call evenings and weekends. Still, a part of me longed to have more people in my life whom I could count on.

I didn't have a lot of options. Since I had proven to myself numerous times that I was incapable of sustaining normal romantic relationships, I knew that dating wasn't the answer. My friends from high school and college had scattered, moving away as I had for graduate school or jobs, or disappeared into serious relationships or marriages. Without intending too, I had worsened my isolation by diving so deeply into my own work. Aside from professional relationships, Simone and Sid were my only two remaining lifelines to any sort of social existence.

The impulse to go downstairs and hang out with Ben nagged at me, but I worried that he might think it was weird. After what had happened with Don, though, I figured I had a good excuse to want some company.

I had fallen asleep in with my hair still in a braid. It had gone askew, loose in some places and tight in others. With a lot of careful unbraiding, I managed to untangle my mass of long, wavy hair without pulling too much out. After realizing how rumpled my clothes were, I slipped out of them and into my bathrobe and headed downstairs.

Ben was standing at the front window, looking out through the blinds. He turned as he heard my footfalls. He had taken off his jacket and laid it neatly over the back of the chair, revealing the Marines insignia on the back of his T-shirt. "Everything all right?" he asked.

At the sight of his face, my anxiety began to melt away. It was replaced by something nice, something soothing. "Yeah. Trouble sleeping, that's all."

"That's understandable." Ben sat down on the couch. He was giving me an odd look—a mixture of surprise and awe, like I was some sort of rare species of bird he hadn't seen before.

"What?" I asked.

"Nothing," he said, shaking the look from his face. "It's just—you let your hair down."

"Oh, yeah." I gave my wild sea of hair a dismissive finger flick. "It's kind of unruly. That's why I keep it up most of the time." Then I noticed that Ben had been playing solitaire on the coffee table… with Sid's racy deck.

He followed my gaze. "Interesting deck."

Perfect. A blush crept onto my face. "They're not mine."

"Mm-hmm," he said, then took mercy on me and changed the subject. "So, what usually helps you get back to sleep?"

"Umm…" I thought for a moment. "Ice cream?"

He nodded with mock-gravitas. "Do you have some or do we need to go out and get it?"

I grinned. "I have some, of course. Besides, I wouldn't ask you to make an ice cream run with me at two in the morning, especially not after everything else you're doing for me." I went into the kitchen. "Any for you? It's peanut butter cup."

"No, thanks. No ice cream while on duty."

I grabbed the ice cream carton and a spoon and sat on the other end of the couch. "Is that some kind of military rule?"

"That's right. Numerous operations have been ruined by the untimely ingestion of rum raisin." He pointed at my carton. "Glad to see you're not standing on ceremony or anything."

"If you want formality, you're going to have to come protect me at a reasonable hour."

The sound of his easy chuckle warmed me. "I'm glad to see this whole thing hasn't made you lose your sense of humor." As I savored the ice cream, he asked gently, "Are you doing okay, Cate? For real."

I decided to dip a cautious toe into the self-revelation pool. "I'm okay about the Don thing, I think. The way you and Pete jumped in, I'm really overwhelmed. And grateful." I paused. "It's just weird. I've been taking care of myself for years and taking care of a lot of other people besides. Having the shoe on the other foot isn't very comfortable for me, I guess."

He nodded. "I get that. But I'm glad you didn't let your discomfort stop you from accepting our help. No one should have to handle a situation like this by themselves."

I felt myself softening. "Thanks."

"Sure thing. I'm still a little worried about you, though."

"Why?"

"Well," he replied with eyebrows raised, "you haven't argued with me about anything in nearly twelve hours. Not in earnest, anyway."

"And this worries you, why?"

"It's not normal from what I've seen."

"Would you like me to argue with you about something?" I offered. "Would that put your mind at ease?"

"I'm not complaining. It's a nice change of pace."

I grabbed a throw pillow from behind my back and lobbed it at his sideways grin, but he caught it easily. "I just wanted to make sure you were still in there somewhere," he said.

"I'm here. I'm just not really myself right now, I guess."

He stood and handed me the pillow, then sat down and stretched his arm along the back of the couch behind me. He sat just close enough that I could feel the edges of the warmth radiating from his body. "You want to talk about it?"

I hesitated, wondering how much I should tell Ben about the reason for my insomnia. I hadn't really talked to anyone about my mother's death. There was something that would make me more comfortable, though. "Ben, would you mind…" I wasn't even sure how to word it. "I mean, it might be easier for me to talk to you…"

"What is it?"

I squinted up at him. "You know that thing I do with my clients?"

"Yes, of course." He nodded. "You want to submerge into me before you confide in me."

"I'm sorry," I said, instantly embarrassed. "I shouldn't have asked."

"Of course you can, and don't apologize," he said emphatically. "You said that submerging gives you a general sense of a person. If it'll make you feel more comfortable with me, I'm all for it. I want you to know that you can trust me, Cate. What do you need me to do?"

I tried to ignore the heat rising in my cheeks. "I don't know. This is kind of an unusual situation."

"Okay, I'll tell you what," he said. "Since you usually do it with clients, let's pretend I'm a client. You can ask me questions, and I'll answer them. At some point, you'll probably start to feel your way along. What do you think?"

I liked the idea of being put back into the therapist role, which was much more comfortable for me than being a patient. However, I wasn't sure if it would work. "That sounds good, I guess. It's just that with clients, they're actually coming to me with a problem. It's usually when they start really talking about the problem that I'm able to fully lose myself in them. I don't know if role-playing is going to work."

He thought for a minute. "I'll tell you what. I'll give you a real problem to work with."

"Really? You would do that?"

"Sure. Anything I can do to help."

"Wow. Thanks." I was once again moved by unexpected generosity from the drill instructor. "Okay, I'll give it a shot."

He straightened himself up on the couch. "Go ahead, Doc."

I grinned at the absurdity of the situation. I also felt a sudden spark of excitement at the thought of doing an actual experiment. "So, you're Benjamin MacGregor, Ph.D. in organizational psychology, ex-Marine Corps, clinic manager. Married? Single?"

"Single."

"And what is your age?"

"Thirty-one."

"Okay." I took notes on an imaginary pad. "What brings you in today, Dr. MacGregor?"

"I'm here supporting a friend," he said, smiling.

"Wonderful. That's very kind of you." I smiled back. "While you're here, is there anything I can help you with? Any low mood, persistent worries? Trouble with sleep or appetite? Anything out of the ordinary?"

"Well, there is one thing you might be able to help me with."

"Oh? And what's that?"

Ben examined his hands. "It's kind of embarrassing."

In that instant, my self-consciousness disappeared. If the eyes were the windows to the soul, it was time to break glass. I focused my attention on him entirely, like a lens zooming in. "Ben, there's no reason to feel embarrassed with me, believe me," I said sincerely, no longer playing a role. "What is it?"

"It's just…" He seemed to be searching for words. "It's a problem I've had since I was a kid, an anxiety thing. I've tried, but I've never been able to shake it."

"Go ahead."

As he spoke, he once again met my gaze. I looked into his eyes, preparing. "I don't like to eat in front of other people," he finally said.

"What?" Utterly taken by surprise, I wondered if I'd heard him correctly.

His brow furrowed. "I can't…I can't eat in front of other people. It makes me nervous."

"Oh." I hadn't known what to expect, but it certainly wasn't that. I felt honored that he'd confided in me about something that was so emotionally raw for him. *Well, therapist,* I told myself, *time to go to work.* I looked into his eyes. All at once I was inside, swimming in a sea of Ben.

Once submerged into his mind, I stretched out my empathic senses. Right away, I picked up on Ben's intelligence, his sincerity, and his desire to help and protect others. But I also became aware of his stubbornness and a near-compulsion to be in control. Ben had that rare integrity, then—someone who was exactly the same on the inside as they appeared on the outside. While there were no surprises, though, there were parts of him that I couldn't quite identify. They were dark and in shadow, but they didn't feel at all threatening to me. That was all I needed to know for the moment.

I found my bearings and focused on the task at hand. As I held his problem in my mind, my attention was drawn to something that looked like a dark pillar. When I moved toward it, the pillar moved away. I followed its movements until eventually it brought me to a place that felt small and confining. Then the pillar disappeared.

Inside the small space I sensed the presence of a young boy. An image flashed through my mind: a small plate of food. I knew that must be what the boy was seeing.

"Eating," I observed aloud. I could sense that the boy felt like a turtle without a shell. "It makes you feel vulnerable."

"Yes," I heard Ben reply, "and I've never understood why."

I felt another presence. Again an image flashed into my head: a small brown dog lying on the ground, foam around its lips, and a half-eaten bowl of dog food by its side. "Your dog. He was poisoned?"

"Yes. How did you know?"

I leaned forward as I experienced the boy's broken heart, his fear, and his terrible guilt. "Someone poisoned him, and you think it was your fault."

"Why would I think it was my fault?" Ben asked, perplexed.

Silently, I held the question in my heart. Moments later, words entered my mind as though they were coming from my own memory: *The neighbor poisoned him for barking too much. It was my job to make sure he didn't bother anybody.*

"No, no," I said. "It wasn't your fault that the dog barked. Dogs bark; that's what they do. It was the neighbor's fault for having unrealistic expectations and for being cruel."

"Oh wow," Ben exclaimed.

I felt a rush of compassion for the boy travel from my heart into the small space. "You and the dog ate together. He died, and you thought it was your fault. Now you're afraid to eat with anyone else for fear that they, too, will die." My desire to heal him unleashed itself, flowing like a torrent out of me and into the boy. "Please let me help you with this."

"Cate," Ben said, and I felt his hands on either side of my face. At his touch, I pulled myself back into my own body, bringing as much of his pain back with me as I could. It dropped down into the center of my being with a sickening thud. Fortunately, I was used to concealing my own pain. I didn't want Ben to feel guilty or have any regrets.

"What?" he stammered. "How?"

Still mildly disoriented, I fumbled for words. "Did it work?"

"I should say so," he said, dropping his hands onto his lap. "I don't know what..."

I looked up at Ben and placed my hands in his. As I saw a child's mixture of pain and wonder reflected in his grown-up face, I felt the impulse to take care of him. "Are you okay?"

"Definitely. More than okay." He squeezed my hands and appeared to regain his composure. "You are incredible. You have an amazing gift. You shared insights that have eluded me for years, not to mention my mother and several psychologists. And," he added, pointing to his chest, "I could feel you. I could actually *feel* you in there, healing me."

I blinked. "Really?"

"Yes, really. It felt like a river of healing energy flowing from you into me. *That's* empath healing, Cate," he said intently. "Is that something you've done before, with your clients?"

Still somewhat stunned, I tried to recall. "No, not that I'm aware of. I think that was a first."

"Well, you're definitely a natural. Right now, if I think about eating in front of people, I can still feel the anxiety, the resistance. But it's much reduced."

"The wound seemed very deep," I said. "If it's been around since you were a child, it will probably take some work to overcome it."

"What did you mean when you asked me if you could help me with it? Were you talking about the empath healing?"

"No. That just kind of happened automatically. What I meant was, let me help you. In real life. Practice eating with someone. With me." I blushed again and looked down at my lap, realizing how inappropriate that might have sounded. I was his client, not the other way around. "If you want to, I mean."

There was a pause. "I would like that."

I looked up, disbelieving. "Really?"

"Sure. We could start with say, lunch tomorrow?"

I was surprised at how much the idea pleased me. "That would be great. Maybe it's some way for me to pay you back for all of this protection you're giving me."

Gold flashed through his eyes again. "If it helps you to look at it that way, go ahead, but no payment is required. It really is our pleasure."

Before I could respond, we heard the rumbling diesel engine of Pete's truck pulling up out front. "Three a.m. Right on time as usual." Ben took me by the hand. "Cate, thank you. I mean it."

"Thank *you* for being willing to share that with me. I know it wasn't easy."

"You made it more than worth it. I hope you'll feel more comfortable confiding in me now." He opened the door.

Pete stepped in and narrowed his accusing eyes at us. "I saw you weren't in your car. What are you two kids doin' in here? Havin' a good time?"

Ben grinned. "Like we'd tell you if we were." He turned back toward me, pointing a thumb at Pete. "Cate, where do you want this one?"

"Oh, he can stay in the living room, too. What the heck, my reputation with the neighbors is already ruined." Suddenly weary again, I yawned.

"So you put her to sleep, I see," Pete teased. "You must not have been having too good a time after all."

Ben smiled easily as he headed for the door. "See you both at eight thirty. Get some sleep, Cate. You'll need it for tomorrow."

"Okay, goodnight," I said as he closed the door behind him. Pete was already sitting on the edge of the sofa and kicking off his boots.

"Go." He took off his hat and used it to shoo me toward the stairs. "I'm on it."

"Thanks, Pete. I really mean it."

"Go on, git."

I barely managed to get out of my robe and under the covers before fading clean away.

CHAPTER TWELVE

Hell Week, Day Two

On Monday morning, in a pleasant surprise, Ben offered me the option of merely observing tai chi for a day so that I could get the general idea of what they were doing. I watched the session, which looked like a cross between ballet and modern dance. At the same time, I became even more certain that I would never be able to master the art, lacking as I was in natural grace.

Afterwards, Ben changed into his business attire and took me back to his office. As we settled into our respective seats, I was surprised to find that after only one day, I already felt much more comfortable there.

"Were you able to sleep after I left last night?" he asked.

"Like a baby," I said, smiling. "I'd guess I've had a lot more sleep than you have in the past twenty-four hours."

"You get used to living on little sleep in the Corps. It sticks with you."

I wanted to know more about his time in the military, but I had never known a Marine before, and I didn't know if it was rude to ask a lot of questions. I figured it was safe to inquire about the issue we had discussed the night before. "Was it hard for you in the Marines? I mean, with your eating issue?"

He thought for a moment. "You know, I never had trouble eating in front of the guys, and I never understood why until last night. If the core problem is that I'm afraid that people I eat with will die, then I wouldn't have that problem with other Marines because we all knew that dying was always a possibility. We signed up for that. Maybe having their consent, so to speak, short-circuited my anxiety in that situation."

"Oh," I said, impressed with his insight. "That makes sense."

"I'm looking forward to our work on that at lunch today, by the way."

"Me too." I was a little surprised at the collegial manner in which we seemed to be interacting. I'd half-expected him to return to drill-instructor mode once treatment restarted.

"About last night," he said, "I know the empath healing was a first, but the way you submerged into me—is that what you do with your clients?"

It was my turn to think. "Well, yes, to an extent," I explained. "With you, as with them, I could only really submerge when you told me what your problem was. And I followed the same process, which is to go inside and look around until I find the source of the pain. The difference is that I wouldn't tell a client what I was seeing. Instead, I would ask them normal diagnostic questions, but subtly direct the conversation toward the problem areas."

"Yeah, it probably wouldn't go over too well if you started discussing things about your clients that they hadn't even told you yet."

"Exactly. They would think I was a freak. But with you…"

"I already *know* you're a freak." His eyes flickered gold.

"Right." I tried, and failed, to suppress a smile.

Ben shifted into serious manager mode, but the change seemed a little less abrupt—or I was just getting used to his quick changes. "What you're describing, having to hide aspects of your gift at work, leads us right into this morning's topic: what we do here at the clinic. Dr. MacGregor set this place up with a couple of goals in mind. The first was to create a space in which alternative healing modalities could be practiced in a safe and supportive environment. Many people in the medical field still view acupuncture and Reiki as nothing but smoke and mirrors, for example. And most don't even recognize the existence of sensitives."

"Sorry, what? Sensitives?"

"Shorthand for people with paranormal abilities. Most people view parapsychology the way you were taught to in grad school—as a pseudoscience, not a serious field of study. The bias is so strong that my mother lost her faculty appointment at Washington Hill when she expressed an interest in doing parapsychological research. That was why she went into private practice. The irony, of course, is that the same doctors who pushed for her removal from the hospital now send her their patients who aren't responding well to conventional treatments."

"That's totally unfair." I grimaced. "So that's who you treat? Patients other doctors can't help?"

"Yes, as well as people from the community who've learned about us by word-of-mouth. We take all patients regardless of their ability to pay, so we get a lot of people who can't afford to go elsewhere and are open-minded enough to try our methods. If they need more traditional medical care, though, we have relationships with certain doctors and clinics who are willing to make financial arrangements for patients we refer."

The MacGregors had bigger hearts than I'd thought. "How many patients do you see in a given day?"

"Fifteen, twenty—it varies, based on demand and everyone's work schedules. But you won't see any patients at the church this week. We cleared our schedules once we knew you were coming."

I did a double-take. "Why?"

"Supporting the healer is our top priority. If the healers aren't doing well, they can't help others. We wanted to be able to focus our energy exclusively on you."

"Oh." I felt guilty for some reason. I looked down and examined my fingernails.

"Which brings us to her second goal for the clinic: research. We also treat research subjects from the National Institutes of Mental Health."

"NIMH?" I couldn't hide my surprise. "Really?"

"Yes. For political reasons, they don't advertise it, but NIMH does research on sensitives. Often their subjects need extra healing or support of some kind, so we provide our services. My mother hopes that joining forces will speed up our progress in demonstrating that these abilities exist and how they work."

My indignation flared on Dr. MacGregor's behalf. "I'll bet Washington Hill will want her back *then*."

"That would bring things full-circle for her, certainly. It's no secret that she'd like to return there someday soon. For one thing, a hospital with their resources would provide unequalled research opportunities. For another—"

"Vindication." I could get behind that. I wouldn't have guessed it from our first encounter, but it appeared that Dr. MacGregor was an underdog, willing to risk her reputation for something she believed in. "So she's not planning to retire anytime soon."

With a rumbling laugh, Ben said, "Oh, no. My mother believes that retirement would bore her to tears, and the women in her family tend to live a long time. I have a feeling she'll outlive and outwork all of her critics."

That was heartening. "Anything I can do to help, just let me know."

"Good. We'll take you up on that. Any questions?"

"Just one." There was something I'd wanted to ask him ever since class the day before. "You mentioned identifying the origins of paranormal abilities. I gather that you're not a big believer in the Bronze Age tribal stuff Vani was talking about yesterday."

Annoyance flitted across his face, but he recovered quickly. "Running the clinic in the here-and-now requires all of my focus. I leave questions of history to those who are interested in that subject."

So I'd been right about Ben's opinion—but he didn't want to directly contradict his mother or his colleagues. "Your mother must believe in it, then," I probed. "I mean, *someone* put it on the orientation syllabus."

There was a slight pause. I could tell that Ben regretted asking me if I had any questions. "My mother finds the theory interesting enough that she'd like to investigate it further," he said coolly. "And Vani and Kai are more than willing to help. Vani has been studying the subject since college, in fact."

"It surprises me that your mother takes it that seriously," I said, genuinely curious. "I mean, she's a psychiatrist doing scientific research, not a folklorist."

Ben stood and retrieved a small plaque from the table by the window. "You'll have to talk to her about that. But I can tell you that Dr. MacGregor and I both see the wisdom in this quote from Jung." He handed it to me. The plaque read, "I shall not commit the fashionable stupidity of regarding everything I cannot explain as a fraud."

"Interesting," I said, trying to hide my chagrin. If he was implying that I was "stupid" for considering the Bronze Age tribal theory to be folklore, I wasn't going to give him the satisfaction of a response. He returned the plaque to its spot on the table.

Skeptic though he might be, loyalty clearly took precedence for Ben. But he'd referred to his mother as "Dr. MacGregor" again, so I must have hit a nerve. They must not be the perfectly united front they liked to present.

Ben sat back down behind the desk and clasped his hands behind his neck. "Any *more* questions?"

His stony expression told me what answer he wanted. I was willing to leave it there for the moment. "Not right now. Thanks," I said lightly. "I was just wondering."

There was a knock on the door, and I heard Kai's voice. "You ready for me yet?"

"Come on in," Ben said, visibly grateful for the distraction.

Kai entered the room in an elaborately embroidered salwar kameez and gave me a low bow. "Orientator person, at your service."

"Thank you!" I stood and did my best to bow back.

"Kai will take you downstairs and tell you more about the people who work here," Ben said. "You'll probably know their star signs and favorite colors by the time he's done with you. Have fun, and I'll see you at lunch."

"Oh, right." I perked up. "Where are we doing lunch?" I was looking forward to our first session to work on his problem.

Kai gave Ben a curious look.

"I think…" Ben looked around the room. "Let's do it in here."

"Okay. See you then!"

"What was that all about?" Kai asked as we headed to the basement. "Ben doesn't eat, or hadn't you noticed?"

"We just have some stuff to go over," I said, trying to make it sound uninteresting.

"Whatever you say." With a shrewd grin, Kai showed me to his desk.

The basement was a long rectangular room that looked as though it may have served as a social hall at one time. At the front of the room was a stage upon which sat a large makeshift altar. Cubicles lined the sides of the room while floor mats and folded chairs were stacked against the walls. The exercise studio and bathroom were in the back.

Kai's cubicle was the one closest to the stage. In addition to his computer, it was filled with all manner of what I silently dubbed "New Age whatnot." Various crystals, stones, incense cones, bundled herbs, and packs of matches were scattered around. Pinned to the walls were images of the Buddha and the chakra system. Kai also had a collection of what looked like sacred objects from various religious traditions.

"Welcome to my lair." With a flourish, he pulled up a chair for me.

My attention was drawn to an assortment of flat, round stones on Kai's desk that had gold symbols painted on them. "What are these?" I picked one up.

"Chakra stones." He reached out and took me by the wrist, then removed the stone from my hand and put it back on the desk. "Ben asked me to give you the lowdown on our crew."

"Sorry…right, the crew." But my attention was drawn to what looked like a short metal staff leaning against the wall. It was covered in elaborate silver and gold carvings and topped with a fan of peacock feathers. "Oh wow, did you make this, too?" I reached for the staff.

Kai lightly slapped the back of my hand. "Didn't anybody ever teach you to keep your hands to yourself? You're getting your chaotic energy all over everything." He waved his hands around me, as though trying to sweep the air clean.

"Sorry," I mumbled as I continued to examine the contents of the cubicle. "Everything just looks so *cool*."

"It's okay. It's only natural to be curious. I'll be showing you all of these things as time goes on."

It seemed like the right time to ask a question that had been puzzling me. "This is kind of a weird workplace. Do you know why the MacGregors decided to set up in a church?"

"It made sense for them to move into a building that was already energized by centuries of sacred activity. There's a lot of divine mojo coursing through this space, keeping it protected and cleansed. But we can talk more about that later."

Obviously relishing his role as official gossip, Kai launched into a description of the group. He said that Dr. MacGregor had recruited him and the others through a newspaper ad asking for subjects in her research study. Many people had been screened, but only the four of them had been chosen.

Asa was originally from Philadelphia, but his father was invited to become head of the English department at a university in Baltimore just as Asa was starting high school. He had stayed in the area for college, joining the campus Wicca Club in the hopes of meeting free-spirited girls. One of their club activities had been a Reiki workshop led by a local instructor. Asa had immediately taken to it and had earned Reiki master certification in less than a year. It was during that time that he had rediscovered his gift for telepathy. He was born with the ability, but had learned to repress it as a child since it kept getting him into trouble. Now he was working to hone it again.

Eve's family had moved to Washington, D.C. from Hong Kong when she was a baby. Her father had studied traditional Chinese medicine before emigrating and setting up a private practice. Eve had been training with him since she was sixteen. According to Kai, she could see the future while in a deep trance—something Eve first experienced while taking a meditation class in high school. She was still learning how to harness her gift, so the future often came to her in impressions and brief glimpses that were hard to interpret. Dr. MacGregor didn't feel it was safe to let Eve stay in a trance state for too long yet. As a result, she primarily did acupuncture—a skill that Kai felt was just as useful as precognition, and needed more often. Apparently, Eve and Asa had become close friends through their mutual interests in computer gaming and attending comic book conventions.

I already knew about Vani's aura-reading gift, so Kai filled me in on the rest of her life. Apparently, she was incredibly busy, dividing her time between her advertising job, aura reading, and grant writing for the clinic, not to mention the evaluation—and so far, rejection—of an endless string of suitors. And that was when she wasn't jetting off to visit family in London or Mumbai.

The multiple suitors part didn't surprise me, but something else did. "You mean people actually give out grant money for the kind of stuff you do here?"

Kai sucked in his cheeks and nodded. "You'd be surprised at how many people are interested in our work, and who they are. Quite a varied crowd. But they keep it on the down low, of course. No one wants to be publicly affiliated with *our* sort," he said with a wink.

For his part, Kai said that he and Pete had met each other after Kai joined the MacGregors' program. We spent most of our time talking about their romance—how they met (Pete came to pick up Kai for an appointment with Dr. MacGregor), Pete's first awkward attempts at courting, and how they had finally moved in together three years before.

Kai's parents had moved from Greece to North Carolina when he was five to help some extended family members run their business crafting jewelry. Kai said he grew up talking to spirits, and his family was well known for having the "sight," as he called it. When Kai had come out of the closet at nineteen, it had caused a huge family rift, and his parents had disowned him. Alone and without resources, he had worked his way up the East Coast and finally landed in Baltimore. As an artisan skilled in fine metalwork, he had quickly made a home for himself in the city's quirky, spirited arts scene.

After Kai and Pete moved in together, Kai and his parents had achieved a fragile reconciliation. Ironically, his relationship with Pete had made Kai's parents much more comfortable with his sexuality. They seemed pleased that at least he was in a stable relationship, and Pete had impressed them with his stoic brand of solidity.

Kai spoke about reading minds, seeing the future, and talking to the dead as though they were entirely ordinary occurrences to be taken for granted. In a way, I envied the ease with which he engaged in magical thinking; Kai's inner world was much more expansive and colorful than mine. To show that I was taking an interest, I asked him what it was like being a medium. He smiled and said, "Oh, you'll find out tomorrow. We're doing something special then, and I don't want to scare you off by telling you about it now."

I shook my head. "You don't have to worry about scaring me, Kai."

"Oh, you just wait, honey." He patted the back of my hand.

Kai appeared so at home in the clinic, truly in his element. "It seems like you've really found your niche here."

"Oh, yes. This is the only place I've worked where I can be who I really am, and help people in the way I was put on this earth to do. I mean, you know the MacGregors can be—" he gestured vaguely—"personality-challenged. But believe me, they are wonderful people to have in your corner."

He proceeded to tell me a bit more about the MacGregors. Dr. MacGregor's family had made their money in Scottish shipbuilding. Her parents had sent her Stateside for medical school where she had met Ben's father. They had been married for thirty-five years when he had died five years before. Soon afterwards, Ben had left the

Marine Corps and moved in with his mother because he didn't want her living alone. That was when they started the clinic.

"Oh." My heart ached for Ben and his mother. "I didn't realize they'd gone through all of that."

"I know Dr. MacGregor seems like the Iron Lady, but she fell apart for a while after her husband died. Ben didn't even hesitate; as soon as he could, he dropped everything to come take care of her. That's kind of his thing, if you hadn't noticed."

"What is?"

"Taking care of his responsibilities, looking out for the people close to him."

"Oh." That certainly explained why Ben had left the Corps when, from what I'd seen, it remained such a strong part of his identity. "And Pete just dropped everything, as well, to come help Ben?"

Kai nodded. "Once he was able. Those two are basically brothers, and Dr. MacGregor is kind of like Pete's surrogate mother. Pete would do anything for those two."

"Wow, so Ben's father must have been relatively young when he died. Do you know what happened?"

"I don't know for sure," Kai said in a low voice, "but Pete says it was probably alcohol-related. Ben used to enjoy throwing back a few, but he hasn't touched a drop since his dad died."

"Oh, that must have been terrible." Substance-related deaths were so often torturesome tragedies. I couldn't imagine the suffering his father must have gone through—not to mention Ben and his mother. And addiction could elicit such complex emotions. If Ben's father had suffered from an alcohol problem, that might be related to Ben's apparent anger toward him.

"I can only imagine," Kai agreed, then glanced at his computer screen. "Okay, honey, our time is up. I better get you back to Ben."

I forced myself to turn off my therapist brain and change the subject. As we headed up the stairs, I asked, "Do you know what Pete and Ben did in the Marines?"

"Hah!" Kai shook his head. "Good luck finding out anything

about that. Pete said it's so top secret he can't even tell me where they went, let alone what they did." I could see from Kai's expression that the subject had been a point of contention between them. "Believe me, if I can't get it out of Pete, you're not going to get anything out of Ben!"

I had no reason to disbelieve him on that point. Kai seemed like someone who could be pretty persuasive when he wanted to be.

The scent of spices wafted through the air. "Indian food is a favorite here," Kai explained. "We get it at least twice a week."

Since I was a big fan, that worked for me. I just hoped it would work for Ben, and for our luncheon.

CHAPTER THIRTEEN

Ben was waiting when we returned to the lounge. We filled our plates with food and retired to his office. I could feel all eyes on us as we did so. Apparently, Ben's reluctance to eat in front of others was well known.

We took our usual places on either side of his desk. Ben looked up at me with an uneasy smile. "So what do we do now, Doc?"

I appreciated his show of willingness. "Well, we could approach this several ways. But rather than starting off with my ideas, I'd first like to hear what you think would be most helpful to you."

"Hmm." He stared at his plate, contemplating. "Well, I like watching other people eat and enjoy themselves, so it might help if you started eating first."

"Sure, no problem." I put a little bit of rice on a fork and speared a small piece of potato, then held it up to my mouth. "Here we go." I slid the food into my mouth, closed my lips, and pulled out the fork. "Mmm, that is delicious."

Ben laughed, a little nervously. "You don't have to oversell it."

"No," I exclaimed, "that really is delicious! Thanks, by the way, for lunch every day. I wasn't expecting that, and certainly not food of this quality." I picked up a samosa and nibbled on the corner. "So." I gave him an encouraging smile. "Your turn."

Ben closed his eyes and took a deep breath. I could see that he was fighting to control his anxiety.

"Okay," I said, "forget eating for the moment. Your job is just to pick out something that looks good and put it on your fork."

Eyes still closed, he said, "Cate, I have to tell you, I feel ridiculous."

"If I flick this piece of cauliflower at you and get korma sauce all over your face, then you'll *really* feel ridiculous," I teased.

"Oh, I see. So this is therapy by threat?"

"You got it," I said, trying to provoke him further. "Come on, you big tough Marine, stick something with your fork. That's all I'm asking."

That broke him out of his paralysis. His eyes flipped open, and he gave me a dangerous look. "You're throwing down the gauntlet then."

"I guess I am, yes."

"Okay, fine." He picked up the fork. He flinched as though he were getting a shot as he speared a piece of broccoli. Then he dropped the fork onto the plate.

"You have to *hold* the fork," I said.

"You didn't say anything about holding the fork." He was smiling, but I could sense the tension flowing underneath.

While I was relieved that he was having fun with the experiment, I also wanted to make sure he made some measurable progress with minimal struggle. "Okay," I said, working on a brainstorm, "fair enough. I have another idea."

He raised his eyebrows.

"Obviously, you're not comfortable holding the fork. How would you feel about it if I…fed you?"

He cleared his throat. "You know, I've never tried that particular approach."

"Would you be willing to give it a go?"

"I'd probably feel even more ridiculous."

"I'm less worried about you feeling ridiculous than I am about helping you move forward with this."

Ben looked back down at his plate. "You really think it will work?"

"As a first step, maybe," I said. "After all, if I'm feeding you, then you're not technically responsible for what's happening. It might be enough to trick your subconscious into letting go of the fear that by eating in front of me, you might cause me harm."

He seemed to release some of his tension as the logic of the approach settled in. Finally he said, “Okay, let’s do it.”

Eager not to squander the moment, I pulled my chair over behind the desk so that our knees were almost touching. “First of all, tell me: did you pick this broccoli because you actually wanted to eat it, or because it was the first thing you saw?”

He gave the broccoli a hostile look. “Definitely the latter.”

“What do you want to eat?”

He contemplated. “How about that piece of potato? That looks pretty good.”

I smiled. “Okay.” I speared the potato, which was steaming. I put it in front of my lips and blew gently on it a couple of times. I didn’t want him to burn his mouth on his first attempt. Then I looked up at Ben.

Our eyes met, and as though I had just jumped into a river, I entered a torrent of emotion flowing between us. My attraction to him, which I’d been trying to ignore; my growing affection for him; and something even more powerful coming from his direction—a chaotic jumble of emotions that I couldn’t quite identify, save one. He was attracted to me, too. The force of the flow held me paralyzed. I froze, fork in midair, unable to speak.

But Ben wasn’t paralyzed. Holding my gaze, he slowly leaned forward and put his lips around the end of the fork. Then he pulled away, taking the piece of potato with him. We continued staring at one another as he chewed slowly and swallowed. “It worked,” he murmured.

“What? Oh!” He had done it! I grinned. “Do it again!”

He broke our gaze, looked down, and took the fork from me. He chose another potato, this time lifting it to his own lips. Looking back into my eyes, he ate.

As he swallowed, I bounced up and down. “You did it! You ate in front of me. And I didn’t die!”

“No, you didn’t. I appreciate that,” he said as a smile slowly spread across his face. He reached down, speared a piece of cauliflower, and munched gamely on it.

I couldn't believe it had actually worked. "Wow." I fell back against my chair.

He set eagerly to work on a samosa. "You were right. Their food is particularly good today."

With some relief, I realized that I must have been the only one who had been hit by the emotional flow between us. Ben was focused on the food, which was what I wanted. "Look at you. You're eating like you haven't had a bite in days."

"I don't know. All of a sudden, I feel fine eating in front of you."

"How about the others?"

Fear flashed across his face. "One step at a time, Doc."

"Sorry. Of course." I nodded. "I'm just so impressed with what you've done today. That's more than enough for now."

He dug in with gusto. I slid my chair back around to the other side of the desk and watched him. Ben seemed oblivious as my eyes wandered hungrily from his hands to his face, finally settling on his mouth. That's when it occurred to me: Ben might not even be aware of his attraction toward me. It was possible that his conscious mind considered it unacceptable, and had therefore buried it somewhere far beyond his awareness. I knew that it would be best for all concerned if I just forgot I'd ever known about it in the first place and let it go.

A deep sense of disappointment began to sink in. I cleared my throat and forced myself back into a clinical mindset. "So, what was it about that exercise that worked, do you think?"

He put down his fork and looked at me intently. I felt the flow between us again, although more gently this time. "It was you. *You* worked."

"Oh." Fighting a sudden attack of shyness, I asked, "You're sure it wasn't that 'big, tough Marine' comment that did it?"

"Oh yeah. You'll pay for that one."

I grinned. "Oh really?"

"Mm-hmm. You'll see. Someday, somewhere, *I'll* throw down the gauntlet. Hey, you should eat something. Your food is getting cold."

Pleased to see how well he was doing, I joined him. For a while, we ate in silence.

Eventually, Ben asked, "So, was your conversation with Kai educational?"

"Very. It sounds like you have a pretty incredible group here. I'm still not sure how much of the *woo-woo* stuff I believe, but that doesn't mean I'm not impressed with the people."

"Well, we're pretty impressed with you, too." He punctuated his remark with another bite of food.

What I'd learned about the MacGregor family that morning had left me with more questions than answers, though. "I was wondering how your mother became interested in studying special abilities."

Ben paused and pushed himself back from the desk. "When she was in her psychiatry residency, she helped one of the attending doctors with a difficult case—a patient who thought he could see the future. He was diagnosed with a psychotic disorder because everyone thought he was delusional. The patient wasn't even certain of his own sanity since most of his visions weren't verifiable. Either they were visions of people he didn't know or of events years into the future. Anyway, they put this guy on a lot of medications—and this was over thirty years ago, when the side effects were brutal. None of them stopped his visions. The patient ended up taking his life."

"Oh!" My stomach dropped. "How tragic."

Ben nodded slowly. "In his suicide note, he said that he just couldn't keep going anymore. He was so tired of being sick and of not knowing whether his visions were real. Then, at the end of his note, he wrote, 'Congratulations, Dr. MacGregor.' He put down that she was going to have a baby boy and the date and time of the birth. She wasn't pregnant at the time, but for some reason, she kept a copy of the note. About a year later, I was born at the exact time the patient had predicted."

"My God!" The hair on my arms stood on end.

"She named me 'Benjamin' after her patient," he said softly. "I think she felt guilty that she hadn't done more for him, and that she hadn't believed in his abilities until it was too late. She wanted to honor him somehow."

"I can certainly understand that," I said with a new respect for Dr. MacGregor's work.

We finished our food in silence. Then, as we cleaned up, Ben took me gently by the elbow. "Hey, thank you for your help with this," he said. "I never thought I'd eat in front of anyone again. You're amazing."

His smile warmed me like the summer sun. "You're more than welcome. Anytime."

"I'm going to take you up on that." He opened the office door. "Now it's time for your first training exercise."

CHAPTER FOURTEEN

Ben led me down to the large room in the basement where the staff cubicles were. It was quiet, and the only person there was Vani. She was barefoot and wore black velvet leggings and an emerald-green tunic with gold embroidery. She sat cross-legged on one end of a large blue mat in the middle of the floor. Her hair was pulled into a ponytail, which told me she must be in serious work mode. Ben directed me to sit across from her, and then rolled a desk chair over next to the mat for himself.

"Welcome, Cate," Vani said warmly.

"Thanks." I was glad that the initial chill between us seemed to have thawed.

"Vani, can you give Cate a little tutorial before we start?"

"Sure." She turned to me. "Everyone has an energy field surrounding their body," she explained. "In physics, this is referred to as a subtle energy body. We haven't figured out how to measure it with scientific instruments yet, so for now, you have me."

Vani flashed us her glamorous smile and adjusted the glass bangles on her wrists with a gentle clinking noise. "To me, your aura is like a manual. It can find out anything I need to know about you at a given moment in time. But in addition to reading auras, I also heal them."

Since she had blown away any doubts I had about her abilities the day before, I knew better than to answer her claim with skepticism. "What needs healing in an aura?"

Ben jumped in. "Many things, potentially. But for the purposes of this afternoon, let's focus on *your* aura. We've discussed how, when you submerge into a client, information about that person flows into you—like you showed me last night—and after a couple of sessions, a filament forms that connects you to the client when you're no longer with them. We call that 'opening a psychic portal.'"

"A psychic *portal?*" He couldn't be serious. "So, what—it's like *Ghost Trappers* meets *Star Trek*?"

Ben's eyebrow arched slightly. "Look, it's just our term for 'filament.' If it helps, think of it as a metaphor."

"Oh for goodness' sake. Okay, fine." Metaphors were safe enough. "But then why do I have filaments—I mean, portals—open to family and friends? I've never submerged into them."

"It happens automatically when you spend time with someone you care about," he said. "Without making any conscious effort, you are constantly connecting with them. Eventually, a portal forms."

I nodded. That didn't sound completely crazy.

"These open portals are like holes in your aura through which energy is always flowing," Ben explained. "Having so many holes in your aura is depleting you by constantly exposing you to other people's emotions. Even when you're alone, energetically, it's as though you're always in a crowd of people—a crowd of at least fifty, if I remember correctly how many clients Dr. Nelson told us you have. So much external energy is entering you right now that you're drowning in it. That's the cause of your depression and anxiety. What Vani can do is temporarily close the portals between you and your clients."

I jerked my head back as though I had been slapped. "What?"

Both Ben and Vani jumped a little. "Only until you finish the program, Cate," Ben said.

It felt as though my filaments were strings connecting me to a bunch of helium balloons, and Ben was yanking down on them violently. "Ben, can I talk to you for a minute? In private?"

"Sure. Over here." He led me to the space beneath the stairs. "What is it?"

I swallowed hard, fighting to keep my breathing slow and steady. "You never said anything about disconnecting me from my clients."

"I understand your concern, but it's only temporary. When

training is over, Vani will reopen all of the portals if you want her to."

"But I *can't* cut them off, not even temporarily!"

Ben leaned down to meet my gaze, but I turned to the side. The corners of his mouth dropped. "Why not, exactly?"

I was starting to believe that I could trust him. Still, my whole body tensed. "If I tell you, you have to promise it won't go any further. You won't tell your mother or Dr. Nelson."

Ben rubbed his forehead for a moment, then quickly raked his hand through his hair. "All right, just between you and me, what is it?"

Why was I hesitating? It wasn't like I had anything to be ashamed of. I cleared my throat. "It's like I said in my intake interview. I use the filaments—portals—to check in on my clients."

His eyes narrowed. "When you were working at the clinic and had a specific reason to be concerned about someone."

"Yes, that's what I told you," I said carefully, "but the truth is, I still check in on my clients every day. If I sense that someone's in crisis, I call Simone, and she looks into it."

Ben did a double-take. "You *what?*"

"That's why you can't tell anyone," I whispered urgently. "I don't want Simone to get in trouble."

His eyebrows forged a straight rod. "How long has this been going on?"

"Ever since I got back from my mother's funeral."

Ben covered his eyes with his hand for a moment. Eventually he spoke, stabbing the air with his finger. "*This* is why you haven't been getting any better. You can't start healing if you're tearing the scab off the wound every day!"

"My clients are not scabs," I hissed, "or wounds, or whatever is it that you're implying!"

"That's not what I meant." Ben blew out a hard breath. "I know how much you care about your clients, but actively connecting with them is harmful to you right now." He added in an almost hostile tone, "Frankly, I'm surprised that Simone has allowed you to stay so involved in your cases when you so urgently need to focus on your own healing."

"It's not her fault! She's been telling me from the beginning to stop worrying about everyone else. But I care too much about my clients. I can't let them go completely. Eventually she gave up fighting me on it."

"I can see why," he said, his voice hardening, "but I think it's about time you let your colleagues do their jobs."

"But—"

"But what?" He arched his most drill instructor-like eyebrow at me. "Don't you deserve a few weeks off—*completely* off—to take care of yourself? What would you advise a client to do in your position? As you've noticed, this program requires all of your energy. You can't spare any of it, not for your clients and not for anyone else. This time has to be all about you. Let Simone and your colleagues take care of your clients, and let Vani close the portals. Otherwise you can't even begin to heal."

So Ben was convinced that I had to do this in order to get better. What if he was right? If I never got better, I'd lose my job; then I'd be no help at all to my clients. It appeared that I didn't have a choice in the matter.

Suddenly close to tears, I turned away from him again and looked over to the spot where Vani was sitting peacefully. There were few things I despised more than having my hand forced. At least I knew that my clients would be in good hands with Simone in the interim. After all, she somehow managed to be a fabulous therapist without using any paranormal abilities whatsoever. I'd have to ask her to teach me how to do that sometime.

I took a deep breath, slowly let it out, and looked up at Ben. "Okay, fine."

"Good. Thank you." As we walked back over to the mat, Ben tried to break the tension. "I don't know what you're letting yourself get so upset about, anyway," he murmured. "Yesterday, you said you didn't even believe in all of this New Age stuff."

"Good point." I gave him a weak smile. "It's all bullshit.

Let's get started."

His eyes flashed gold, but his expression was somber. "You'll be fine, I promise. Okay, Vani, we're ready."

Vani appeared to be deep in meditation. She spoke so softly that I had to strain to hear. "Cate, make yourself comfortable."

Ben and I took our seats. Vani stood and walked toward me. "Now close your eyes and breathe normally. Gently draw your attention to your breath as it flows in and out of your body."

I recognized the relaxation technique and did as she instructed.

"I don't need to touch you, but I do need to touch your aura, which surrounds your body. You may hear or sense me moving around you, and you may also feel some emotional or physical sensations as I work. Some people do, some don't. Either way, don't worry about it. If you do feel something, I promise it won't hurt." There was kindness in her voice.

"Thanks for that." All I could feel at that moment was the anxiety that had been swirling inside of me ever since the concept of closing the portals had been introduced. But it diminished as I turned my attention away from my thoughts and toward my breathing. Of course my clients would be okay without me for a few weeks. I wondered where this inflated ego of mine came from, the one that made me think I was so critically important to their well-being. I breathed in…and out. In…and out. In…and I drifted softly away.

"Cate?" I heard a man's voice calling me from a long way off. "Cate?" The voice was getting closer.

Something was pressing against the back of my head, against the back of my entire body. Was I lying down?

I felt a hand prop up my head and put something soft beneath it. I heard a female voice next. "I don't know. Nothing like this has ever happened before."

My eyelids fluttered open, and I felt as though I were coming out of a deep sleep. Ben's face was right in front of mine.

"Cate, can you hear me?" His brow was creased with worry.

"Yes, she can hear you," Vani's voice cut in. I heard the clinking of her glass bangles. Then Ben's face was gone, and Vani's appeared. "Cate, you fainted at the end of our session. You're lying on the floor in the church basement. Are you all right?"

"Oh wow," I said, doing a quick mental scan of my body. "Yeah, I'm okay. Can I sit up?"

"Yes," they said in unison, both sounding relieved. Ben took one of my hands and put his other arm around my back.

Vani cautioned, "Slowly, slowly."

"I think I should take her upstairs," Ben said.

"Yes, and I'll get her some tea."

I felt myself being lifted up off the ground. "I'm really okay," I mumbled, but between being in a weakened state and being pressed up against Ben, I couldn't bring myself to object too strenuously. As he carried me up the stairs, my impetuous arms slid themselves around his neck. With a soft grunt, Ben tightened his hold on me, and I barely fought off the urge to wrap myself around him completely. My body sighed with disappointment when we entered the lounge and Ben laid me down gently on a couch.

Vani approached with a cup of tea. Finally, my head began to clear. "I'm fine, really."

"Pete!" Ben barked. Within a minute, Pete appeared in the doorway. He and Ben spoke in low tones. Then Pete disappeared again.

Ben was back at my side. "Cate, I don't know what happened. Are you sure you're all right? Can you look at me?"

"Ben, really, I'm fine. I hate being fussed over."

"Too bad," said Pete, who came back into the room carrying an army-green bag with a red cross on it. He pulled out a blood pressure cuff.

"Pete's a paramedic," Ben explained as he stepped back, giving Pete room to work. Pete's taciturn cowboy and teasing prankster personalities disappeared, and I found myself in the presence of a practiced medical professional.

A stethoscope, blood pressure monitor, and thermometer later—and something shining in my eyes and something poking in my ears—Pete patted me on the arm and declared, "She's okay."

Only then did Ben seem to relax a bit. I could tell that he was working to regain his composure.

Meanwhile, Vani came over and placed the mug of tea in my hands. "I'm glad you're okay. That was quite a session, huh?"

The more my head cleared, the more annoyed I became with being the center of attention. I was also embarrassed about having passed out in the first place. "What happened? I mean I know I fainted, but what happened before that?"

Ben paced up and down the lounge. "I don't know. Honestly, nothing like this has ever happened before. Has it, Vani?"

"Ben, relax. She's fine." Vani waved him away. "Cate, when I went into your aura to close the portals, there were so many of them, and the energy flow coming in was much stronger than I was expecting. I had to work hard to close them. It took much longer than usual."

"Is that why I fainted?"

"It's possible," she acknowledged. "I've closed a lot of portals before, but I've never seen a situation quite like yours. It was a significant amount of work. Maybe we should have taken it in stages."

Then it dawned on me what she was saying. "You mean all of the portals are closed?"

"Yes, the ones you had opened to your clients. Your connections to friends and family, I left intact."

I closed my eyes and turned inward. Almost all of the filaments had disappeared. My heart was cavernous, empty. A wave of panic swept over me. I immediately tried to connect to Elana. Where there had previously been a warm pulse of life, there was nothing but cold and silence. I couldn't help it; I started to cry.

Vani said, "It's okay. I know it feels strange."

Ben rushed over. "What is it? Are you all right?"

"They're…*gone*," I whispered.

Ben and Vani exchanged a meaningful glance. She stood. "I'm going to go back downstairs. I'm glad you're all right. Let me know if you need me." Then she disappeared.

I couldn't stop the tears. It felt like fifty deaths had occurred all at once. Ben sat down next to me and put his arm around my shoulder. "What have I done?" I whispered. "Where did they all go?"

He gave me a light squeeze. "They're all fine, Cate. They're fine, and they're out there living their lives. Nothing has changed for them, only for you."

"You mean, they can't feel—"

"No. This only affects your aura, not theirs. None of them will know that anything has changed."

Oh thank God, I thought. "But it hurts!"

"It's going to be okay, Cate. I promise."

My head fell against his chest. Feelings of grief pounded at my heart like hard rain against a window. Ben rested his hand on my forehead as I cried. After what seemed like an eternity, my tears finally began to slow.

"I'm sorry," he murmured, smoothing my hair back. "I didn't know it was going to be that intense."

I saw that Ben's shirt was stained with my tears. Suddenly self-conscious, I pulled away and dried my eyes. "What's it normally like?"

"We've worked with empaths before, but I've never seen anyone have such an extreme reaction to a portal closure," he said. "You're one of a kind, Cate."

I rubbed my face with my hands. "In that case, I hope you're documenting this for science."

"Don't worry." As he smiled, I saw some of the worry leave his face. "I'm starting to figure you out now, though."

"Figure me out?"

"Your heart, your strength. I'm starting to get it."

"Meaning?"

"Meaning, now I know to expect the unexpected. I have a feeling that nothing is going to go as planned when it comes to you."

"Oh," I said, unsure what to make of that. I sighed heavily. "Did we really have to close the portals?"

"Yes, we really did," he said without a hint of hesitation.

"But why?"

"We went over this under the stairs, remember?"

"Yes, but I didn't believe anything was actually going to *happen* then."

His eyes widened. "Are you blaming me for that?"

"Well, you didn't try very hard to convince me, did you? 'Think of it as a metaphor,' you said."

"And if I had tried harder to convince you, you would have believed me. Is that what you're saying?"

"No, that's not what I'm saying."

"Then what are you saying?"

I paused to think. "I don't know," I admitted.

Ben took my hands, which like the rest of my body felt like lifeless lumps of clay. "I hate that this was so hard for you. But believe me, it's for the best. We had to do this before we could make any further progress. I know you won't believe this now, but you may come to *prefer* being the only person living in your own body."

I was far from convinced. The emptiness inside of me howled softly.

"Look," he said, "I think you've had quite a day already. I don't think we should push it any further." He turned toward the hallway and called out Pete's name again.

Pete rejoined us in the lounge. "Hey, you alert now? Because I have good news."

"What is it?" I could use some good news.

"While you were downstairs, the police called," Pete said. My heart jumped into my throat. "I knew what you were doing down there, so I didn't interrupt. But they wanted me to tell Cate that they caught that Don guy."

My heart flip-flopped. "They what?"

"They caught him—get this—on a routine traffic stop. Turns out he was out hot-roddin' around last night and got pulled over. He had a bunch of old unpaid tickets and a few outstanding bench warrants, so they took him in. He's going to be in there for quite a while until all of that gets sorted out." Pete grinned and hooked his thumbs into his belt buckle.

Ben grinned back. "He must be mighty pissed off right about now!"

Pete chuckled. "Yeah, maybe we should go pay him a visit!"

I was still trying to wrap my brain around the facts. "You mean he's in jail? For a while?"

"Yeah," Pete said, "a couple of weeks at least, the police said. Enough time to figure out what to do with your complaint. They'll probably be callin' you in to pick him out of a lineup or something."

The idea of seeing Don again made me shudder. Still, relief engulfed me—Elana and I were both safe, at least for a couple of weeks.

Ben put his hand on mine. "Listen, this is good news, but if it would make you feel more comfortable to keep us around, Pete and I will be glad to stay on guard duty until you feel better about things."

Pete nodded. "No problem at all. We don't want to intrude, but you only have to say the word and we'll be there."

Deep down, I liked the idea of having them continue to guard me. My previous assumptions about safety and security had been shaken by Don's visit the night before. But the stubborn part of me was unwilling to give in to Don's bullying by falling victim to irrational fears. "No, thank you. Having you there last night made all the difference. But the threat is gone, thank God, and if you keep watching over me, I'm going to start to feel a bit silly."

"You're sure?" Ben asked.

"Yes, I'm sure," I said, trying to sound confident.

"All right, but keep the panic button just in case."

I nodded. "Thanks so much. I mean it."

Pete said, "Okay, Cate, saddle up. Time to go home and bed down."

Overwhelmed by exhaustion, I barely managed a wave to Ben as I followed Pete out to the truck.

Chapter Fifteen

Midnight found me lying in bed awake. I had slept for a few hours, but after a siren awakened me, sleep refused to come. I held my eyes closed and turned my attention inward.

In my heart, there was no more tugging. First my mother, then my clients. They were gone. The portals had been closed. I had never felt so lonely for connection, so forced into solitude. My whole purpose and reason for being—the relationships I had worked so hard to build—had been taken away from me. And in their place was nothingness.

Sharp points of grief scraped along the walls of my heart, but I had cried so much that I was out of tears. Ben had said I might come to prefer the feeling of being alone in my skin, but what did he know? He hadn't expected me to react the way I had to the portal closures. I was "one of a kind," he'd said. In other words, no one else was like me, so no one else could know the desolation I was feeling.

I felt an acute longing to call my mother and ask for her advice. But she had chosen to remove herself from my life. The dry heat of unshed tears burned my eyes. I would have to figure it out on my own.

I wrestled with myself. I was really growing to like Ben in spite of how difficult he could be at times, and I liked the others as well. I was genuinely interested in Dr. MacGregor's work and in what she was trying to do. Certainly, she and Ben seemed to "get" what was going on with me more than anyone else ever had. It would be nice to have someone I could lean on. But the truth was that eventually the training program would end, and I would go back to my regular life.

Dr. Nelson had said he didn't want me to give up on the program after one day. Well, I had given it two days; that would just have to be good enough. After all, in only forty-eight hours, they had already taken much more away from me than I could afford to lose. Who knew what would happen if I stayed even longer?

A quiet knowing settled upon me: There was only one thing to do. I had to get out.

• • •

Hell Week, Day Three

When Pete arrived Tuesday morning, I was showered and dressed in yoga pants and a fitted T-shirt. My hair was in a neat braid, my pills taken, breakfast eaten. I heard Pete's truck pulling up and decided to shock him by opening the door before he knocked.

Standing on the front stoop, Pete looked impressed. "You're ready to roll this morning."

"Yes," I said brightly, determined to start the day off looking professional and competent. I had worked out a plan, and looking like an idiot was not part of it.

As we pulled away from the curb, I realized that our commute presented me with the perfect opportunity to learn more about my opposition before going into battle. "Pete," I inquired lightly, "what would you say Ben is like?"

He pushed his hat back a bit. "Meanin'?"

"I don't know." I made an effort to sound as though I had no ulterior motive whatsoever. "Like, if you had to describe him, how would you do it?"

He chuckled and rubbed his hairline. "Oh, well, in the Corps, we called him Rottie."

"Really? What does that mean?"

"Rottie, short for Rottweiler. You know, those big black-and-brown guard dogs. Our unit worked with one named Tank for a while, and Ben really bonded with him. They were a lot alike—

both always barkin'."

"All bark, but no bite?" I asked hopefully.

"Hell yeah, he could bite," Pete said with admiration. I decided to assume he was talking about the dog. "You surely don't want to be anywhere near a Rottweiler when they get worked up. But really, Tank was just a big softie like all dogs. All he wanted was for us to throw him a ball, wrassle with him, scratch his belly. You know."

"Yeah," I said, although I had no experience with Rottweilers. I would have to take his word for it. "So Ben's like that, too? A big softie?"

"Oh yeah," Pete said, "and you can tell him I said that, by the way. Just be sure he's got his shock collar on when you do!" He tilted his head back and laughed, taking one hand off the wheel to slap his thigh.

I laughed tentatively. Unsure when I would get another chance to be alone with Pete, I figured I had better take full advantage of the situation. "Hey, do you know anything about Ben's father?"

The jovial mood disappeared instantly. Pete pushed his hat back down into place. "Now, that's maybe somethin' you should ask Ben about, don't you think?"

I looked down at my hands. "He doesn't seem to want to talk about him."

"There you go, then."

"I'm sorry. I shouldn't have asked. It's none of my business."

"It's all right." Pete rubbed his chin. "I know you don't mean any harm. I'll tell you this, though: Ben joined the Corps to get away from him. Beyond that, you'll have to talk to the big dog."

"Okay. Thanks."

I looked out the window and watched the empty streets and boarded-up houses pass by. As we got closer to the church, I summoned my courage once more, figuring that it was as good a time as any to test Kai's claim that what Pete and Ben had done in the service was all some sort of big secret. "So, you guys had a guard dog in the Marines? Was he guarding you or helping you guard something else?"

"Oh no." Pete smiled and shook his head. "You're gonna have to wake up a bit earlier in the mornin' to catch *me* out, girlie."

I feigned innocence. "What do you mean?"

"Kai told me you asked him about that. You know full well what we did was a couple of notches above top secret, and we can't talk about it, not to anyone. And that includes you."

How thoroughly annoying. I smirked. "I think you're making that up. I bet you guys spent all of your time in some red-light district somewhere, and you just don't want anybody to know about it, so you say it was 'top secret.'"

"Well then," Pete said, grinning widely, "if you're wonderin' how Big Ben is in the sack after all those sessions with the pros, I'm afraid I can't shed any light there. You'll have to find that out all on your own."

A fierce blush exploded across my face. I quickly turned to look out my window again. *Goddamned Pete,* I thought—and not for the last time.

• • •

Ben asked me to join him in his office after tai chi, which had been a little less embarrassing than before. I had skulked around the back of the room, trying to go unnoticed and doing my best to go through the arm motions. Thankfully, Ben had stayed in the front of the room, which had improved my concentration.

He had changed back into his usual suit and button-down shirt with the collar undone. "So." Ben clapped his hands together, radiating good health as he took his seat behind the desk. "How do you feel this morning?"

"Okay," I lied, taking my place in the usual armchair. "Well-rested."

"Glad to hear it. How about emotionally?"

"Oh…well…" I looked up at the ceiling.

He rubbed his jaw. "Still trying to get used to the portals being closed?"

"Um..." I tried to remember how I had decided to start my speech. "About that."

"Yes?"

Here goes, I thought. "After I got home last night, I had time to think over everything that's happened over the past two days, and I realized that it could all actually be explained without resorting to a belief in auras or portals or any other New Age stuff. I mean Vani could easily be a very perceptive person and a good guesser."

"Ah." Ben's expression was inscrutable as he leaned back in his chair.

"And I could have passed out from, I don't know, dehydration or nerves or something."

"Mm-hmm." Ben brushed an invisible piece of lint off of his knee.

I was getting much less resistance than I had expected. A seed of suspicion formed in the back of my mind that Ben's calm wasn't what it appeared to be. Still, I pushed onward. "And as far as not being able to sense my clients anymore, who knows? Maybe the filaments were all in my head. Maybe we never really were connected like that, and the 'evidence' I thought I was seeing was merely due to coincidence. Coincidences do happen, after all."

I gave Ben a professional smile. *He hasn't disagreed with me yet,* I marveled. *Could it really be this easy?*

"Yes, they do," Ben said. "So what you're saying is that all of the problems you've been having could be the products of an overactive imagination."

"And probably some anxiety," I tacked on to add clinical legitimacy.

"Of course, and some anxiety. And all of those symptoms you told us about in your intake interview...they've all disappeared?"

"I just needed to get a handle on them, that's all—which I have done now with your help." I made an effort to project a combination of gratitude and confidence.

"I can see that you're a person of intellectual integrity. That's a quality I respect a great deal."

I couldn't tell if he was being sincere or sarcastic, but I decided to go with the former presumption. "Thank you," I said, trying to appear humble. There was no need to burn bridges; the MacGregors were colleagues of Dr. Nelson's after all.

He leaned forward, put his elbows on the desk, and regarded me thoughtfully. "Cate, I don't care how you fit what we do here into your belief system, if at all. The important thing is that you learn the skills we have to teach you."

I felt almost relieved that he was finally pushing back. I was also glad that I had anticipated what he might say and had a ready answer to his argument. I maintained a polite tone. "But now that I have a better idea of what you do here, I don't think I can learn the skills you want to teach me without completely abandoning my belief system—a system I've been carefully developing my entire life—and that's just not something I'm willing to do. Things that don't fit into my belief system don't really hold any value for me."

"I see." A shadow fell across his face. "So in spite of the commitment you made to stay for the entire program, you've decided to leave us."

Well, since he'd brought it up…time for the diplomatic grand finale. "I'm very grateful for the help you've given me. What we've done so far has really brought me back to reality and helped me to see things clearly. Please don't misunderstand; I think the work you're doing here is interesting, and I'd love to keep up with Dr. MacGregor's research. But to be honest, I don't see any point in staying. I think it would be a waste of your time and mine." I covered one hand with the other and crossed my hidden fingers.

He held my eyes for an uncomfortably long moment. "You're sure? Your mind is made up?"

"It is. I spent a lot of time considering this."

Ben leaned over and started rummaging around in his briefcase. "I can't tell you how sorry I am to hear that."

He sounded even sorrier than I was expecting him to. "Like I said, I really appreciate everything you've tried to do for me."

He pulled a piece of paper from the briefcase and slid it across the desk to me. "You're leaving me no choice then."

Oh for God's sake, I thought. "Look, if that's the contract I signed, I really don't think—"

"Read it." His eyes hardened.

I picked up the paper. It was a note, handwritten on a piece of paper from…Dr. Nelson's prescription pad? I looked up at Ben. He gestured toward the paper. It was dated the day before, and it read: "If Cate Duncan leaves the MacGregor's program after Day Two, she will not be returned to work but will be placed on indefinite suspension until I decide what to do with her. Affectionately, Dr. Nelson."

I stared at the note. I double-checked the date. I analyzed the handwriting and signature. I couldn't believe what I was seeing.

I heard Ben's voice. "I told my mother about your reaction to the portal closure yesterday. We were both concerned, so we had Dr. Nelson over for dinner to discuss things."

My eyes closed. They'd had Dr. Nelson over for dinner? *This cannot be happening,* I told myself.

"Don't worry, I didn't tell them that you've been secretly checking in on your clients and working with Simone," he said. "We just talked in general terms about how you're doing. Dr. Nelson really cares about you, you know."

They weren't going to let me go. I put the note back on the desk, leaned back in my chair, and covered my face with my hands.

"It's obvious to all of us that you could not be better suited to our program. However, I know better than anyone how challenging all of this has been for you, so I expressed some reservations about your staying power."

I bet he did. I felt like I was starting to drown.

"We all agreed that after what happened yesterday, it was likely that you would come in today and try to reason your way out of continuing with the program." He tapped the note on the desk with his finger. "So Dr. Nelson provided a little insurance in case you tried to leave. Feel free to call him if you would like to verify any of this."

I pulled my hands away from my face. Ben's formerly handsome face suddenly appeared tyrannical to me. The straight dark line of eyebrows resembled a billy club, and the square corner of his jaw was evocative of a prison cell. "You son of a bitch."

"That's fine," he said, meeting my challenging gaze with his own. "Be angry at me. But you should know that it was out of respect for you and confidence in our program that Dr. Nelson only stipulated that you have to stay beyond Day Two. He's aware that the first few training exercises can be a bit of a shock, but he also has faith that given the opportunity to rethink things—and giving us another opportunity to win you over—you will choose to honor your commitment." The corners of his eyes creased with concern. "We all care about you, Cate."

So the MacGregors and Dr. Nelson were thick as thieves. "Dr. Nelson is *very* familiar with the program then," I observed bitterly.

Ben appeared implacable. "He certainly is. He helped my mother develop it. That's why he's so confident this is the right thing for you."

I struggled to absorb what I was hearing. I had actually thought that I was getting to know Ben. I'd submerged into him, for God's sake. But now…who *was* this person? "I can't believe you did this to me! How could you, after everything we've been through over the past couple of days?"

I thought I saw him flinch slightly. "I'm sorry you feel that way, but my priority is to keep you in the program. You don't understand how important that is yet, but we do. It's not just about training you at this point. It's for your own safety."

"My *safety*?" More desperate bullshit. Something inside of me went very cold. I willed it to grow and spread itself over the wound Ben had inflicted, to dull the pain. "I don't know you at all, do I?"

Ben ignored my question. "Our next meeting is with Kai in the basement. Shall we?" He stood up and opened the door.

Snookered again. I swallowed hard to keep tears from rising to the surface. The walk to the basement felt like a walk to the gallows.

Chapter Sixteen

The basement was humming with activity. Kai was on the stage busying himself around a makeshift altar. Vani was standing in the middle of the room tapping on her phone. Eve and Asa appeared to be locked into an intense computer gaming session, sitting in their respective cubicles wearing high-tech looking headsets and exacting punishment on their consoles. Though surrounded by people, I felt acutely alone.

I heard the familiar ambient music from our tai chi sessions playing in the background. When she spotted us, Vani came over and squeezed my hands. "How are you today?"

"Fine," I lied. I told myself that if I was going to be stuck there for the rest of the day, I would have to find some way of making things bearable. I decided to show Ben how agreeable I could be when people treated me reasonably. I forced myself to smile back at Vani. "How are you?"

"Great," she chirped. "Looking forward to your initiation ritual."

"My what?" I asked. She gestured toward the stage where Kai was donning some kind of elaborate robe.

"We're all going to participate. Hopefully, the extra bodies will help contain the energy so we don't have a repeat of yesterday's… well, you know." She shrugged apologetically.

"Right, I remember. But *what* kind of ritual?"

Vani gave Ben a puzzled look. "You didn't explain it to her?"

"We had other things to discuss," Ben said impassively. "Why don't you do the honors?"

As Vani gave us a curious look, Kai shouted, "Oh no, honey, leave it to me. I'll take care of Cate. Come on over here!" I was all too glad to leave Ben's circle of influence and climb onto the stage.

Kai was really decked out. He wore Cleopatra-style eyeliner and a long crimson robe covered with embroidery and fastened at the neck with a gold clasp. On his head was some kind of elaborate headdress with feathers, a cross between a Catholic bishop's hat and something you might see on a Rockette.

"Wow, Kai," I said, "you look stunning!"

"Thanks, hon. I could wear jeans and a T-shirt, but what fun would that be? Plus, I think the Divine appreciates it when you put in a little effort out of respect."

I couldn't help but smile. As much as I hated having to be there, I loved being around Kai. I remembered what he'd said that first day about coming to him if Ben ever gave me a hard time. I figured it was as good a time as any to find out if the offer was genuine. "Kai, can I ask you something?"

"Anything," he said as he arranged some two foot-long pink and white crystals in a square on the stage floor.

"Is Ben *always* a pain in the ass?"

"Always, always." He placed two chairs facing one another on either side of the crystal configuration, appearing completely unsurprised by my question. "That's like death and taxes."

"That's what I was afraid of," I muttered.

"Don't worry." Kai straightened up and put a hand on my shoulder. "He's a good boy at heart. He means well. But you know, we are what we are. Nothing can change that. And what Ben is, is definitely a pain in the ass!" Kai shouted the last four words in Ben's direction.

Ben shot us a scowl.

Kai chuckled and patted my arm. "He's a pussycat, baby. This ritual we're going to do today is going to blow your mind! Are you excited?"

Kai certainly looked excited. I decided to reserve judgment so as not to insult my new ally. I searched for words, finally settling on, "I have no idea what to expect."

"What we're going to do is open you up so you have easier

access to all of your gifts. We'll blow your doors off their hinges. You are going to be humming and churning with power when we finish with you. Are you up for that?"

I was hit by a sharp wave of panic. After my portal closure fainting spell, I wasn't sure I could handle any more "mind blowing." But as I looked around, everything I saw reminded me of nothing more than the prop room at a middle school play. Surely there was nothing more to it than a bit of amateur theatrics. There couldn't be any harm in humoring him. "Sure, I'm up for it."

"Great!" He clapped his hands several times. "Okay, everybody, we're ready. Come on up."

With reluctance, Eve and Asa dragged themselves away from their computers, but they greeted me warmly once on stage. Eve wore the dark multi-textured and carefully put-together uniform of the style-conscious punk, while Asa was casual in khakis and a T-shirt emblazoned with the slogan User Friendly.

"What were you guys playing?" I asked.

"*Apocalypse Slaughter Death House Five!*" Asa announced.

"Yeah, we were just destroying a couple of tweakers in Moscow," Eve explained.

"Congratulations!"

"Thanks," Eve said. Then she added quickly, "But your ritual is going to be much cooler."

"Oh yeah," Asa nodded. "Much cooler."

"That's good to hear," I said, touched by their efforts to reassure me.

"Okay, enough nerd talk, children," Kai said as he gestured for me to sit in one of the chairs near the crystals. He took the chair facing me while Vani, Asa, and Eve sat around us like points on a triangle.

Ben stood awkwardly on the floor in front of the stage. "Do you need me?" he asked Kai.

"No, Benjamin," Kai said sternly, "I get the impression you've done quite enough this morning. I think we'll do better without your energy mussing things up."

I could hardly believe my eyes: Ben actually looked chastened. He took a seat in Vani's cubicle. I gaped at Kai, who seemed to take his power over Ben entirely for granted. He was already giving out instructions to the people on the stage.

"You all," Kai gestured to Eve, Vani, and Asa, "you got my back. If anything goes wrong, you know what to do." They all nodded, looking completely confident and at ease—and why shouldn't they? What could possibly go wrong? It was all make-believe. Robes, crystals…no ritual knives or goat heads. There was nothing to worry about.

Then Kai turned to me. "So this is what's going to happen. Don't worry; all you have to do is sit here. I'll invite the Other Side to join us. Then I'll see who shows up for you and ask if they have anything to say."

I blinked. "What do you mean, 'who shows up for me?'"

"You know, spirits. Dead people," he said casually, as though mentioning that he were left-handed. "We'll see who accepts our invitation to show up from the other side to support you. If they want to talk to us, I might ask you some questions to verify the information they're giving me. In that case, answer me briefly, yes or no. Got it?"

I loved Kai, but he truly was a crackpot. "Okay," I said, hoping to conceal my disbelief. "Then what?"

"Then, kaboom!" Kai moved his hands as if to illustrate an explosion. "We'll blow those doors off of their hinges like we talked about, and your gifts will be fully accessible. It will be earth shattering. Just you wait."

I could feel Ben's eyes on me, but I refused to look his way. "Sounds good."

"Wonderful!" said Kai. "Everyone, prepare yourselves."

Vani, Eve, and Asa sat cross-legged with their eyes closed and their hands on their knees, palms up. Kai closed his eyes and pressed his hands together, placing them in front of his forehead. I closed my eyes as well, not wanting to be disrespectful.

When Kai spoke, it was with the deep tone and rhythmic

cadence of a televangelist. "I ask the gods and goddesses, spirit guides, and guardian angels, spirits from beyond the veil, and all those who wish to support Cate Duncan in this opening ritual to be in attendance with us now."

I felt a chill go down my spine. *Kai is great at this*, I thought. *He would be a hit in Vegas.*

There was silence for a few moments before Kai spoke again. "Spirits, I feel your presence. If there is one among you who would like to step forward and communicate with us in support of Cate, please make yourself known to me."

I felt a cool wind start to blow gently on the crown of my head. I wondered if I might be sitting under an air conditioning vent.

"Cate, who is Rhona?"

My heart leapt and my eyes flipped open. I looked at Kai; his eyes were still closed. "What did you say?" I asked, trying to control the alarm in my voice.

"Rhona says she has come here for you. Is this someone you know?"

Is this some kind of a sick joke? I wondered. Rhona was an unusual name, and one that I had never mentioned to anyone. "My mother's name was Rhona."

"Thank you," Kai acknowledged matter-of-factly. "Your mother says she is here today to support you in this ritual." His eyebrows knit together as though he were listening carefully to something. "I hope you understand this, because I don't. She says she's glad you're taking good care of the blue turtle. Do you know what she means?"

The blue turtle. A gold brooch in the shape of a turtle, inlaid with blue opal. It was one of the few things I'd kept of my mother's. It sat in a red-velvet jewelry box on my dresser. "Yes, I know," I whispered.

"Okay. She mentioned that as a way of letting you know it's really her. She says to tell you she loves you very much, and she apologizes for crossing herself over."

All at once, I felt my mother's presence. I caught the faint aroma of her coconut hand cream. My throat felt like it was closing up.

"Rhona says that you two are very similar. She was an empath, too, although she tried not to use her gifts. She feared them, so she suppressed them, ignored them. Still, she couldn't stop absorbing negative emotions, and eventually it got to be too much for her. She began to envy her dying patients, how close they were to a release from the pain. Her thoughts became distorted. She wasn't in her right mind when she took those pills." Kai paused as though listening to a voice that no one else could hear.

So my mother *had* been an empath? My eyes swelled with tears. The cool air blowing on my head became icy and strong. What the hell was going on?

Kai continued. "She has seen everything you've been through since she passed, and she is sorry. She's been working to protect you from toxic surges for the past couple of months, but if she'd had any idea how much you were struggling while she was alive, she would have stayed here and tried to help you. But since you never told her about your gifts, she was able to remain in denial. She didn't want to admit to herself that you were like her, because she didn't want to imagine that you might suffer like she had. Where she is now, though, she is healthy, happy, and at peace. She doesn't want you to worry about her."

I closed my eyes against the room. I wasn't sure how much more I could take.

"Okay." There was a pause as Kai appeared to be listening for something. "She's telling you that it's important to stick with the MacGregors. She knows that you think about following in her footsteps. If you don't accept Ben's help, she's afraid you'll end up like her."

A sob caught in my throat.

"Oh, honey, much sorrow," Kai said, his tone grim. "She would have much sorrow if you joined her now. Much greater things are meant for you in your life. Wonderful things."

Tears were dripping onto my T-shirt, but I couldn't make my arms move to wipe them from my cheeks.

"Cate, she is pulling her energy back now, but she is going to stay close by as we do the ritual. She will be supporting you, and she says don't be afraid of your power. Okay everyone, it's time."

I sat perfectly still and tried to push down the rising sobs with deep breaths.

Kai stood up and held his hands palms down over the crystal configuration on the floor. "Ultimate Divine, we invite you to release your servant, Cate Duncan, from her human limitations and open her to the source of all power so that she may fully experience her gifts and embrace the destiny you have set forth for her in this lifetime."

I opened my eyes. Kai had moved his hands over my head and was chanting something silently. The air in the room began to hum and vibrate. Suddenly he clapped his hands three times over the crown of my head. The cold air that had been blowing on the top of my head turned into freezing water. It flowed in, filling me like a glass. My whole body felt icy. I started to shiver.

Kai lowered his hands to his sides. "Thank you, spirits, for attending today to support us in this ritual. Please hold us all in the palm of your hand and continue to give us your guidance and support. Amen."

"Amen," the others chimed in. As everyone's eyes opened, Vani, Eve, and Asa exchanged looks of wonderment. Kai smiled excitedly at me, but his face quickly twisted with worry. "Good lord, someone get this girl a blanket."

Ben was already on his way, taking the steps up to the stage two at a time. He unrolled a wool blanket and wrapped it around me. My teeth started to chatter. "Get away from me," I managed to whisper.

Looking startled, Ben gestured to Vani who took over blanket duty.

Kai pulled a chair up next to me and put an arm around my shoulders, rubbing to warm me up. "That was amazing. Your mother is such a clear communicator. Don't worry; you'll warm up in a minute. Spirit energy is cold. There must have been some powerful ones here to freeze you up this good."

I gave Kai a pleading look. "What just happened?"

"Oh no! You look terrified! Relax; there's nothing to be afraid of. It's like I told you, very simple. We invited some spirits to support you, and we opened you up. Like an auric steam bath. Your energy is as smooth and clear as a baby's bottom now." He smiled. "Using your gifts will be a snap."

My skin started to tingle painfully, like a limb that had been asleep and was finally waking up. "My skin hurts."

"I know," Kai said sympathetically. "Like when you overuse a loofah. It doesn't last very long, maybe a few minutes. I think we should take you upstairs where you can rest." He turned to Ben. "Can we put her in your office?"

"Of course," Ben said.

That was the last place I wanted to go, but I didn't have the strength to object.

"Can you take her, Vani? I've got to straighten up down here," said Kai. Vani held the blanket around me as we made our way off the stage and upstairs to Ben's office.

She sat me in one of the club chairs and brought me a mug of tea. "That was fascinating," Vani said, closing the door. "We don't usually have a spirit come through as clearly as your mother did, and the energy in the room was really powerful."

Tears filled my eyes again. Vani put her arm around my shoulders. "What is it? Are you okay?"

"I'm not sure," I whispered. "I guess I'm just freaked out."

She gave me a knowing smile and retrieved some tissues from the desk. "I'm not surprised. Kai is really talented. The abilities the rest of us have can potentially be explained away. That's why I get so frustrated with skeptics—not *you*," she clarified quickly. "I mean other people."

I nodded, grateful for her kind distinction.

"But when Kai connects with someone as clearly as he did this morning, it's really hard to find a way to dismiss what he does."

"It's not even that so much, although it's partially that. It's more than that." My voice came out in a whisper as I asked, "I mean, do you think that was really my mom?"

Vani tilted her head to one side. "Can you think of anyone else it could have been?"

I started to cry again.

"Cate, I'm sorry. Maybe I'm saying the wrong things."

"No, it's not you." I took a deep breath and let it out slowly. "But if it *was* her…she was a home hospice aide. If she was an empath, too…"

Vani's eyes widened. "Oh, I see what you mean. That must have been unbelievably hard, especially if she didn't have any paranormal training or supports."

I tried to imagine what it must have been like for my mom, spending every day absorbing the emotions of people who were dying and the loved ones who were losing them. A sob caught in my throat.

"Oh no. Now I've done it. Do you want me to get Ben?"

"No!" A surge of anger cauterized the flow of my tears.

Vani shook her head. "What is going on here? You two seemed okay yesterday, but today, it's like there's a layer of frost between you."

I dabbed my face with a tissue. "I guess you could say we had a fight."

"Oh." She took a seat in the other armchair. "I can't say that I'm surprised. He can be difficult."

"He's using blackmail to keep me here. I'd say that's being difficult."

"I see." Vani's wide brown eyes grew wider, and I could tell that she was reluctant to get in the middle of our dispute. "Well, all I can say is that Ben may stick his foot in it from time to time, but it's always with the best of intentions. If you can find it in you to give him the benefit of the doubt—"

"And why would I do that?"

"Because he might be trying to protect you. He's kind of chivalrous like that, even if he's clumsy about it."

What in the heck was she talking about? "What could he possibly need to protect me from—besides himself, I mean?"

Vani took a seat in the chair next to mine. "Look, life in general isn't very easy for sensitives, especially right now. At other points in history we were more highly valued as healers. We were taken care of by the societies in which we lived. As it is now, we're forced to live like everyone else in the modern world. The Western lifestyle in particular is quite incompatible with who we are. That's why sensitives have such high rates of addiction, mental illness..."

And suicide, I thought. My head began to throb.

Vani took my hand. "Ben and Dr. MacGregor understand all of that, which is why they try to help people like us."

Whether or not what she said was true of the MacGregors, as far as I was concerned, it still didn't excuse Ben's behavior. "I understand your point, but I'm a therapist, Vani. I think I would know if my problems were that serious."

She shrugged. "Maybe, maybe not. No offense, but this isn't exactly your area of expertise, Cate, and it isn't child's play. The things you're going to be learning here are very powerful. They can be wonderfully healing—or incredibly dangerous if you don't treat them with respect."

The more she sounded like Ben, the more irritated I felt. "I know you're trying to be helpful, but I've taken care of myself for a long time, and I've managed to survive so far."

"I get it," she said gently. "I do. You're a grown woman. You don't want to admit that you need looking after. But you do, for a while anyway." She shrugged. "I did, too, in the beginning. It won't be like this forever though."

Just as I opened my mouth to argue, there was a knock on the door. Vani leaped up to open it. As she let Ben in, she headed out, saying, "Get warm, and I'll see you later!"

I really, really didn't want to be alone with Ben. I fixed my eyes on my mug of tea.

He sat in the armchair Vani had vacated. There was a long pause and though I didn't look at him, I could sense that he was struggling to find the right words. "Cate."

"Please don't talk to me."

"All right." There was another long pause. I slowly took a

sip of tea.

He spoke again. "I just wanted to say—"

I shot him a warning look, but he was determined. His voice was ragged with emotion. "I'm sorry. Normally spirits don't communicate with Kai until at least a year after they've crossed over. If I'd had any idea that your mother might come through today, I would have warned you. I can't imagine what a shock that must have been." His expression was sharp with pain, and I could tell that he was being honest.

Not that it mattered, after what he'd done to me earlier. "You would have warned me? Well, thanks for that," I said coldly and forced my eyes back to my mug. "I'd like to be alone now if you don't mind."

"Okay, sure." He stood and headed for the door. "We'll talk later. I'll be in the lounge if you need anything."

Once he was gone, I put the mug on the desk and curled into a ball on the chair, glad to finally have a moment to myself.

I closed my eyes. "Mom, was that really you?" I whispered. Silence. "If you can hear me…" The tears started to flow again. "I'm sorry that I was so clueless. I had no idea how much you were suffering. Thank you for letting me know that you're okay." My shoulders started to shake. "I really wish you were here."

And then I didn't know what else to say. I let the tears take me.

Chapter Seventeen

I must have fallen asleep because I was awakened by the sound of lowered voices coming from the lounge. I heard one of them say my name, so I stood up and crept over to the door, which stood slightly ajar.

As I walked, I felt something hanging around my neck. I looked down to find that I was wearing a silver pendant. I held it up for a closer look. It was stunning: round and slightly convex with concentric circles carved into the surface. Two overlaid strips of silver formed a cross. When I let it hang down, the pendant fell just over my heart.

I figured it must be the totem Kai had promised me. Someone had slipped it on me while I slept. I strained to hear the voices outside.

"—sound asleep in there," I heard Vani say.

"All right, Benjamin Angus MacGregor, what did you do to her?" Kai stage-whispered.

"Only what I had to do to keep her here," Ben muttered.

"And that was what, exactly?"

I could hear Ben speaking, but his voice was too low for me to make out words.

"Well, good lord," Kai exclaimed, "no wonder she's mad at you! You couldn't have tried a box of chocolates? We can't lose her, Ben!"

"I know that," Ben said, "but not for the reason you're thinking!"

Kai sounded wounded. "I'm not just thinking about us. I'm thinking about her, too. And you can believe what you want, but I know what your father told me."

His *father*? I figured I must have misheard Kai. As I leaned in closer to the door, I heard a loud thud as though someone had kicked something. Then silence. I stood stock-still, afraid to make a sound.

After a moment, Vani spoke. "Ben, not to get too personal, but your aura is all lit up like a Christmas tree."

"That's enough, Vani," Ben warned.

"I'm merely pointing out that your feelings for her might be clouding your judgment."

"I said that's enough!"

"Color me surprised," Kai said dryly.

"My aura is not the issue here!"

"I knew you wouldn't be able to resist that juicy *Kama Sutra* figure of hers," Kai said. "Well, that explains a lot. No offense, Ben, but we all know that when it comes to women, you're like a bull in a china shop."

"And what would *you* know about women?" Ben growled.

"If you're going to go *there*, then *some* kind of feelings are definitely clouding your judgment!"

Vani interrupted. "Can we please sit down and take a deep breath before you two wake her up?"

I heard the telltale clunk of Pete's boots entering the lounge. "All right, all right, break it up," he said good-naturedly. "Kai, have you been gettin' Ben all riled up again?"

"Would you please do something with your boy?" Kai said. "He's acting so bullheaded, he's about to drive Cate right out the door!"

"Well now," Pete said patiently, "how do you know Cate's not actin' as bullheaded as he is?"

Thanks a lot, Pete, I thought.

Thankfully, Kai replied, "If she is, she's certainly justified."

"I'm sure you're right, darlin'," Pete said, "but you know the best person to talk to a jarhead is another jarhead. Maybe you and Vani should give us a minute—go downstairs and polish some rocks or somethin'."

"Fine, you talk to him," Kai said. "And they're diaspore crystals from Mulga, not rocks." I heard what sounded like an air kiss then two sets of heeled shoes clicking slowly away. "Semper Fi," I heard Kai call back down the hallway. I stifled a laugh.

I heard bodies settling into seats. "What's the story?" Pete asked.

A heavy sigh. "I think I screwed up."

"Nothin' new there," Pete said. "What happened?"

Another sigh. "She was trying to leave, so I pulled out the big guns. Maybe too big," Ben said.

"What'd you use?"

"Nelson."

"Hmm, yeah," Pete said. "I bet she didn't like that."

"No, she didn't." There was a moment's pause. "Kai thinks I should have used chocolate."

Pete chuckled. "That would have worked—on Kai."

"You're right. That's the problem," Ben said, his voice a rumble. "I don't know what's going to work on Cate. She's so…"

After a pause, Pete suggested, "Stubborn?"

"Yeah."

"Like you, you mean?"

"Well, yeah. I'm sure that's one reason we keep butting heads."

"You know, when you're breakin' a horse, you can't come at it head-on," Pete pointed out. "You gotta come at it from the side, talk real gentle, rub its neck, then slide the harness over its head so it hardly knows what happened."

While I got the impression that Pete was trying to help me in some twisted way, I wished that he had found some way to do it without comparing me to livestock.

"If I could use a harness," Ben grumbled, "we wouldn't need to have this conversation."

I resisted the urge to bang my head against the wall.

"True, true," Pete said with a hint of amusement. "All I'm sayin' is, she's a good filly. She might just need a softer hand. Like that saddle-shy first lieutenant at Quantico."

I scowled as this comparison was followed by chuckling from both men.

"I understand what you're saying," Ben said, "and you're

probably right. But I don't think we have time for that. It's not only that she's stubborn; she's also dangerous. Left alone, I'm afraid she might hurt herself." I could almost hear him running his fingers through his hair.

"What makes you think that?"

"I had reason to suspect before, but in this morning's ritual, her mother confirmed that Cate thinks about suicide. And you know when someone's both stubborn and self-destructive—"

"That's a highly combustible combination," Pete said. "I see what you mean. Well, if that's the situation, you'd better get a handle on it."

"Who do you think has been keeping a handle on her this whole time?" Ben asked.

I dug my fingernails into my palms.

"So just keep doin' what you're doin' and stop worryin' about it! What's the problem? You sweet on her or somethin'?"

There was another pause. I held my breath.

"It wouldn't matter if I was," Ben said. "She's off limits."

"Why?"

"Because I'm her superior, that's why."

My superior? Who the hell did he think he was? I bit my fist to keep from shouting.

"Hah!" Pete guffawed. "I wouldn't tell her that if I were you. She may be off-limits, but you're still crushin' on her, aren't ya?"

"I said it doesn't matter," Ben muttered.

"That little girl got you roped, flanked, and tied in record time," Pete marveled.

Ben's voice took on a dangerous edge. "Are you done having fun yet? Because Nelson only bought us one day. I have to figure something out quickly."

"Okay, okay. You're right. Let's think this through." There was a pause, then, "Did you try telling her?"

"Telling her what?"

"That you're sweet on her, dumbass!"

It wasn't possible—was it? I pressed my knuckles against my

lips. I knew Ben was attracted to me, but I couldn't be sure that *he* knew. After all, he hadn't shown any signs of interest whatsoever. Was Pete just needling him?

Ben's voice grew taut. "Even if she weren't off-limits, telling her I had feelings for her would just send her running as fast as she could in the opposite direction."

"I don't know about that," Pete replied. "If you *don't* tell her, she might start feelin' all rejected and go runnin' the other direction anyway. I've seen her lookin' at you. I know you're her superior and all, but she's a grown woman. I mean, if the feelings are mutual…"

"The feelings are *not* mutual." Sounding dejected, Ben added, "She hates me right now."

Had Ben just admitted that he had actual *feelings* for me? I leaned in closer still, trying to get a better look through the opening in the door. But my knees had gone weak. I slipped and fell against the wall with a loud thud.

I heard footsteps quick-march toward me, followed by a soft knock on the door. I was busted. "Cate, are you awake?" Ben asked.

I did my best fake yawn and eye-rub as I opened the door. "Yeah, I just woke up," I said in my sleepiest voice.

Ben appeared to have fallen for my act. Pete, on the other hand, had clocked my guilty expression. He grinned at me as he called out from the sofa, "There's blanket creases on your face."

I glowered at him. "Thanks, that's very helpful." I ran my hand over my face. Sure enough, blanket creases.

Ben looked me over from head to toe. "How are you feeling now?"

I was in such a tangle of emotions that I had no idea how to answer him. Finally, I just said, "Better."

At that moment, Asa and Eve bustled into the room carrying plastic-wrapped trays of food. "Lunchtime!" Eve announced as she and Asa began to set up the food.

Ben leaned in close to me. "I'm glad," he murmured. "You had me worried."

I smiled to reassure him that everything was okay. I didn't know *why* everything was okay, since I was sure that I still had every reason to be mad at him. I just couldn't seem to remember what those reasons were at that precise moment.

"Hungry?"

I nodded. Ben took me by the elbow and we walked out into the lounge together.

Chapter Eighteen

With the unexpected news that Ben might have real feelings for me, I found myself warming to him again. That would explain why he'd gone to such lengths to keep me from leaving. While that didn't excuse his blackmail stunt, at least there was some kind of reason behind it.

Still, I decided it was wise to keep my guard up, at least for the moment. I wanted to know why Kai had said that they couldn't lose me—although I didn't know how to find out without revealing that I'd been eavesdropping. Besides, I still planned to leave the program at the end of the day, which might kill any feelings Ben had for me stone dead. I'd already seen how he could turn on a dime from warm and intimate to cold and distant. I would have to keep watching my back.

Meanwhile, there was lunch to distract me. Everyone seemed energized after the morning's ritual. Ben hung in the background, once again not eating. Pete kept shooting me knowing looks, which I studiously ignored. Once the lunch gathering started winding down, Ben motioned for Kai and me to join him in his office.

Kai had changed out of his stage clothes and into jeans and a saffron-colored blouse. He still had a glow about him, pleased with the way the ritual had gone. "How are you feeling?" he asked me as we settled into the armchairs.

"Back to normal body temperature, I think."

Ben had once again switched back into manager mode. "So the purpose of this meeting is to talk about the ritual this morning and to answer any questions Cate might have. Cate?"

Was he serious? I had nothing *but* questions, like why I had turned into a human ice cube, for one thing. I didn't want to say anything that might offend Kai, though. "Honestly, I don't know where to start."

Kai smiled. "Well, how about we start with do you like your totem?"

I fingered the pendant. "It's gorgeous, Kai. Did you put this on me?"

"Mm-hmm. And yes, I know it's pretty, but it's also very important, honey. We opened you wide up this morning, but you do *not* want to stay that wide-open all of the time. You'd be like a big exposed net, walking around and catching all the emotional energy around you—positive and negative. More than you can handle, believe me."

"And potentially dangerous," Ben added in a warning tone.

"Don't worry, though," Kai reassured. "As long as you're wearing the pendant, your aura will be sealed up tighter than a drum. You're still vulnerable to toxic surges until you learn that meditation next week and we clear out whatever negative emotions you're still carrying. But this pendant will at least keep any new ones from coming in. I tailor-made it for you."

My mouth fell open. "Wow, you did? Thank you! It's beautiful. I love it."

"I'm glad." He beamed. "It's a replica of a Scottish Bronze Age pendant that had powerful protective properties," he explained. "I connected with the spirit of the original designer while I was making it, so it's a darn nigh perfect copy."

"You talked to a Bronze Age jewelry designer?" I asked, making an effort to sound curious instead of dumbfounded.

"That's right. He was also a mystic, and he was really annoying. Couldn't keep his mouth shut about life on the Other Side. Trying to get detailed instructions out of him was like pulling teeth. But I digress." Kai leaned over and lifted the pendant off of my chest. "The cross marks your heart chakra, and the circles represent the never-ending circle of life. I also infused it with my energy, so it's potent. But you have to wear it all the time until we close you back up at the end of the program, okay? I mean, sleep in it, shower in it, have sex in it, everything."

At the mention of sex, Ben pressed his eyes closed for just longer than a blink. Then he cleared his throat and added, "Except when I instruct you otherwise. You'll want to take it off when we're doing certain training exercises so you can fully access your gifts."

"Right. Only then, take it off," Kai agreed as he released the pendant, "but then put it right back on."

"Can I still…access my portals?" I asked, trying to get used to the new terminology. "The ones I have left, I mean."

"Absolutely," Ben said. "It won't affect your portals at all."

"Okay." I reached up and ran my fingers over the ridges of the design. "It protects me from absorbing negative emotions, so don't take it off except when you tell me to." I shook my head, not quite believing that those words had come out of my mouth.

Kai looked at me and laughed. "Good lord, girl! You look about as confused as you did during the ritual. You turned three shades of white this morning, you know."

"Yeah, it shook me up a bit."

Kai gestured for me to lean in closer. "All right, let's start there. What scared you?"

But I didn't want to talk about it. My emotions still felt as though they had been put through a blender. I wanted to put the focus on Kai by asking him more about his gift. What was it like to talk to the dead? What were his beliefs about the afterlife?

I really didn't want to ask those questions in front of Ben, though. I was afraid that if Ben got the idea that my skepticism was softening, he would start trying to push me into things I wasn't ready for. I'd had enough shocks to my system over the past couple of days. I needed some breathing room.

Something in my face must have given me away. Kai gave me a broad wink. "Benjamin, dear," he said, "would you mind terribly going and getting us two cups of tea? And take your time with it."

Ben appeared to get the message. He cleared his throat. "Uh, sure. No problem. I'll be right outside."

"Thank you." A smile slowly spread across Kai's face. "Okay, so now that we got rid of Soldier Boy, what scared you so bad this morning?"

I didn't want to offend Kai. I clasped and unclasped my hands. "To be honest, until this morning, I didn't believe in life after death."

Kai nodded sagely. "But you do now."

"Well, I can't say that for sure, but I guess I believe it's possible now. I mean after what you said, especially about the blue turtle."

"I'm sorry, baby." Kai patted my hand. "When I'm channeling, I act as a conduit. I don't often remember all the details of what I said. A blue turtle?"

I told him about my mother's brooch.

"Oh, I see. Yes, that was a pretty powerful validation. Sounds like she didn't want to leave any room for doubt—although I can't imagine why she'd be worried about that with *you*!"

I smiled at his dramatic hand-flourish. "I guess there's a part of me that still can't believe it was really her. I don't know what to think."

"Give yourself some time," Kai said gently. "For somebody who didn't believe in life after death when she woke up this morning, you've traveled a long distance in a short amount of time."

"Thanks. I guess you're right." I shifted uncomfortably, both wanting and not wanting to ask a question.

"Is there something else?"

I pressed my fingers against my mouth so I wouldn't bite my lip. "Do you think dreams can be, you know, real? Because I dreamed about my mother recently, and she said she'd be visiting me soon. Then this morning happened."

Kai took both of my hands and squeezed. "Yes, honey. Dreams can be real, and the dead often come to us in dreams in order to communicate. But I think we should talk about that another time—maybe when Ben's not sitting in the lounge feeling like a third wheel and holding two cups of tea."

I smiled weakly. "Okay. Thanks."

"Don't worry, baby, everything's going to be fine. I'll send him back in." Kai gave me a warm smile before heading out into the lounge.

Within moments, Ben appeared and handed me a cup of tea. "Everything okay?"

"Yeah, everything's fine. Thank you." I sipped quietly as he took his seat behind the desk.

"You're welcome." He leaned forward and put his elbows on the desk. "So we have acupuncture with Eve in a little while. But first, there was one part of your ritual I think we need to talk about, if it's okay with you."

It only took me a second to guess which part he meant. I couldn't believe he'd told Pete that he thought I was suicidal. Humiliation and anger sent my pulse racing. That was my business—and my mother's, apparently—and I had no intention of discussing it with Ben or anyone else. "Well, I *do* mind, as a matter of fact. That was *my* ritual, not yours. And since you didn't even find it necessary to prepare me for what might happen ahead of time, guess what? I get to decide when to talk about it, if ever!" I punctuated the last word by pounding my fist on the arm of my chair.

All of the blood ran out of Ben's face. "I apologize, Cate. I shouldn't have pushed."

I blinked in surprise, unprepared to deal with an apology from Ben. What if he did have feelings for me, and was genuinely worried…? I felt myself softening. I sighed. "It's okay. It's just been a lot this morning."

Ben held up his hand. "No need to explain. We'll talk about it when you're ready." He ran his hand through his hair. "I'm sorry, Cate. I can be a real clod sometimes."

In spite of the seriousness of the conversation, I had to suppress a stitch of amusement. Had he really just called himself a clod? "That's true. You *can* be a real clod."

He squinted at me. "What?"

"Very clod-like." I grinned. "I'm glad to hear you realize that."

Relief washed the lines from his face. "So we're okay?"

I considered. It was probably my last day in the program, and therefore, my last chance to find out if there could potentially be something between us. I closed my eyes and decided to take the leap. "Well, that depends."

"On what?"

As the next words came out of my mouth, I couldn't quite believe I was saying them. "On whether you'll hold my hand while Eve sticks needles into me."

• • •

That evening, I floated around my house in a warm haze. Worries and unanswered questions still sat in the back of my mind, and the constant ache in my chest where the portals had been closed had not gone away. But something had shifted between Ben and me, and it had left my whole body deliciously warm and humming. The sensation was so pleasant that I allowed it to push everything else into the background—at least for one night.

Eve's touch with the acupuncture needles had been so light that I couldn't even feel most of the insertions. She had worked primarily on my ankles and wrists, putting a few needles in my midriff, too. The placement of the needles had prohibited any actual handholding, but Ben had sat right next to me the whole time while I stole occasional glances at him.

The consummate professional, whatever else he may have been thinking about, Ben had kept our conversation focused on what Eve was doing. He was determined to make sure I learned something no matter what.

Eve explained that by placing the needles where she did, she was correcting imbalances in the flow of my *chi*, or life force. As unlikely as that sounded, I knew that acupuncture had really helped some of my clients. It was even covered by a lot of health insurance companies, so I figured there must be something to it.

Pete and I hadn't said much on the drive home, but he'd worn a stupid grin on his face the whole way. When he dropped me off and said, "See you in the morning," I didn't argue. He was right, after all; I had decided to give the program one more day.

• • •

As I lay in bed trying to sleep, my mind drifted to the blue turtle. My mother had lived simply and hadn't accumulated many possessions. Most of her estate had been sold to help cover her final expenses.

A thread of longing pulled painfully at my chest. I got out of bed, walked over to the dresser, and opened the red-velvet jewelry box. Inside lay the gold turtle, its blue opals shining in the moonlight. Mom had never told me much about it, other than that it was a gift my father had given to her when I was born. I picked it up and pressed it to my lips, then carefully put it back in the box. I made a silent wish that I would dream of her again soon.

Chapter Nineteen

Hell Week, Day Four

Wednesday morning found me sitting on a chair in the church basement with my eyes closed. I was feeling that sensation of cool air blowing on the crown of my head again. Ben assured me that since it was October, they did not have the air conditioning on. According to Asa, the cool sensation was due to spiritual energy entering my body.

Asa was in the midst of what he called giving me a Reiki attunement—my second that morning—which was supposed to open me up to a certain vibration of healing energy. That sounded to me like something he must have seen in a science fiction movie, but after my fumble with Kai the day before, I had decided to wear my skepticism on the inside for a while. I could hear Asa breathing deeply, and I was aware that he was moving his hands around my head. I kept my eyes closed and waited patiently until he said, "Okay, done."

Pete was napping in a chair off to one side with his hat drawn down over his face. I had been wondering what he was doing in the basement with us. For the most part, Pete seemed to disappear until he was needed. My question was answered when Asa placed a chair on the floor in front of me facing in the same direction as mine and called Pete over. "Okay, Cate, I'm going to show you something really cool now," Asa said, beaming.

As Pete came over and sat in the chair, Asa drew what looked like a strange doodle on a piece of paper and handed it to me. "This is called the Talking Symbol." Asa drew it in the air. "Try it."

Tentatively, I drew the doodle in the air. "It looks like a dinosaur."

"That's good! It's good to come up with your own ways of remembering the symbols," Asa said. "Normally when I'm teaching Reiki, I have a whole four-day curriculum that I follow. I would be giving you a lot more history, background information, and other stuff. But since we're sort of putting you on the fast track here and you already have empath abilities, we're just going to go for it. Okay?"

I nodded, grateful that I would only have to sit through the short course.

"So, the Talking Symbol lets you communicate with people's subconscious minds, to help them heal deep emotional stuff. I know you know all about that, though, 'cuz you're a therapist." He smiled brightly. "So what you're going to do is draw the symbol I taught you earlier—the one you called Curly-Cue—over Pete's head, followed by the Talking Symbol. Then rest your hands on his head and ask him—silently in your mind—if there is anything you can help him heal."

Pete removed his cowboy hat.

I suddenly felt awkward. "I'm going to do what now?"

Asa clarified, "You've had the attunement, so now the healing energy is flowing through you. You don't have to do anything to make it happen. You just have to open the communication, and the Reiki will do the rest."

I thought I understood, even though it didn't make any sense. "So I draw the symbols in the air, put my hands on Pete's head, and then ask silently if there is anything he needs healed? And then it gets healed?"

"Right, you got it!" Asa clapped. "Oh, and his subconscious might talk to you. You might hear it in your mind like a conversation. You'll know the healing is done when you feel his energy starting to pull away from you."

"I'll hear him talking in my head?"

"Maybe, maybe not. If you do, you can tell Pete what you heard afterwards, and he'll either verify it for you or tell you it was all in your imagination."

"Oh good." I was grateful to hear that someone else was leaving open the possibility that this could all turn out to be completely imaginary.

"Okay," Asa said, "go for it!"

I leaned forward slightly and murmured behind Pete's ear. "Pete, are you ready for this?"

"I'm ready for anything." I heard the smile in his voice.

"Okay, here goes!" I studied the doodle again for a minute then started to blush as I felt Asa and Ben looking at me. "Don't watch, you guys. You're making me nervous." They muttered their apologies and obediently wandered off.

I took a deep breath and closed my eyes, then drew the doodles in the air over Pete's head and placed my hands on his hair. I noticed that Pete had mean hat head. *Remember what you're supposed to be doing,* I admonished myself. I figured I'd better give it an honest try so that I could have something to report back to Asa.

I did my best to think at Pete: *Pete, this is Cate. Is there anything that I can help you heal today?*

There was silence. I waited a few moments. I felt a bit silly, but I knew it would be bad form to give up right away.

Then out of nowhere, the middle of my chest filled with a screaming pain. I fought to catch my breath and wondered if I was having a heart attack. Then a quiet sense of recognition overcame me. I knew that feeling very well. It was grief, but it didn't belong to me.

A wailing sound filled my head. *Pete? Is that you?*

Images flashed through my mind. A man who looked like an older version of Pete. A sweet-looking middle-aged woman. A bright-eyed girl of about sixteen.

Your family. You lost them?

Yes, I heard Pete think.

What happened? I tried to breathe through the pain.

They're fine. They're alive, he thought, *but they don't speak to me.*

I'm dead to them.

Why? I pleaded. Their faces looked so full of affection; I couldn't understand.

Because I'm with Kai, he thought. The grief in my chest began to mix with other feelings: warmth, devotion, love.

Oh. I gasped as the meaning of what he was saying branded my heart. *Pete, I'm so sorry.*

I felt his energy pull away from me. The wailing sound grew softer, and the pain in my chest started to abate. Eventually, I removed my hands from his head and collapsed backward into my chair. Asa and Ben walked back in our direction as Pete turned his chair around to face me. He was smiling until he saw the stricken look on my face. "You okay?"

I threw my arms around Pete and squeezed him hard. "Oof," he said, and I heard Asa and Ben's footsteps quicken.

Tears started to fall from my eyes. "Oh, Pete, I'm so sorry!" I clung to his flannel shirt as Asa and Ben worriedly asked what was going on.

I felt Pete's arms tentatively go around my shoulders. "Whoa, whoa, whoa," he said, "stall the waterworks! What are you sorry for?"

He gently pushed me away from him. Ben and Asa stood over us, waiting to hear my answer.

I recalled that according to Asa, I had been talking to Pete's subconscious. He might not even have been aware of what he was feeling. Suddenly feeling very protective of Pete, I wondered whether I should share anything about what I'd seen and heard, particularly in front of Asa and Ben.

Pete seemed to understand my hesitation. "It's all right, Cate. Go ahead and tell us what happened. This isn't my first stint as guinea pig."

Ben handed me a tissue. "Yeah," he chimed in, "this is all part of your training. Besides, Pete volunteered."

Well, he was asking, and it was supposed to be healing. Maybe it would actually help him. I did my best to dry my eyes, then took Pete's hands between mine and looked up at him. "I'm so sorry,

Pete. About your family."

His blue eyes darkened. "Oh yeah. That."

A lump formed in my throat. "Does it always feel that bad?"

He sighed, and I knew that he understood the question. "It's always there, but probably more so today. It's Lydia's birthday."

Lydia, his little sister. My muscles seemed to lose all their tone, and my torso fell forward until my head was resting on his shoulder. "Oh, Pete."

He patted my hair. "It's okay, Cate," he said, but his voice was particularly raspy. "I've learned to live with it. It's like everything else. Some days are harder than others."

"Right." I realized that I had better pull it together before I made Pete feel worse. I forced myself to sit back in my chair and tried to rub some life back into my face. I did my best to smile. "Thanks, Pete."

"Thank *you*," he said, and there was real gratitude in his eyes—for what, I didn't know. I felt like all I had done was dredge up his pain. I could tell he was putting on a brave face. He put his hat back on, pulling the rim down a bit lower than usual. "Ben, you done with me? I got some stuff to do."

"Sure," Ben said. "Thanks, Pete."

As Pete walked off and up the stairs, Asa sat in the chair facing me. His mouth was hanging slightly open. "Are you okay?"

"Yeah, sure," I said. And to my surprise, it was the truth. Aside from feeling sympathy for Pete, I felt unexpectedly light. Pete's grief and pain had left me completely the moment I removed my hands from his head. I tried to explain to Ben and Asa that when I submerged into clients, I always carried some of their pain back with me, but that hadn't happened this time. Discovering that Reiki had no unpleasant side effects was a welcome revelation.

"Exactly!" Asa said. "This time, you weren't doing the healing. The Reiki energy was doing it. With these techniques, you shouldn't have any hangovers."

"But I'm not really sure I *did* any healing," I said. "I think I made him feel worse."

Asa shook his head. "No, believe me, what you did was healing. You brought his grief out into the open where he can deal with it. Plus you shared his burden, and that's always helpful."

I smiled at Asa. I wasn't sure I believed him, but I was touched by his optimism.

Ben couldn't resist putting in his plug for the program. "This is why you're here, Cate. You can learn how to use your gifts without hurting yourself."

"Okay," I said softly. "I'm starting to get it."

Asa turned to Ben. "Do we have time to teach her another technique?"

"I don't know." Ben turned to me and murmured, "Do you feel up to another one?"

"Yes," I said, not wanting to disappoint Asa. "Sure."

"Oh good. You'll love this one!" Asa started drawing another, more complex doodle. "You take a photo of the person you want to heal, or write their name on a piece of paper. Then you draw this symbol over it, hold the piece of paper in your hands, and send a healing intention out to them. It's called Distance Healing."

Ben shot Asa a warning look. "Wait a minute—"

What Asa was saying would have sounded totally crazy to me had it not been for what had happened with Pete. Like a heavy door slamming into place, my mind locked immediately onto one person: Elana. "You mean, you send them Reiki, and they receive it no matter where they are?"

"That's right."

"Since you're doing it from a distance, is it psychokinesis, like empath healing?"

"No," Asa explained, "because it's not something you're doing under your own power. Reiki is an independent energy source. You're just channeling it."

This time, Ben's interruption sounded final. "Okay, slow down." He placed a hand on Asa's shoulder. "This isn't a good technique for Cate right now. She can open portals, remember?"

"Oh right. I forgot." Asa nodded. "Cate, when you use this

technique, you could open a temporary portal to the person you're trying to heal. It would only stay open while you were actually doing the Reiki, but depending on who you connect to—"

"It could still be too much for you to handle right now." Ben retrieved my protective pendant from Asa's desk where we had put it for safekeeping. "I think we should save that technique for later, when she has more of the basics down."

Asa shrugged. "Sorry, I get ahead of myself sometimes."

"No problem," I said casually, trying to conceal my emerging larcenous intent.

I thought of Elana sitting in Washington Hill Hospital, trying to deal with all that Don had put her through. I couldn't help feeling somewhat responsible. If I hadn't been so broken that I'd had to take so much time off, or if I had been a better therapist to her in the first place, perhaps I could have helped her avoid the pain she was in.

And as things stood, chances were that I wouldn't even get back to work in time to help support her when she got out of the hospital. Who knew what further damage Don had done when he had visited her? The thought made me vaguely ill.

From the way he reacted to Asa even bringing up the Distance Healing technique, however, it was clear that Ben would not support any attempt by me to use it. I decided to grab what might be my only chance to get a few moments alone with Asa's notebook.

"That was amazing, Asa," I cooed. "You're a great teacher. Thank you so much!"

"I'm glad you liked it," Asa said with a shy grin.

Ben fastened Kai's pendant back around my neck. "Okay, Asa, go get some lunch. We'll be right up."

Asa started toward the stairs. "Awesome, today is Thai day. I can smell it from here!"

Ben's hand fell to my elbow. He stared intently at me. "What you said about when you submerge into your clients, how you bring some of their pain back with you. Did that happen with me that night? Did you take on some of my pain?"

I pressed my lips together and tried to decide whether to tell him the truth.

"Tell me the truth," he said.

That convinced me: Ben *must* be at least partially telepathic. "All right," I said, resting my hand on his arm. "Yes, it happened with you that night. But it's just part of the process. I knew exactly what to expect. Besides, it was my idea, remember? I asked you to let me do it for my own purposes."

A deep indentation formed between his eyebrows. "Cate." He sighed heavily. "I had no idea. If I had—"

"Don't." I squeezed his arm. "I was happy to take some of that burden from you. It meant a lot to me to be able to help."

He ran a hand roughly through his hair. "I appreciate your willingness to do that. You helped me more than you know, and for that I'll always be grateful. But no more empathic submergence, okay? Not until you've finished your training." His voice became gruff. "And no more submerging into me, ever. I don't want you taking on anything more of mine."

I mentally kicked myself. I should never have said anything about the effect submerging had on me. I'd let my enthusiasm about Reiki get the better of me, and now Ben felt guilty. "Okay, understood."

It only took a second for Ben to dial his emotions back down. "You need to be protecting yourself from negative emotions right now, not absorbing more."

"I got it," I said softly. "I *am* really encouraged by this Reiki stuff, though. I don't feel any after-effects at all."

Ben tried to smile, but couldn't quite pull it off. "I'm glad to hear that."

A break in the conversation: that was my moment. It was time for my secret mission. "Listen, go ahead without me. I'll be up in a minute. I just need to use the ladies' room."

"I can wait here…"

I gave my best eye roll. "I know how to find my own way up the stairs, Ben."

He managed a genuine smile. "All right. See you upstairs."

I waved as I walked toward the bathroom. But as soon as I heard his feet hit the second floor, I crept back to Asa's cubicle. I tore a blank piece of paper out of his notebook, wrote Elana's name on it, and folded it in half. Then I carefully removed my necklace and placed it on Asa's desk.

I took a deep breath and gathered my courage. I sat in the chair with the folded paper in my lap and put Asa's notebook on the floor next to me, opened to his drawing of the Distance Healing symbol. Then I traced the symbol in the air over the folded paper and held it between my hands, closing my eyes.

"Elana Bruter," I whispered as I tried to picture her in the hospital. "I am sending you Distance Healing."

Before I could form another word, it was as though I had been swallowed by an icy tsunami. I felt my whole body turning to stone: my arms and legs, my head, my torso. My lungs were cold and unmoving; I couldn't breathe. My stone heart stopped beating.

What's going on? I thought desperately as I tried to pull air into my lungs. Nothing. As I struggled to make sense of what was happening, my limbs felt heavier and heavier. It was like I had been dropped into a deep, inky pool of water, but rather than swimming, I was falling, falling…

There was no pain when I hit the floor, only a jolt and a loud crashing sound. I heard voices and feet running down the stairs. I couldn't open my eyes.

I'm dying. The realization washed over me in a cold wave. *Ben…*

I heard Ben's voice shouting, "Cate, can you hear me?" Someone rolled me onto my back and straightened out my stone limbs. "She's not breathing. Pete, get the defibrillator! Come on, let's go, let's go!" Something sharp pressed into my forehead, and I heard what sounded like Kai's voice, chanting. I felt a light pressure on my feet.

My whole body lurched as something pounded into the stone of my chest. "One! Two!" I heard Ben count with each blow. As the seconds flowed by, the voices and sensations seemed to grow farther and farther away. *No, please. No, no, no…*Suddenly, a point of pure pain formed in my chest and opened like a flower.

"There's a pulse!" I heard Pete shout. The pounding and Ben's counting stopped, and I heard sounds that didn't make sense: the whisper of scissors cutting cloth, a whining beep. "Clear!"

My icy self shattered as pain screamed along my limbs and life exploded back into my body. I gasped air violently into my lungs, and my heart lurched into an excruciating beat.

I wanted to cry out, but breathing was a more urgent need. I swallowed mouthfuls of air and reached out to hold onto something, anything. My hands found someone's arms. I clutched at them and held on for dear life.

The sharp object was still pressing into my forehead close to where Kai was chanting. I became aware that there were hands on my shoulders and feet. After what seemed like an eternity, my breathing and heartbeat began to resemble their usual rhythm. I was able to open my eyes.

The first thing I saw was Ben. He was kneeling at my side, and it was his arms I was clutching. His face hovered above mine, cracked with heartbreak.

My heart hammered, and I knew in that moment that more than anything else, I never wanted to see such an expression on his face again. Tears formed in my eyes and rolled down the sides of my face. Barely able to find my voice, I whispered, "Sorry."

Ben sat motionless for a few moments, staring at me as though seeking reassurance that I was really back. Once he was satisfied, he straightened up and rocked back onto his heels. I let go of his arms and my hands fell to my sides. Ben rested his hands on his thighs and closed his eyes.

"It's okay, everybody. She's okay," he said, his voice hoarse.

Pete knelt on the other side of me and began poking and prodding. I tore my eyes away from Ben and looked around.

Kai was kneeling at my head with a red scarf wrapped around his neck. He stopped chanting and removed what turned out to be a crystal from where he had been pressing it against my forehead. Asa was sitting at my feet, which he was cradling in his hands. He looked stricken as he slid away from me. Eve was standing to one side of

Ben, looking down at me with her mouth open in horror.

I slowly took in the rest of the scene. A chair had fallen over next to me, presumably the one I had been sitting in. I saw that I had knocked over the standing lamp that had been near Asa's desk. The light bulb flickered erratically. Vani was over by the stage and appeared to be looking for something.

Ben ran a hand through his hair. Then he stood up and did a quick scan of the room. His expression darkened as he spotted my necklace on Asa's desk. He pointed it out to Kai. Then he looked around at everyone but me. "All right, let's give her some air." As one, the others slowly pulled away, and I became aware that my shirt and bra had been cut down the center and were hanging open. Mortified, I grasped for the edges of the fabric and tried to cover my chest as a painful flush heated my cheeks.

Vani appeared at my side, wide-eyed and pale, and quickly draped a blanket over me. "Sorry about that," she whispered.

I felt Kai's fingers fumbling as they fastened my necklace back around my neck. "What happened?" he asked.

"Leave us," Ben barked. Vani, Eve, and Asa melted away from me and up the stairs. Pete walked over to the stage and began packing his medical equipment into a bag. Kai stood up but lingered nearby.

Ben pushed himself up and stepped over to the fallen chair. I awkwardly pulled myself into a seated position on the floor while keeping Vani's blanket wrapped around me. My body ached all over, and it felt like someone had kicked me in the sternum. Not knowing where to look, I stared at my hands as they clutched the blanket closed.

Out of the corner of my eye, I saw Kai take Ben by the arm and pull him aside. Although his voice was low and intense, I could just make out his words to Ben: "I don't know what happened here, but if you yell at her right now, I will *skin* you."

Ben looked at Kai for a moment, then nodded and made a conciliatory hand gesture. Kai walked over to me, gave my shoulders a light squeeze, and whispered in my ear: "I'll see you later, baby."

I nodded but still didn't have the courage to look up. Kai turned and followed the others up the stairs.

Out of the corner of my eye, I saw Ben looking around on the floor. He picked up Asa's notebook, which was still open to the Distance Healing symbol. Then he found my folded-up piece of paper.

"Who's Elana Bruter?" he demanded in a tone that brooked no opposition.

I struggled to speak. "I can't tell you."

"I can't hear you."

I cleared my throat. "I can't tell you," I managed with a little more volume.

"A client, then." He walked back around and sat down on Asa's other chair, facing me. His voice was biting. "For the record, as the clinic manager, I'm bound by the same rules of confidentiality that you are, so yes, you can tell me. Do you understand what just happened?"

I looked down and shook my head. Of course I had some idea, but I figured it was safer to claim ignorance.

"I think you do, but I'll explain anyway," he said, the emotion in his voice intensifying. "You nearly died is what just happened—and you *would've* died if we hadn't heard the lamp fall over."

I didn't move. There was a long pause. I sensed that Ben was working hard to exert control over himself.

"So you tried the Distance Healing technique on this Elana person, am I right? And you opened a temporary portal."

I still didn't move.

"As I warned you, that was an extremely dangerous thing for you to do at this point in your training," he said with cold fury. "Judging from the profound effect this had on you, your client must be very ill."

I closed my eyes.

"The Distance Healing technique opens portals much larger than those you've encountered before, so you felt the full weight of this client's emotional toxicity. Are you listening to me?"

I looked up at him. His eyes were like flames burning into me.

My tears started to flow again. "Yes, but Ben—"

"No, Cate. No 'buts.'" He closed his eyes and appeared to be trying to decide what to say next.

Pete stood up, slowly walked over to where Ben sat, and murmured something in his ear. Ben thought for a moment and nodded. "Pete will take you to the Urgent Care Center to make sure you're all right, then he'll take you home. He'll stay on your couch tonight."

"But—"

Ben silenced me with a look. "You're going to need to sleep this off." He made it sound like an order. "We'll talk tomorrow morning. In the meantime, don't try any more *stupid stunts.*" The last two words exploded from his mouth. I felt like I had been punched in the stomach.

Ben nodded to Pete. Then he stalked up the stairs.

By that point, I was crying in earnest. Pete held out a hand to help me up. His voice was gentle. "C'mon, sis. Let's go."

Only because I knew somewhere in my mind that I couldn't sit there on the floor crying forever, I held out my free hand and let Pete pull me to my feet, clutching the blanket closed around me.

CHAPTER TWENTY

Hell Week, Day Five

When Pete and I arrived at the church on Thursday morning, he walked me all the way from the parking lot to the door of Ben's office. I felt about as fragile as I had the morning after I had discovered vodka and orange juice, multiplied by a factor of ten.

I had awakened to the sound of Pete yelling up the stairs, "Get up, get up, get out of the rack!" I begged him to let me stay home for one day at least, but he kept saying in different formulas of words that it would only make matters worse. Finally, I gave in. I only had the energy to throw on sweatpants, a T-shirt, and sneakers and toss my hair into a sloppy ponytail. I figured it was just as well; if I looked as miserable as I felt, I might garner a little more sympathy.

My phone vibrated on the ride to the church: a voicemail from Simone. The anticipation of hearing her voice felt so good I nearly cried. Then I *did* cry as I listened to her message. "Hey Cate! I heard they caught that asshole who threatened you. Thank God, or I was going to have to go all vigilante on him. Anyway, I know you're busy with your program and I probably shouldn't bother you with work stuff, but just I had to tell you, I got the weirdest message from Elana. She called from Washington Hill, said she was in a meditation group yesterday and she had a vision that you appeared and hovered over her like a ghost or something, and that you smiled and put your hand on her heart, and this purple light filled her…I don't remember the rest, just that she said you healed her, and she's been gradually feeling better ever since. She hasn't even needed any of her 'as-needed' medications since she had the vision, and she was taking all of them before. Isn't that wacky? I know you love wacky stuff, and you were worried about her, so I just had to tell you. Everything's fine here. I hope you're taking good care. Call me soon, okay?"

I listened to the message twice, sniffling and drying my face on my sleeve. Pete asked if was good news or bad news; I told him good. He seemed satisfied with that. For my part, I was overjoyed to learn that Elana had received the Reiki energy I'd sent her before I collapsed, and that she was feeling so much better. It also buoyed my spirits a little to know that everything I'd gone through the day before—and whatever I was about to go through—hadn't been for nothing.

As we approached Ben's office, I could see Dr. MacGregor through the door, wearing a sharp gray suit, sitting in one of the armchairs and listening intently to someone—presumably Ben—sitting behind the desk. I felt a flash of panic: why would *she* be there unless they were kicking me out of the program?

True, I'd been trying to get out of the program since day one. But I didn't want to leave anymore. For one thing, I had begun to learn some useful skills. And then there was Ben…

My stomach sank as I reminded myself that after the previous day's disaster, there probably *wasn't* Ben anymore—at least, not in the way I had hoped. I would be surprised if he could even stand to look at me. I swallowed hard. As we reached the door, I gave Pete one last pleading look. "Come in with me?"

"Chicken. Get in there." He propelled me through the door by the elbow and closed it behind me.

Dr. MacGregor and Ben both turned to look at me. "Cate, you look terrible," Dr. MacGregor said. "Sit down."

Ben was dressed more formally than usual, in an expensive-looking black suit and a crisp light blue shirt—sans tie, as usual. After giving me a disapproving look, he turned back toward his mother.

"Benjamin here tells me you have been giving him a hard time," Dr. MacGregor said. "I can't say I'm terribly surprised. As they say,

'Doctors make the worst patients.' That's because they think the rules that apply to everyone else don't apply to them." She smiled. "I'm a terrible patient myself."

I felt a momentary pang of sympathy for her doctor, whoever that might be.

"So tell me," she asked, "what is it going to take to make this work?"

I blinked in surprise. "What?"

"I mean, what is it going to take to keep you in the program *and* to convince you to follow the rules?"

"You mean you're not kicking me out? You actually want me to stay?"

Dr. MacGregor smiled indulgently. "Of course we're not kicking you out. Whatever gave you that idea?"

"I don't know," I muttered. "I guess I thought, after what happened yesterday—"

"Oh no, dear. My goodness. We all make mistakes, and besides, from what I heard, you made yours with the best of intentions. Isn't that right, Benjamin?"

Ben gave a stiff nod.

"We would very much like for you to complete the program. You have a rare combination of talents. We would never go to all of this trouble to train you otherwise." She picked up a pen and began tapping it on the arm of her chair. "However, we do need you to follow the rules. As Ben has explained—and as you saw yourself yesterday—they are there for your safety."

"I know," I said quickly, trying to show how cooperative I was before she had a chance to reconsider. "I get that now."

"Good. To be sure that we're clear, Benjamin and I have created a new, simpler set of rules for you that should obviate the risk of any future misunderstandings." She laid her pen on the desk with a decisive click. "You will do what he tells you to do, and you will refrain from doing what he tells you not to do."

Hearing the rules expressed in those terms made them seem much more difficult to follow. At least they were letting me stay.

"Okay," I muttered.

She leaned forward. "What was that?"

"Yes, okay."

"All right then." Dr. MacGregor smiled and began to stand.

"Um, Dr. MacGregor, before you go—"

"Yes?"

I pushed through my ambivalence about whether I really wanted to know the answer and forced myself to ask the question that had been on my mind. "I was just wondering, what happened to me yesterday?"

"Oh, yes. Well, you've heard the expressions 'died of a broken heart' and 'paralyzed by fear?' Those are actual medical conditions. The first is called stress-induced cardiomyopathy, or broken-heart syndrome. And several conditions can induce temporary loss of muscle control. In your case, acute stress probably induced either hysteria or cataplexy."

"You can actually die of a broken heart?" I asked in disbelief. I remembered feeling as though I might a few times after my mother passed away, but I never knew that it was a real possibility.

"Of course. Surely you've heard of the mind-body connection."

"Yes, but I didn't realize it was so strong."

"That's why you're here, dear, to learn new things." Dr. MacGregor glanced at her watch. "So apparently, in spite of multiple warnings," she gestured toward Ben, "you chose to bite off a good deal more than you could chew. Your body is only designed to handle *your* emotions—and also because you're an empath, very small amounts of emotion from other people. But by opening that portal yesterday, for those few moments, you essentially asked your body to handle not only all of your emotions but all of your client's, too—a client who I gather is not well. Your body is not equipped to handle all of that, so it responded by shutting down. Perfectly simple."

"Oh," I mumbled.

She peered at me over her glasses. "You have a sharp mind, Cate, and I appreciate your eagerness to learn and understand. All will be explained eventually, but we simply can't teach you everything at once. You can't explain heat conduction to a child, for example, but you can still instruct him to keep his hand off the stove, correct?"

"Yes." I bristled at the comparison.

"Good. I'm glad we understand each other. I'm afraid I have private practice patients to attend to this morning." She stood and gathered her coat and purse. "We're glad you're here. You're a unique young woman, and you'll be a great asset to our team. Benjamin, are you still taking Eve to Rockville this afternoon?"

He nodded.

"All right then," Dr. MacGregor said, turning back toward me. "If neither of us are here, do whatever Peter says. Benjamin, call me when you get there."

"Will do," he said. She left the room, closing the door behind her.

All at once, I was alone with Ben. Afraid to make eye contact with him, I stared at the front edge of the desk and fingered my pendant.

The room was ominously quiet. It became evident that Ben wasn't going to be the one to break the ice. *The longer you stay silent,* I thought, *the more uncomfortable you're going to feel.* Tentatively, I asked, "So, you and Eve are going to Rockville?"

"To visit a sick colleague."

"Someone you're close to?"

"No."

I bit my lip. So it was going to be like pulling teeth. I figured I'd better get directly to the point. "Look, Ben, about yesterday—"

"What about it?" His voice was cold.

I wanted to ask him if he was still angry with me and if we were going to be okay, but I was too afraid of what his answers might be. So instead, I tried to explain myself. "Elana Bruter, she's the girlfriend of Don, that guy who threatened me."

I paused to let that sink in. Although Ben's expression remained unchanged, at least he was listening.

"She checked herself into the hospital last week," I continued. "I was really worried about her, even more so after Don told me he'd been over there to see her. That's why I tried to send her… you know."

"Flowers? A card?" Ben raised an eyebrow. "You know, you *could* have told me that you were worried about your client. We could have asked Asa to send her Distance Healing, or the whole group could have joined in for greater effect. But that's not what you did, is it? Which raises the question: are there any other clients you're worried about that you'd like to discuss, or are we going to have to keep pulling out the defibrillator every time you have a bleeding-heart moment?"

Tears pricked the corners of my eyes. I dropped my head into my hands.

Ben leaned over me and put his hands on the arms of my chair. "Pete told me you overheard the end of our conversation in the lounge the other day. You remember, the one you claimed to have slept through."

Of course I remembered. My face burned. Goddamned Pete. "So?"

"So you must have some idea of what it was like for me to come downstairs and find you nearly dead yesterday. What is it going to take for you to start trusting me?"

"It's not that I don't trust you," I muttered.

"Cate, look at me." He spoke the words gently, so I looked up and met his gaze. Once our eyes locked, I couldn't turn away, even though it felt like he was reaching inside of me and giving me a shake. "I know you've had to rely on yourself for a long time. It shows. You're creative, independent-minded, and resourceful. I admire those things about you. But we can't work in isolation here. The work is too complex and high risk. We have to work together."

If my near-death experience the day before hadn't taught me that, nothing would. "I understand that now."

"I'm glad to hear that, but I need you to do more than understand. I need you to start acting like it. Honestly, Cate, I don't think I can take another day like yesterday."

As he spoke, the agonized expression I had seen on his face the day before returned. "Ben, I'm so sorry."

"I don't need another apology. I need you to promise me that you're never, ever going to put your safety at risk like that, ever again. And since you don't know where all of the risks lie, that means following my instructions to the letter as long as you're in this program."

"Okay, I get it," I said, trying not to sound reluctant. "I really do. I promise."

He looked at me for a long moment as though he were trying to decide whether he believed me. "All right then," he finally said. Ben stood up and handed me a tissue from his desk.

I took my first full breath since Ben had begun hovering over my chair and dabbed the moisture from my eyes. "So everyone pretty much hates me now, right? I mean, I wouldn't blame them. Or you."

Ben paused, looking as though he were trying to think of the right thing to say.

My eyelids flew wide open. "Oh my god, I'm right, aren't I?"

"No, of course they don't hate you. Everyone was a little frustrated with you after they pieced together what happened, but only because they hated to see you get hurt. But that quickly changed into admiration for your compassion and your dedication to your client, qualities that are highly respected here." Ben frowned. "Then Kai decided the whole thing was *my* fault, somehow. I don't know what's gone on between you two, but he certainly seems to take your side a lot."

It was comforting to hear that the others understood my motivations. That gave me some hope at least. But I noticed that Ben had carefully skirted the issue of whether *he* hated me. I pressed the tissue against my eyes to staunch a fresh threat of tears. "I'm really good at ruining things, aren't I?"

"I won't disagree with you there."

I looked up in alarm, but his eyes flashed with amusement. "I've been told recently that I should try to be less argumentative," he explained.

"How thoughtful of you," I said dryly.

"But I do have to contradict you on one point."

"And what's that?"

"I don't hate you."

My heart gave a small leap. "You don't?"

"No."

"Oh." I screwed up my courage. "Well, that's nice to hear, but it doesn't really matter, does it? Because I'm 'off-limits,' right?" I put the offending phrase in air quotes.

Ben arched an accusing brow, but a smile played at the corners of his mouth. "So Pete was right. You *were* listening in."

I bit my lip. The time had come to go for broke. If Kai was right and they could teach me how to have a normal relationship without freaking out, then why not give it a try with Ben? There was a mutual attraction; I had my protective pendant; and after all, it wasn't like I had anything left to lose. I stared at my hands as they worried the tissue in my lap. "Look, we're both adults here. I know you probably have some policy about managers not dating clients. But policies are made to protect the vulnerable, and I'm not vulnerable like that." I looked up and waved the tissue at him. "I'm not even sure why any of the usual policies would apply here. I've never heard of a program like this. I don't even know what to call it. It's more like a series of workshops—"

"ParaTrain."

I blinked, then blinked again. "What?"

"I'm thinking of calling it ParaTrain, a paranormal skills training program."

I grimaced. "ParaTrain?"

Ben's brows knit together. "You don't like it?"

"It just sounds a little…military, don't you think?"

He appeared confused as to why that should surprise me. He had a point. But I refused to be derailed by some side conversation about what they named their program. "What I'm saying is that if we like each other, don't you think it's a little silly to let some policy dictate our, you know…behavior?"

"Cate," he said in a rough whisper. He stepped forward and held his hand out to me. I took it, and he helped me out of the chair. As we stood there facing one another, Ben brought his hand up to my chin. His eyes flashed gold like the Vegas strip. For a moment, I felt certain he was going to kiss me. My heart stumbled.

"Yes?"

"First of all," he murmured, "we don't actually have a policy on this, since it's never come up before. But while I find your argument very compelling, you're more vulnerable than you know, and I'm—" He screwed his eyes shut. "Look, you can ask anybody. I'm no good at this kind of thing. I don't trust myself not to do anything that might hurt you, or interfere with your training in some way. And that's a risk I'm not willing to take."

Had he just said *no*? I jerked my chin away from his hand. "Did you seriously just give me the 'It's not you, it's me' speech?"

His face contorted with confusion. "The what?"

Pain and humiliation sliced through me. Fortunately, they were easily funneled into anger. I put my hands on his chest and shoved him back against the desk. "If you don't feel the same way, just say so! Don't pretend you're some white knight trying to ride in and protect me! And for God's sake, don't make up some story about how you're bad at this kind of thing—"

Ben froze, as though he were watching a train wreck happening in slow motion and there was no way to stop it. His words tumbled out. "But I *am* bad at it! I didn't make up—what story? And I never said I didn't feel—"

There was a knock on the office door. "Ben?"

It was Vani's voice. I walked over to the bookshelves, turning my back to the door.

"What is it?" Ben barked.

Vani took his words as an invitation to enter. "Oh, sorry. I didn't realize I was interrupting—"

"It's okay, Vani." I heard Ben take a deep breath and exhale slowly. "What do you need?"

"Nothing important really. Hi, Cate!"

I turned toward her just enough to give her a wave and a half smile.

"Just a question about Rockville. It can wait, though. Again, sorry for barging in." She quickly slid out the door, closing it behind her before Ben could reply.

My whole body stiffened as Ben walked up behind me. "Cate, please, I'm sorry. I told you I'm bad at this. Obviously I'm doing this wrong."

I whipped around to face him. "Oh, don't worry," I snapped. "There's no right way to reject someone."

To my surprise, instead of retreating, Ben took another step toward me. I backed up to find myself pressed against the bookshelf. He was standing close enough that his scent surrounded me, filling my senses. Ben reached out as though to touch my arm, my cheek, my hair—but stopped about an inch away each time. Finally, his wandering hand grabbed onto the shelf beside my head. "Cate."

Once our eyes met, his gaze had me pinioned. In an instant, the portal between us opened, and the rush of his emotions poured into me. The intense tenderness he felt toward me made my whole body go weak, while the force of his desire was so strong that it held me upright. Stunned, I tried to control my ragged breathing.

He searched my eyes like a dog on the hunt. "Has a portal opened between us yet?"

I managed a small nod.

His voice rumbled. "Can you feel what I'm feeling, then, or do you need me to tell you?"

My voice came out in a squeak. "I can feel it."

"Good." He kept his eyes locked on mine for a few more moments. My face grew more and more flushed as my breathing grew shallow. Afraid that I might faint, I pulled together every thread of willpower within me and forced the portal to close. I gasped with relief and struggled to remain standing.

Ben quickly grasped the situation. With one hand holding my elbow and the other pressed against the small of my back, he helped me back to my chair. As I tried to breathe normally, he went to get a cup of water from the lounge. I gulped it down while he watched.

"Are you all right?" he asked.

"Mm-hmm," I said, testing my voice. It seemed to be working. Ben took his seat behind the desk.

I coughed and forced myself to speak. "So…what happens now?"

Ben leaned back, clasping his hands behind his neck and appearing to consult the ceiling. "I don't know," he said, as though speaking to himself. "I've never been in this situation before."

"We're *both* in the situation," I reminded him. I knew how *I* wanted to proceed, but I figured that Ben would be more likely to go along with a plan that he came up with himself. "How do you usually find your way through new territory?"

He blew out a hard breath, then rocked forward and leaned his elbows on his desk. "Well, normally I take a wait-and-see approach."

Of course he does, I thought.

"And as regards clinic-related questions, I consult with our medical director."

He hadn't actually just said—? Mouth agape, I asked, "You mean, you want to talk to your *mother* about this?"

"Now that you mention it, that's not a bad idea," he said. "I trust her to evaluate the situation objectively—whether there would be a chance of a relationship between us harming you in any way, or interfering with your training. And whether I'd be violating any ethical boundaries, of course."

I gritted my teeth. "I wasn't actually *suggesting*—"

"Oh, I know, but you helped guide me to my own solution. You're a very good therapist." His lips swung into a teasing smile.

The glare I gave him could have stopped a meteor. "Don't I have any say in the matter?"

"No."

"Why not?" I snipped. "Because you're my *superior*?"

That caught him off-guard. He skewered me with an incisive look. "How much of that conversation did you hear?"

But there was no way I was laying down my trump card. I just shrugged and pulled at an imaginary thread on the hem of my shirt.

"Hmm." He tapped his pen on the desk. "Your eyes turned grey again, by the way," he said, "over by the bookshelf. I think I'm starting to see a pattern here."

Damn him, I thought as I started to blush again. I tossed my hands in the air. "Fine!" I blasted. "Talk to your mother if it'll make you feel better."

"Thanks. I will." He stood, slapping his palms on the desk. "Now that we've got that settled, can I get you something else to drink?"

Chapter Twenty-One

I took Ben up on his offer and asked him to make me a cup of tea, hoping for a few moments alone. I paced around his office, looking at but not really seeing his books, the window, the pictures on the wall. Ben's feelings for me were much more powerful than I had anticipated. I still didn't know how to handle that revelation—or the fact that as his emotions flowed into me through the portal, my own feelings rose to meet his, answering with the same level of intensity. Whatever was happening between us might be a new situation for him, but it was an entirely new universe for me.

I couldn't keep thinking about that, though. I only had a few minutes to pull myself together before he returned. Besides, Ben had made it perfectly clear that our relationship was not going to change unless his mother gave us the go-ahead. Incredulous about that aspect of things, I flopped down in my chair and rubbed my face with my hands, trying to even out the blood flow. At least I'd expended some of my nervous energy. I forced myself to focus on something else.

So the MacGregors wanted to keep me in the program, but I had to follow Ben's instructions from there on out. I knew that shouldn't have bothered me so much, but the idea of obeying orders—especially his, for some reason—really rankled me. It was a relief to know that the rest of the group didn't want to tar and feather me, at least, so I'd have some chance of repairing those relationships. And Ben was going to Rockville that afternoon. That would give me a little space in which to think things through.

As I tidied my braid, something that had been lingering in the back of my mind worked its way forward. Ben came back into the office with a mug for me and a bottle of water.

"Thank you." Once he was comfortable behind the desk, I took a sip of tea and asked, "Hey, what did your mother mean earlier when she said I'd be 'an asset to your team'?"

Ben stiffened. "That's a discussion for later."

My curiosity was officially piqued. "Why later? Why not now?"

The telltale muscle in his jaw twitched. "She spoke prematurely. Do us both a favor and forget she said anything."

I gave him my best "you have *got* to be kidding" look. "Surely by now, you know that I'm not going to be put off with a ridiculous non-answer like that."

"We'll talk about it when the time is right."

"But she's the one who brought it up!"

"Well, she shouldn't have."

"Fine then! Don't tell me. But you can't seriously expect me to be okay with the fact that you're keeping a secret that obviously has something to do with me!"

"I'm not keeping a *secret*," he said as though the idea were absurd. "I'm just waiting for the appropriate time to discuss it."

I imagined flying Ben in a helicopter over the mouth of an active volcano, then dangling him over the churning lava below. "If you don't explain what your mother was talking about *right now*, I'm going to call over to her private practice office and ask her myself."

Ben rubbed his forehead. "You're really not going to let this go, are you?"

I glared at him.

He closed his eyes, looking as though he were deep in meditation. Finally he looked up. "All right. I'll tell you, but I'm warning you right now, you're not going to like it."

"I don't care."

"Fine, but I have two conditions."

"Which are?"

He held up one finger. "You have to promise to hear me out." Then he held up finger number two. "And you have to promise not to overreact."

Oh god, this must be serious, I thought. *I have to know now.* Pushing aside a creeping feeling of trepidation, I nodded.

"Okay then." He clasped his hands on the desk. "The reason my mother said you would make a great asset to our team is that it has been our intention all along to recruit you to work for us."

"To *recruit* me?" I leaned forward to make sure I was hearing him correctly.

"It was Dr. Nelson's idea," Ben explained. "As you know, he referred you to us because he's familiar with our program. He knows all about sensitives and the dangers they can face. Even before your mother passed away and things took a downhill turn, Dr. Nelson saw the signs that you were an empath in trouble—how unusually in tune you were with everyone, how overwhelmed you were after a day at work, and how your clients kept getting better while you appeared to be feeling worse. Obviously, we agreed to help. But over the past few months…Let's just say Dr. Nelson thought you might benefit from being involved with us over the long term, so the subject of recruitment came up."

"Oh." I was touched that Dr. Nelson had been so concerned about me. However, it was disconcerting that they'd been having all of these conversations about me behind my back. And there was something else that bothered me. "So this is some kind of charity hire? You want me to work here as a favor to Dr. Nelson because he's a friend of yours?"

"No, of course not." Ben pushed a hand through his hair. "It just turned out that by coincidence, we were looking for an empath."

"What? Why?"

"We wanted to be able to offer to our clients empath healing. It's an effective, efficient tool for dealing with emotional and psychological wounds. Also, it's important to my mother's research that all categories of paranormal gifts be represented on our staff. Otherwise, her study would be incomplete."

"So since you couldn't find anyone who could levitate a pencil or bend spoons with their mind, you needed an empath to slot into the psychokinesis category."

As his eyebrow arched dangerously, Ben replied, "I wouldn't have put it quite like that."

"It's true, then," I said with grim satisfaction. But after a moment, confusion set in. "Wait a minute, though. There must be other empaths running around who already know what they're doing. Why bother with me, someone you have to train from scratch?"

"We did consider others," Ben acknowledged, "but none of their gifts were as strong as yours. For example, the ability to open portals is quite rare, and almost always comes with strong empath healing abilities, as you have demonstrated. Also, just as the other staff members bring added value in addition to their paranormal gifts, my mother wanted to find an empath who could be an asset to our clinic in multiple ways. When Dr. Nelson told her about your therapeutic skills, she was intrigued. We don't have anyone with the training to help clients manage the mental health aspects of their healing, which in some cases are quite significant."

That didn't make any sense. "What about your mother?"

"She's very busy between her research and her private practice."

Something still wasn't adding up. "I don't get it," I wondered aloud. "There must be a lot of empaths who go into mental health. And maybe it's rare to be able to open portals, but you and Vani have been telling me that I shouldn't do too much of that, anyway." Then it dawned on me: Dr. MacGregor was interested in the Bronze Age tribal mythology. "Oooh!" My hands flew up. "You were missing both an empath *and* a Caledonian, and bringing me on board kills two birds with one stone! Is that it?"

Ben reminded me of one of those giant heads on Easter Island—stoic, stony, and expressionless. "I won't lie to you. My mother believed that adding a Caledonian would be beneficial to our group."

"Ah-hah!" Gratification surged through me. "So I was *right* in Vani's class when I said that with me here, you'd have a complete set. And everyone clammed up because you weren't ready to talk to me about it yet! I *knew* something else was going on in there."

"Yes, you were right." But the strain on Ben's face told me that he was still holding something back.

I was almost afraid to ask. "There's more, isn't there?"

Ben nodded, but didn't say anything.

"Well?"

With an air of weariness, Ben continued. "Kai claims that a few weeks ago, the spirit of my father came to him and foretold the arrival of a Caledonian empath. His spirit allegedly said that it was of critical importance that once you arrived, we convinced you to stay. He said you'd be in danger without us, and that we needed you to make our group whole—something about having to fight a rising darkness in the near future." He rubbed his forehead. "I know how crazy that sounds, but if Kai is to be believed, it was the first time my father's spirit has appeared since his death. As you can imagine, my mother was very compelled by his message."

So *that's* what Kai had been talking about, that day I overheard their conversation in the lounge: "We can't lose her…I know what your father told me." It was all so bizarre, and the part about the rising darkness was downright creepy. Thankfully, Ben's dry tone told me that he put no stock whatsoever in his father's advice from beyond the grave. To reassure him that we were both on the same page on that, at least, I said, "That is supremely weird, Ben."

He nodded. "I know. I'm sorry. I don't even know what to say about that, or the Caledonian thing. The point is that there are multiple reasons we want you to come to work for us. Admittedly, some of them are weird, but hopefully the others make sense to you."

I paused to consider his offer. In spite of the superstitious beliefs some of them held, I liked everyone at the MacGregor Group so far, and I was definitely interested in Dr. MacGregor's research. It was certainly a unique opportunity, and I could easily see myself working there a few evenings and weekends. The idea was even kind of exciting, and it wasn't like I had a life outside of work anyway. And—bonus—it would mean more time with Ben, who for some reason looked positively grim.

"For a recruiter, you don't seem very enthusiastic about this idea," I observed. "Is that because of your dad's…involvement?"

"No, it's nothing to do with that," he said, harshly dismissive.

After everything he'd told me, I couldn't imagine what additional bombs Ben might still have to drop. "What is it then? Do I have to take a blood oath? Get a Caledonian tribal tattoo?"

"Hear me out, Cate," he said, his face a somber mask. "I told you, you're not going to like this."

Bracing myself, I sat back, folded my arms, and listened.

He paused, and I could tell that he was bracing himself, too. "You have to leave your job at Dr. Nelson's clinic."

I leaned forward, squinting. "What?"

"You can't go back to being a psychotherapist."

I definitely couldn't have heard him correctly. "Wait, what? You said everybody here works part-time. They have other jobs, or they're in school."

"You can hold a second job if you want to, but not as a therapist." He spoke slowly and with care. "It would be impossible for you to do two jobs simultaneously that require the use of your empath abilities. You would burn out in no time."

I started to jump in with an objection, but Ben held up his hand. "I know, I know. You would never leave your job. But there's something else you don't know." Darkness clouded his expression. "I hate being the one to tell you this—this isn't how we planned it—but once you've finished the training program, Dr. Nelson only wants to have you back at the clinic for a month or six weeks, however long you need to wrap things up with your clients."

"Wha—? No, that's wrong." I shook my head. "You're wrong. The whole reason he sent me here was to get better so that I could come back to work. Obviously there's been a misunderstanding."

The lines in Ben's forehead deepened. "Dr. Nelson didn't want to tell you the truth until after you'd completed our program. He thought you would be more likely to understand his decision and go along with it once you had the training under your belt—not to mention a new job offer. We all agreed that would be the best approach, which is why I didn't want to have this conversation with you yet."

"You all *what*?" A fist of anxiety clutched at my chest. No, there was no way Dr. Nelson would do that to me. In any case, there was no way Ben would do that to me—was there? "I don't believe you," I said resolutely, as though saying the words could stop it from being true.

"I'm sorry. I know it's a lot to take in." Ben's sympathy appeared authentic. He picked up the phone handset. "If you like, we can call Dr. Nelson and talk to him about it. He cares a lot about you. We all do. If it helps, none of us enjoyed keeping this from you." He must have seen the blood draining from my face, because he added, "While I know this might not mean much to you right now, we *will* double your salary, and we offer flexible hours with a top-notch benefits package."

I felt like I had just stepped off of the Tilt-A-Whirl at the carnival: dizzy, disoriented, and nauseous. "But, Ben, my clients…"

His voice was gentle. "I know that leaving them is going to be the hardest part for you. We'll be right here for you, though, giving you all the support you need."

Ben's words landed like stones in the pit of my stomach. "Hang on. When you closed the portals to my clients, you had no intention of opening them back up, did you?" I rose halfway out of my chair. "Oh my god! You don't give a damn about the relationships I've formed with them, all of the work that we've done…"

Ben gestured for me to sit back. "I know this will be hard for you to accept, but everything that we did, we did to help you."

The calmer he sounded, the more I panicked. "No you didn't! You did it because you and your mother wanted a full set of paranormal action figures to play with!"

Ben's jaw tightened. "That is not—"

But I was no longer interested in anything he had to say. I stood up. "I can't believe you lied to me. You all lied to me!"

"Only because we thought it was necessary for your own good." He stood up, too, speaking as though he were presenting a courtroom defense. "In retrospect, I still think we made the right decision. You would never have come to the program otherwise."

My panic began to transform into fury. "Well I wish I had never come, and I'm certainly not going to stay!"

Ben pinched the bridge of his nose. "I know you're upset right now, and that's understandable. But you did promise not to overreact."

He thought *that* was overreacting? I jabbed an accusing finger at him. "I can't believe I ever thought you cared about me!"

The ridge of his eyebrows formed a firm line. "There is no need to be melodramatic."

"How dare you!" For a moment, my outrage was so complete that I couldn't form words.

Ben took advantage of my temporary speechlessness. "Cate, I know how much being a therapist means to you, but you simply couldn't go on the way you were. It was hurting you."

I paused for a moment to marvel at the fact that he was still trying to justify what he had done, instead of groveling on the floor and begging for forgiveness. I planted my hands on my hips. "So what if it was? What business is that of yours?"

He extended a hand to me. "You know how I feel about you."

"Oh no you don't!" I backed away from him. "You don't get to play the 'I care about you' card, not after what you did! You have exactly no right to express an opinion about the choices I make and whether or not they're hurting me! What I do is none of your goddamned business!"

Ben's arm dropped to his side. "Dr. Nelson evidently felt it was *his* business, as someone else who cares about you—and as your boss."

Dr. Nelson. The mention of his name brought with it a stabbing pain so sharp that for a moment, it took my breath away. If Ben was to be believed, Dr. Nelson had been the author of the whole deception. He had been lying to me the entire time and I hadn't even picked up on it. Some empath I was.

Well, I didn't give a damn about their Machiavellian plans. There was simply no way I was leaving my clients. I would just have to convince Dr. Nelson to let me keep my job. But as far as I was concerned, both he and the MacGregors had lost any authority they might have claimed. I was done playing by their rules.

"You know what? It's none of his business either," I countered. "I should never have accepted his offer to take more time off. I'm going back to work tomorrow, and if he asks me how I'm doing, I'll tell him I'm fine. I'll just take a few of those pills he gave me. If he tries to make me go home, I'll go straight to Human Resources. I'm sure that what he did must have violated *some* personnel policy." I knew that plan was shaky at best, but at least it was something—enough, anyway, to propel me out of that prison of a church and as far away from Ben as possible. I reached down to pick up my purse.

Ben's tone took on a hard edge. "I know this has been difficult for you to hear, and I understand that you're upset, but you might as well take a seat. Even if you do decide to leave the program, you can't walk away just like that—not until we take care of a few things."

"Still giving orders? Really?" I threw my hands up in disbelief. "Don't you get it? I'm done here! It's not up to you whether I stay or go!"

"Maybe not, but it is up to me to ensure that if you go, you do so safely. I've said from the beginning that it would be dangerous for you to leave in the middle of the program—which you agreed not to do, by the way."

"Under false pretenses!"

I could sense that Ben was shifting into drill instructor mode. "The work we've done so far has stripped you of your former protections, leaving you extremely vulnerable. I can't let you out of here on your own until we've at least put those protections back in place. Without them, the cardiac arrest you experienced yesterday is only one of the many things that could potentially go wrong."

The turning-to-stone incident was still fresh in my memory. On the off chance that he was telling the truth, I gingerly sat down again, but I was in no mood to be accommodating. "Then put my protections back already!"

Ben pulled out his tablet and appeared to be reading something. "Let's see. Since Eve and I will be in Rockville for the rest of the day, tomorrow morning is the absolute earliest we could do the closing rituals."

So he was resorting to stall tactics. "If it's liability you're worried about, give me a release and I'll sign it, absolving you and your mother of any and all responsibility. Give me ten damn releases if you want to. I'll sign them all right now!"

He shook his head. "Nice try, Cate, but that's not going to work. You're going to have to stay with us for at least one more day."

"I'd like to see you make me!" My voice rose to a semi-hysterical pitch.

The edge in Ben's voice sharpened. "It's not optional. I'll have Pete stay with you until we get back tomorrow afternoon."

"A *babysitter*?" I slammed my fist on the arm of my chair. "Are you out of your *mind*?"

"Fine, then." He leaned back in his chair and folded his arms across his chest. "What do you do when you're worried about someone's safety? Put them in the hospital?"

I couldn't tell whether he was being serious or sarcastic. Either way, his words felt like ice water being thrown in my face. "What the hell is that supposed to mean?"

He spoke with the gruffness of a determined Marine. "You're a clinician. Let's look at your risk factors. Labile mood—"

"You're making my mood labile!"

"—active suicidal thoughts—"

"Oh, so you listen to my dead mother, but not your dead father?"

"—impulsivity as demonstrated by engaging in risky behaviors without regard to personal safety—"

"Nobody warned me that Reiki could give me a heart attack!"

Ben opened his desk drawer, pulled out a piece of paper, and flung it onto his desk. "And then we have this."

I gasped. It was a folded-up piece of marbled blue stationery with the name "Simone" written across it. I didn't have to look any closer; I knew instantly what it was.

"Eve found it this morning on the floor of the bathroom downstairs. Don't worry," he said in response to what must have been a look of horror on my face. "She said she didn't read it. She brought it straight to me."

The note must have fallen out of my pocket that first day, while I was changing clothes after tai chi. I thought about trying to snatch it off of his desk, but given how fast his reflexes were, I didn't rate my chances. "That's private," I said to no effect. I cringed as he unfolded the paper.

"Dear Simone," he read, his voice straining under the effort to speak calmly. "I know you're already blaming yourself, so just stop. It's not your fault; this was my decision. There's so much I want to say, but the first thing is, if you were the one they called to identify my body, I'm so terribly sorry. That's not how I had it *planned*." Ben emphasized the last word. The way he looked at me then made me shudder. "Would you like to tell me what you have *planned*?"

My chest heaved with the struggle to take in air. Unevenly, I said, "It was a writing exercise. I never intended to act on it."

He kept his eyes on mine for a moment. Then he looked down and refolded the note. "That may be what you tell yourself," he said, "but self-deception is a dangerous game. My mother can have you admitted to Washington Hill with one phone call," he continued. "Of course, if you don't want Pete to look out for you, and you don't want to go to the hospital, we always could just handcuff you and keep you downstairs until we get back."

"*Handcuff* me?" I began to think that he might actually be serious. My heart fluttered against my ribcage. I summoned my most biting tone and asked, "Who's overreacting *now*, Rottie?"

To my disappointment, the use of Ben's old nickname caused only a slight ripple in his composure. "If I've learned anything over the past several days," he said, "it's that when it comes to you, it pays to err on the side of caution. I'm going to keep you safe, Cate, one way or another. What's it going to be?"

"None of the above!" I declared, again standing up to leave.

Ben leaned forward on the desk and gave me a look so intense that it felt like he could see through to the back of my head. "I can choose for you, if you like. I'll warn you right now, though, that I like the simplicity of handcuffs."

Something in his voice made me freeze in place. It occurred to me that I had only known Ben for a few days and really had no idea what he was capable of. Blood pounded in my head, but I knew better than to show any fear. "You don't scare me with your little drill sergeant act!"

Ben slowly stood up. "Well *you* scare *me*, and I'm not going to allow you destroy yourself," he said with steel in his voice. "Not on my watch."

My sense of control over the situation was slipping away. I had to get out of there. I grabbed my purse and ran for the door. But Ben moved faster than I did. He blocked the door with his body and grabbed the handle. "Sit down," he ordered.

"Get out of my way!"

"Sit down, Cate."

"Move!" I put both of my hands on his chest and pushed as hard as I could.

The next thing I knew, Ben's arms were around me, squeezing tightly. I pushed against his hold, trying to free myself, but he was like a vise. Waves of outrage overtook me, inspiring me to tell Ben again and again how much I hated him and what an asshole he was. I tried to kick my way out and pounded my fists against him, but he didn't budge or react in any way. He just held me there while my anger spiraled into despair.

I was losing my job and my clients. I couldn't even trust Ben anymore. I hadn't felt so helpless since the doctor had taken me to my mother's hospital room to say goodbye…

Sobs rose up again and again from a bottomless well. For a while, I believed they would never stop. But after what seemed like an eternity, out of sheer exhaustion, my body quieted. I felt like a field after a brush fire: scorched, dry, and desolate. My muscles were so tired that I could barely stand. Ben loosened his hold and led me back over to the chair. I sank into it, and he took a seat in the chair beside me.

Completely spent, I stared at a random spot on the floor. When

Ben spoke, he sounded troubled, his tone unexpectedly affectionate. "Are you okay?"

No, I was definitely not okay. In fact, I had never been so *not* okay. "I hate you," I said, repeating my new favorite mantra. "I never had any intention of hurting myself, but even if I had, I can guarantee you that I would never act on it, if for no other reason than to spite you." I dried the last of my tears on my sleeve.

He examined me for a long moment. "Even though that makes no sense, I believe you."

I looked at his lips—those lips that I'd thought about kissing—and willed them to be magically sewn together so I wouldn't have to hear another word out of them.

"I wish I didn't have to go anywhere this afternoon, but it's unavoidable. We'll continue this discussion when I get back." He pulled a business card out of his wallet. "In the meantime, here's Pete's cell phone number. Eve and I will be in a hospital, so I'll probably have to keep my cell phone turned off. I'll tell Pete to keep his distance, but if you need anything while I'm away, you can call him."

No babysitter; that was something, at least. I pressed my palms against my eyes.

"I promise that after you've had a good rest and some time to think things over, you'll feel better." He reached over and gently tugged my arms away from my face so he could look me in the eyes, then asked softly, "Can you do that for me? Stay home tonight, eat something, and get some sleep?"

I gave him a deadeye stare. "If I say yes, will you let me go?"

He removed his hands from my arms and held them up in a gesture of surrender.

I took Pete's card and tucked it into my pocket, although I had zero intention of using it.

Ben followed me into the lounge. Pete was stretched out on the couch reading a newspaper.

"Pete, Cate would like to go home now."

Pete stood up slowly. "Sure thing."

"And pick her up tomorrow at, say, two p.m.?" Ben turned to me and gave me a look freighted with meaning. "Does that work for you, Cate?"

He was trying to get me to agree to come back in front of Pete. All right, I would agree, but they couldn't hold me to it. After all, that was more than twenty-four hours away. By then, I could be in another country. "Fine."

"I'll see you tomorrow then," Ben said, his voice pressing home that he would, in fact, see me. I pointedly did not reply.

"All right, saddle up," Pete said. I could feel Ben's eyes following me as I walked away. *That's right, take a good look,* I told him silently. *It may be your last.*

Chapter Twenty-Two

It was early afternoon and I was lying on my back across the bed, watching sunlight flicker on the ceiling as it filtered through the tree outside my window. With my arms up over my head, I held onto the smooth wood of the bedpost with both hands in an attempt to grip something solid and familiar.

All the way home in the truck with Pete, I had stared out the window in silence. Thankfully, he hadn't asked any questions about what happened between Ben and me. I had found his presence surprisingly calming.

Once home, I tried to make sense of everything that had happened over the past few days, but every time I began to reach some conclusions, they hurt too much—conclusions like, I am pathetic. I am a failure. I'm no good to anyone.

I had failed my mother, obviously. Her suicide had proven that. As close as we were, somehow I had missed how much she was suffering, probably because I was so wrapped up in my own problems that I hadn't been able to see beyond my own nose. She had been on the edge of catastrophe, and I had been utterly useless to her—the person I loved most in the world.

According to Ben, I had apparently failed Dr. Nelson, too. If I was really a decent therapist, Dr. Nelson would have found some way to keep me on—empath or not—rather than enlisting the MacGregors to help him get rid of me. As much as I hated to admit it, Ben must have been right about one thing: Dr. Nelson must really care about me if he'd gone to the trouble of arranging a soft landing for me, instead of firing me outright. Even if he had done it through deception, I should be grateful for that at least.

And if I had failed Dr. Nelson, that must mean I had been failing my clients as well without realizing it. I hadn't been there for over ten weeks, but even before that, I wondered how long everyone had been humoring me, telling me that I was doing a good job.

My clients trusted me. They put so much of themselves into our work, and they expected me to come back and pick up where we left off. Well, it looked like that wasn't going to happen. It was true that I might be able to fight getting fired, but my long absence didn't exactly strengthen my case. If Dr. Nelson really wanted me gone, he could find a way. I should be grateful that he was going to let me come back long enough to wrap up my cases.

I was no use to my boss, no use to my clients, and no use to my friends it seemed. Simone would never admit it, but rather than a true friend, I was becoming the shut-in whom she visited out of the goodness of her heart. Even Sid had said that he was beginning to worry about me.

And then there was Ben. I didn't know *what* to think about him anymore. Was I just a trick pony to the MacGregors, someone who conveniently fit all of their program needs and checked all of their weird, superstitious boxes? I was still so furious with Ben for lying to me—not to mention threatening me with hospitalization and handcuffs—that as far as I was concerned, Rockville wasn't nearly far enough away.

In spite of my outrage, though, I couldn't quite convince myself that the feelings between us weren't real. All I had to do was picture the look on his face when he had seen me nearly dying, or remember how it felt earlier that day when I was in his office, backed up against the bookshelf, and the portal between us had opened…

Disappointment hung like a millstone around my neck, and I knew that I only had myself to blame. Despite all evidence to the contrary, I had allowed myself to hope for a few moments that someone could actually fix whatever was wrong with me and I could have a normal life, maybe even a normal relationship. The final verdict was in: happiness and contentment were for other people, people who weren't weak, broken, and freakish.

My mood was scraping bottom. I thought about writing some more practice suicide notes; that had proven oddly soothing in the past. But having Ben read one of them back to me made me realize what an unhealthy and macabre coping mechanism that was. I decided to act as my own therapist for once and try some of the self-care techniques I had recommended to my clients.

I tried unsuccessfully to distract myself by reading. Then I tried watching TV. Then I fixed myself my favorite dinner of steak and cheese, since I no longer felt any obligation to stick to the program's vegetarian requirements, or any of their other rules for that matter. I enjoyed the meal for as long as it lasted, but once I finished, my misery reasserted itself.

If the techniques I usually recommended weren't working, it occurred to me that I should try some more conventional means of numbing emotional pain. They might not be healthy, but at that point I didn't much care as long as they were effective.

Alcohol? No. I had tried that before, so I knew it didn't work unless I drank a lot—and if I had more than two or three drinks, I would wake up hung over and feeling worse than ever.

Drugs? Thanks to some of my clients, I knew where to get them. But thanks to the same clients, I knew that drugs bought off the street could be laced with anything from rat poison to cyanide. I didn't have any prescription drugs other than the pills Dr. Nelson had given me, and while they put a damper on my anxiety, they didn't lift my mood.

There was always my usual go-to: ice cream. But the steak and cheese had more than filled me up, and my stomach felt like lead. I didn't think I could eat more if I tried.

"Argh!" I yelled in frustration, not even caring whether the neighbors heard. I felt like I was going to climb out of my skin. I decided a hot bath might help. I made it scorching hot and threw in some vanilla-scented bubbles. I lowered myself in like a lobster into a pot. The sensory overload distracted me, giving me some relief—that was, until the water grew tepid.

I dried myself off and wiped the steam off of the bathroom

mirror—then jumped, thinking for a moment that I'd seen my mother's ghost. Then I realized that I was just coming to resemble her more and more as time went on.

I opened the mirror to examine the contents of the medicine cabinet, thinking that I might give myself some kind of spa treatment. But there, next to the assorted samples of mud masks and cucumber peels, I saw it—my suicide kit. The two bottles of over-the-counter pills my Internet research had told me would do me in, especially when combined with the pint of rum I had stashed in the kitchen.

The pill bottles just sat there—unopened, seemingly benign. *But what are they doing there?* I forced myself to consider the question. They weren't medications I needed. I remembered tossing them into my cart during my last two a.m. grocery store run, but I couldn't pinpoint the thought process behind that decision. It was one thing to research suicide online, but quite another to actually go about procuring the means.

Maybe Ben was right. Maybe I *had* been deceiving myself, thinking that those suicide notes were just for practice. Maybe my mother's spirit was right, too, and I was actually at risk of following in her footsteps.

Maybe I did need help, after all.

Feeling vaguely nauseous, I double-timed it down the stairs and sat on the couch, wanting to put as much space as I could between myself and those pill bottles. I felt like I should call someone—but who? Certainly not Ben—not after what had happened that morning. I wouldn't give him the satisfaction. Besides, even if I did call him, he'd probably tell Pete to hogtie me and throw me in the back of the pickup truck until he got back from Rockville.

I could call Simone, but it was Thursday afternoon, which meant that she was leading back-to-back groups—and she was doing it solo, thanks to the fact that I was too pathetic to work. I called her cell anyway, knowing it would go straight to voicemail. I didn't leave a message because I couldn't think of anything to say that wouldn't worry her, but it helped a little to hear her voice.

There was only one other person I could think of to call. I got Sid's voicemail, too, so I decided to try texting him.

me: *hey sid*

Proving to me that there was in fact a God, Sid replied immediately.

sid: *hey sexy*
me: *whatcha doin*
sid: *inventory, yawn*
me: *sorry…can you take a break to talk?*

There was a long pause, and for a moment, I was afraid the connection had been dropped. Then, a reply:

sid: *would you rather i come over? it would be a good excuse for me to get out of counting rugs. i could say i have a friend in crisis…*

A strangled laugh escaped my throat.

me: *you kind of do*

The next thing I knew, my phone was ringing. The second I answered, Sid asked, "What's wrong, Cate?"

"Hello to you, too." I swallowed hard. "Nothing's wrong, it's just…I don't know. That program I started isn't really working out."

"You don't sound good," he said, his voice low and intense. "It'll take me an hour to get there. Will you be okay until then?"

"Sure, yeah."

"Still have that card deck?"

In spite of everything, I smiled. "Yeah. Thanks for that, by the way. Now everyone thinks I'm a perv."

"As well they should." I could tell he was trying to make me laugh, but worry had sucked the humor out of his voice. "Just stay put. I'll be there in no time."

I went up to my room just long enough to put on my bathrobe and slippers. Then I lay on the couch and tried to meditate, focused on holding body and soul together until Sid arrived.

Chapter Twenty-Three

As soon as I opened the door, Sid was inside, shutting it quickly behind him. He looked me over like he was examining his car after a fender-bender and didn't like what he saw. Then he pulled me into a tight embrace and placed a decidedly platonic kiss on the top of my head. "Hey, sexy," he said with about as much erotic charge as I would have expected if he were visiting me in the hospital. "You had me worried."

"Sorry," I said as I slipped my arms around him and squeezed back. Wearing jeans and a t-shirt, he was more casually dressed than I'd ever seen him—inventory-taking clothes, I guessed.

After a few more moments, Sid walked over to the bay window, separated the blinds with his fingers, and peered outside.

"What is it?" I asked. "Are they ticketing cars?"

"No, no." He waved me over and pointed out the window. "But I think that cowboy might be stalking you."

"What?" I leapt to the window and pulled the blinds open. Sure enough, there was Pete's truck, steer horns and all, parked on the corner of the cross street at the end of my block. I could just make out the shadowy shape in the cab: a tall, thin figure wearing a cowboy hat.

"Goddammit!" I yelled.

Sid straightened up and squared his shoulders as if preparing to go into battle. "I'll go have a word with him."

"No!" I grabbed him by the arm. "Thank you, Sid. I mean it. But there's no need. He's not stalking me." I nearly spat out the words: "He's *babysitting* me."

"What? Why?"

My hands fisted. "Because Ben—the manager of that program I was going to—told him to, evidently."

"Hmm." Sid studied me as he ran a finger up and down the bridge of his nose. "And why would he do that?"

"Why does it matter?" I flung my arms into the air. "Whose side are you on?"

"Yours, of course." He came over and took my hands. "Yours, always. But first you call and tell me you're in crisis. One look at you tells me that is clearly the case. Then I find out that the people who are supposed to be taking care of you are concerned enough that they've put you under some kind of surveillance." His eyes narrowed. "You want to tell me what's going on?"

The defensive part of me wanted to be angry at Sid, but I couldn't quite manage it. After all, he had just dropped everything and driven an hour to check on me—*and* he'd offered to go confront a man he knew nothing about on my behalf. I interlaced my fingers with his and squeezed. "Yes," I said. "I *do* want to tell you. But there is no way I'm going to be able to talk about anything until I get rid of that goddamned cowboy!"

Sid frowned. "You sure you don't want any help?"

"No, thank you. I prefer to deal with this myself." I scanned the room for a weapon, finally settling on the broken umbrella hanging from the coat rack.

"Uh, Cate," Sid ventured, "you do realize that you're wearing—"

But I was already out the door. Sid stepped out behind me.

"Okay, bathrobe it is!" he called.

"Back in a minute," I shouted over my shoulder. I stalked down the street, swinging the umbrella. Pete must have seen me coming, because he climbed out of the truck and was closing the door when I arrived.

"Afternoon, ma'am," he said, tipping his hat at me.

I smacked the umbrella repeatedly against my palm like a teacher with a ruler. "Don't give me that crap!" I shouted. "Ben told me he told you to keep your distance!"

Pete wore the wounded expression of the falsely accused. "I'm all the way at the end of the block! I can't watch you from any further away. What do you want from me?"

"I want you out of here!" I whacked the umbrella on the truck's bumper—which just further injured the umbrella.

Pete rubbed his chin. "I was wondering what you were plannin' on doin' with that."

"Go! Away!" I pointed the umbrella at him, opening and closing it rapidly like I was trying to scare away a flock of pigeons.

Pete jumped and backed up toward the driver's side door. "You know I can't do that," he said, holding his hands up defensively. "Ben told me to keep an eye on you!"

I twisted around and pointed at Sid, who was standing on my stoop watching the whole spectacle. "Well, as you can see, I have someone else to keep an eye on me now, so you are off the hook!"

Pete frowned in Sid's direction. Then he pushed his hat up and rubbed his hairline.

"No, Pete," I barked, "you do *not* get to think about this! This is *not* your decision!" I slapped the umbrella against my palm again. "If you don't get out of here right now, I swear to God I'm going to call the police and tell them I have a stalker. That'll put you at the station for a few hours at least. You won't be able to keep any eye on *anything* from there!"

Pete spoke in a soothing singsong voice, the same one I imagined he used on nervous horses. "Now, Cate, come on—"

"I'm serious!" I took a step toward him and poked him in the chest with my finger. "You go back to the church and you tell Ben I said to stay the hell away from me, do you hear me?"

His eyes narrowed to slits as he looked up again at where Sid stood. "All right, sis." Pete pushed his hat back into place. "Long as you got somebody here with you. Just take care of yourself. You know if anything bad happens, Ben'll blame me."

My anger ebbed slightly. Pete and I had sort of become friends over the past few days, and after all, he wasn't the one I was really mad at. I reached over and opened the door of the truck. "I'll be fine, Pete. I promise."

He looked down at my umbrella. "Remind me to get you a can of mace."

I gave him my best death glare. "Go!"

He tipped his hat to me again before climbing into the truck. I stepped back onto the sidewalk as his diesel engine rumbled to life and he disappeared down the street.

My task accomplished, I suddenly became self-conscious about the fact that I was standing outside on a clear day, wearing a white fuzzy robe and slippers and carrying an umbrella. I'd been so caught up in my showdown with Pete that I hadn't noticed if there were any witnesses. I made a point of not looking into any of my neighbors' windows as I padded back up the street, resembling nothing more than a gigantic, red-faced, poorly armed marshmallow.

Sid was smiling proudly as I walked up to the house. "I'm impressed," he said, opening the door for me with a flourish. "I had no idea you were so lethal with an umbrella."

I used the embattled weapon to smack him lightly on the leg, then put it back on the coat stand. I knew I should have felt some satisfaction at having got rid of Pete, but my earlier gloom began to overtake me again. I flopped down in the middle of the couch.

Sid's playful expression quickly disappeared. He sat next to me, then invited me to lie down and rest my head in his lap. "Come, my dear. Talk to me."

Even though that was why I'd called him in the first place, I hesitated. I hadn't yet confided in Sid about the severity of the problems I'd been having since my mother's death, and I wasn't sure that I wanted to burden our relationship with such heaviness. I also wasn't sure how much I wanted to tell him about the program. Maybe it was the caring in his voice or the way he looked at me, but in spite of my reservations, something loosened the hold I had been keeping on my misery and the words began to pour out.

Sid stroked my hair as I told him about the anxiety and depression I'd been fighting and confessed that I'd become a virtual recluse. I told him about some of the mind-blowing experiences I'd had at the program—minus the more bizarre details—and how they made sense to me and confused me, all at the same time. Pushing through my embarrassment, I even shared what I'd learned about empaths and catalysts, and how that might apply to Sid and me. I figured he had a right to know.

Then I told him about Ben. Sid listened in silence as I described how Ben and I argued frequently but still had feelings for each other—even though we hadn't acted on them yet. I shared how devastated I'd felt that morning when I learned that Ben and the others had lied to me, and that I was being forced to leave my job and my clients. I explained how that conversation had ended badly, which was probably why Ben had asked Pete to keep an eye on me.

Sid's hand stopped in mid-hair stroke. "What was he afraid might happen?"

"I don't know," I lied, not wanting to worry him even more. Besides, the point seemed moot. Being with Sid seemed to have chased away my dark mood and morbid thoughts—temporarily, at least. Maybe his catalyst energy was working its magic. Or maybe it was just the everyday magic of actually breaking down and confiding in someone who cared about me.

"I see." I could tell from his tone that Sid knew I was keeping something from him, but he opted not to press me further. "That's quite a tale, my dear. Fortunately, you happen to be talking to someone who is remarkably open-minded. Still, I had no idea that your life was so full of drama and intrigue—outside of our entanglement, that is."

"It wasn't…not until recently."

"I'll have to take your word for that." He winked. "I'm just glad that you finally told me what's going on. You've certainly been holding your cards close to the vest."

I nestled in closer to him. "I didn't want to worry you."

"What worries me is when I can tell something's wrong but you're not talking about it—and make no mistake, I can always tell."

"Okay. From now on, I promise to tell you if something's wrong." I smiled up at him.

"I'll hold you to that." He brushed a piece of hair away from my face. "How are you feeling now?"

"Much better, thanks to you."

"Glad to hear it." He squeezed my shoulder. "There is still one thing that concerns me, though."

"What's that?"

"It has to do with matters of the heart," he said gently. "You and I have been carrying on for several years now, and in spite of the fact that talking is not how we spend the bulk of our time, I like to think that I know you pretty well. After all, I am your…catamaran? Catastrophe? What am I again?"

"Catalyst." I batted him on the arm, then felt another pang of guilt as I realized what conclusions he might have reached. "You know you're much more than that, right?"

"Don't worry," he said, looking darkly amused. "Your body tells me frequently and in convincing detail."

My face flushed with heat. Sid placed his hand on my forehead for a few seconds as though checking for fever. "As I was saying, as your *catalyst,* I probably know you better than most people do. My point is that it sounds to me as though this Ben person cares about you quite a bit. I mean, he must, if he sent this cowboy to watch over you."

"Very funny," I said dryly. "Maybe he does care about me. He could also just be a control freak."

Sid took the point of my chin between his fingers and tilted my head so that he could look at me more directly. "Either way, he's only been in the picture for a week, and already you're crying into my arms over him instead of riding me like a mechanical bull. If you try to tell me that's not a sign that something serious is going on, I'm frankly going to be offended."

Sid wore an expression of hard-earned wisdom, like an ancient statue that had watched civilizations rise and fall. "I don't think I like where you're going with this," I said.

"Nor do I, my dear, nor do I." He caressed my cheek. "But as a friend who cares an awful lot about you, I think you should give this Ben thing an opportunity to play out. You never know, a relationship with him might be able to give you all of the things that ours can't—all of the wonderful things you deserve. And we both know you can't really give him a fair chance if you're spending every weekend with me in the garden of earthly delights."

I moaned. "*Siiiiid...*"

"I know, I know. It's tough," he said in mock sympathy. "Just think, though. Some women go their whole lives without ever getting to sleep with me."

Self-pity threatened to drown me. I felt like I was losing my only friend. A round of tears threatened to break through. "I refuse to give you up, especially for him! He's taken too much away from me already!"

"Now, now," Sid murmured, stroking my hair again. "No one said anything about giving anyone up. I know it's twisted and scandalous, but we could actually be 'just friends'—at least until this Ben character screws things up, which for my sake I certainly hope he will."

That did it. The tears started to fall. I rolled over and wrapped my arms around his waist. "But what if nothing happens with Ben?" I found that I was barely able to speak the words. "Or what if something does happen, but then he breaks my heart?"

"Then you'll call me, and I'll call the office and tell them I've contracted a horrible, highly contagious illness, and I'll come over and spend as much time with you as it takes to pick up all of the pieces. Very slowly. With massage oil."

A bittersweet ache settled into my chest. Sid and I, just friends. I tried to imagine it. Certainly, it would be strange at first. But we had grown so comfortable with each other, we cared about each other, and in many ways we probably did know each other better than anyone else. "So I can still call you," I said tentatively. "Just to talk."

He smiled and nodded. "You can call me anytime, day or night. And now that I know you're at the epicenter of so much drama, I'll be checking in on you a lot more frequently."

I considered. "And we can still see each other."

"Of course, although I think we should hold off for a little while. Give you a chance to explore things with Ben without any distractions."

A gentle certainty settled upon me—I could trust Sid not to abandon me. "Okay. If you insist, I'll give it a try."

"That's my girl."

He leaned down and kissed my forehead, inspiring instant melancholy. "Sid," I whispered, "I'm going to miss this so much I don't think I can stand it."

"I'll miss it too, babe." He ran his finger along my jaw line. "I'll tell you what. You look exhausted. Let's go upstairs, and I'll hold you on the bed until you fall asleep. I know how you like that."

"Okay," I nodded, touched by his gesture. Even though I knew he'd refuse, for old times' sake, I asked, "Can you hold me on the bed…naked?"

He sighed heavily as he helped me up off the couch. "And that is why they say, 'Never volunteer for anything.'"

Chapter Twenty-Four

It hadn't taken long for me to drift off into a blank sleep. Sid was gone by the time I rose into wakefulness. Judging from the darkness of the sky and the slant of the shadows from the streetlights, I guessed it was approximately seven p.m.

As my brain slowly creaked into gear, I remembered what had happened earlier in the day. Piece by piece, the whole week started to snap into place, and my mind was wrenched out of its peaceful state and cast back into the fray. At that moment, every cell in my body longed painfully to be somewhere else, living someone else's life. I tried to satisfy the longing by doing a little empath surfing. I lay flat on the bed and closed my eyes against the night, feeling around for portals that were still open—not Ben's, of course. Maybe Sid's, or Simone's.

The moment I turned inward, though, I felt something coming at me like a tornado. It was off in the distance but closing rapidly. Within seconds, a wall of fear slammed into my chest, knocking the breath out of me. It was burning hot and icy cold at the same time, and painful with urgency.

My eyes flew open and I shot up in bed. I looked around and listened. I heard no sounds and saw nothing obvious to be afraid of.

I crept downstairs and checked the door and windows. I peered through the blinds on the front window and saw my car parked out front. Nothing was out of the ordinary. But the terror did not abate.

It occurred to me that it might not be my own fear that I was feeling. It might be coming to me through a portal—which meant that someone close to me was afraid. I turned my attention inward again. I held the terror in my heart and asked, *Whose emotion is this?*

One word surfaced softly in my mind: *Elana*.

What was wrong with Elana? I tried to concentrate, tried to think, but the fear I was receiving was so overwhelming that I couldn't tease out any useful information.

What if they'd let Don out of jail for some reason? What if he was with her at the hospital? Or what if she had gone home? What if he was hurting her?

I ran to the coffee table and pulled my laptop out of the drawer. Unless Dr. Nelson had disabled my login for some reason, I knew I should still be able to get into our database and see if there were any updates on her case. I knew I wasn't allowed to log onto the clinic server while I was technically on leave, but I didn't care. This was an emergency.

As the laptop started up, I tried to figure out what to do next. I couldn't call the police. What was I going to tell them? That I had a psychic impression that my client was in danger?

And I couldn't call Dr. Nelson. Given how close he was to the MacGregors, he might actually believe me about the psychic impression thing. But given what a stickler he was for procedure, I knew he wouldn't do anything about it. If Elana were still in the hospital, he would say it was the hospital's responsibility to keep her safe. If she had been released, he would say it was Elana's responsibility to call someone for help if she needed it. In any case, he would probably insist that I was worrying over nothing since Don was in police custody.

I couldn't call Washington Hill. They wouldn't give me any information about Elana without confirming who I was, and everything I told them would be documented in their records. I couldn't risk Dr. Nelson finding out that I was snooping on my clients.

Workable options were shrinking. I thought about calling Simone, but I knew that if I did, she would have to call Dr. Nelson, which would only create the same problems. If I asked her to keep my call a secret, I would basically be asking her to choose between me and her professional ethics, and I would never ask her to do that.

The very last thing I wanted to do was ask Ben for help with anything, but at least he would take me seriously if I told him that Elana was in trouble. I just couldn't be sure what he would do about it. After all, he had apparently become obsessive about my safety, and I knew that he wanted me to keep my distance from my clients for the moment—Elana in particular, after the Reiki/heart attack incident. Plus, Pete might have already told Ben that Sid was at my house, which would likely put him in an even less cooperative mood. So while it was possible that Ben would help me, it was equally likely that he would try to stop me from intervening—possibly by handcuffing me and tossing me in the church basement. That was a risk I couldn't take.

I would just have to put everyone else out of my mind and focus on Elana. I managed to get into the clinic server and open her file. No one had entered any updates on her case since she went into the hospital. If I called her and there was no answer, it might mean she was still at Washington Hill. I jotted down her phone numbers—and address, just in case.

Her landline had been temporarily disconnected. I tried her cell. After a few rings, her voicemail picked up with the tinny chorus of a pop song. Then Elana's voice came on, sounding tired. "Hi, I'm home from the hospital. Leave a message, and I'll call you back when I get some minutes on my phone. Bye."

Oh, hell. She was out of the hospital, she was terrified, and she wasn't picking up her phone. If by some chance Don *had* been released from jail, what if he'd taken her phone away from her? It wouldn't be the first time; it was one of the control tactics he used. Then Elana would have no way to call for help.

Stop it, I told myself, *you're getting yourself worked up over nothing. Don is in jail.* To prove it to myself, I decided to check the police database. As a supervisor, Simone had access, and she had given me her username and password. I logged in and searched for Don's name. To my horror, I discovered that in spite of the reassurances we'd been given that he would remain locked up "for weeks," Don had been released the previous day. No explanation was noted.

Well, that settled it. Elana could be in danger. There were no options left, and the longer I waited…I would have to do something on my own, without anybody's help. I just didn't know what.

I took a deep breath and tried to think rationally. In terms of violating clinic policy, taking Elana's personal information off of the server while I was out on leave was bad enough. Checking the police database was even worse. But if I actually went over to her house, especially uninvited, and Dr. Nelson found out, he might fire me on the spot, giving me no chance to even say goodbye to my clients. The thought made my anxiety spike.

It's okay, I told myself, *no one ever has to know you were there.* I could just stay out of sight and try to look in on her from outside her apartment. If she was in trouble, I could make an anonymous 911 call. At least then I'd have some concrete information to give the police—something more than a psychic impression.

The drive-by plan seemed reasonably workable, and it was the only one I had. I dressed quickly and as nondescriptly as possible: jeans, sweatshirt, sneakers, hair in a ponytail.

As I checked to make sure that my cell phone was charged, the thought occurred to me: *You know this could be dangerous.* But I also knew it didn't matter. If something happened to Elana, I would never be able to forgive myself.

Chapter Twenty-Five

It was nearly eight o'clock when I reached Elana's address. She lived in a maze of low-rise apartment buildings on a sketchy block near Dr. Nelson's clinic. I sat in my car, spying on her and trying to decide my next move.

Elana was alone in her apartment. I could see her through the window, milling around in her kitchen. I wondered for a moment why I was able to feel her emotions so strongly. Then I remembered—I had opened a portal to her when I used the Distance Healing technique. Everyone had said that the portal would only stay open as long as I was sending her Reiki energy. But maybe it hadn't closed after all, or not fully. Ben had mentioned that I was reacting in unexpected ways to a lot of the exercises we'd been doing. Maybe this was just another example.

It looked like Elana was preparing dinner and setting the table... for two. Through the portal, I felt that her terror had become mixed with frenzied anticipation. I couldn't be sure who she was expecting, but I was willing to put down money that it was Don. At least I'd beat him to her apartment. But as I sat and thought things through, I began to see the holes in my plan.

Option one was to wait until Don showed up, then call the police if he did anything suspicious. But if he was determined to hurt Elana, it might be too late for her by the time the police arrived. Even if I ran up to the apartment the minute I saw him do something suspicious, what would I do once I got there? Don had already threatened to kill me if I got anywhere near Elana, so I could be in just as much danger as she was. It wasn't like I had the means to defend either of us.

Option two: I could go up to her apartment and try to talk her into leaving with me. I could tell her…what? That Simone had told me she'd been in the hospital, and I was worried about her? It would be weird, certainly, but at least being there in person, I could gauge her reaction. If she were really scared of Don, maybe I could talk her into going to a women's shelter. I'd take her there myself. By the time Don arrived, we would both be safely away.

Option two seemed imperfect, but better. Elana could always refuse to go with me, but there was at least a chance she would listen. If not, I could return to the car and go back to option one.

Worst-case scenario: I would get into the apartment and Don would arrive while I was talking to Elana—and the longer I sat there trying to decide what to do, the higher the chances were of that happening. I said a silent prayer and got out of the car.

• • •

Here goes nothing, I thought as I knocked on the door. In a matter of seconds, Elana opened it. Her already large eyes widened. "Cate?"

"Hi, Elana!" I was surprised by how relieved I was to see her. I had to fight the impulse to reach out and hug her.

She held her hand out as if to touch my shoulder, but quickly pulled it back. "Are you here for real?"

"What?" I asked, then realized that she might have thought she was having another vision of me like the one she'd had in the hospital. I decided the less said about that, the better. "Yeah," I said, forcing myself to smile. "Can I come in?"

She poked her head out, looked left and right, and then opened the door. "Sure, I guess," she said, looking as though she was trying to figure out what the heck was going on.

As we entered her living room, I could see that Elana's hair and make-up were carefully done. She was wearing tight jeans with rhinestones glued to the back pockets, a form-fitting yellow tank top, and a delicate gold necklace with a letter "D" charm hanging from it. The room was brightly lit, with a yellow rug that matched the walls and furniture made of white leather and chrome.

"I'm sorry to bother you so late," I said. "Simone told me that you had discharged from Washington Hill. I was in the neighborhood, so I thought I'd see how you were doing." I hoped that sounded legitimate.

Elana closed and locked the door behind me, looking confused. "You were in the neighborhood? *This* neighborhood?"

I did my best to sound casual. "Yeah, so I thought I'd check in. I'm going to be away from work for another couple of weeks, but then I'll be back. I didn't know if you'd heard."

"They told me you were at some kind of conference. I've been seeing Simone once a week."

"Oh good," I said as brightly as I could. "Simone is great. I just wanted to make sure you were okay."

"Yeah, I'm okay." She nervously played with her "D" charm. "I wasn't for a while, but I'm doing better now. They put me on some new medication."

"I'm so glad to hear you're feeling better." I plucked up the courage to be even more intrusive. "Elana, pardon me for asking, but is everything okay here tonight?"

"Yeah, everything is fine. In fact, I'm having someone over for dinner. To be honest, I don't think you should be here when he gets here."

"Oh? Why is that?"

"Don's coming over." She smiled shyly. "You know how it is."

I deduced that Elana didn't know about Don's little visit to my house. "So everything is okay between you guys?"

"Yeah, everything's fine." She walked toward the front door. "Listen, I, um, appreciate your coming by, but I think you should go now. Don is going to be here any minute, and he kind of doesn't want me to be talking to you."

"Really? Why not?" I tried to sound innocent.

"Please," she said with growing agitation, "we can talk about it later. But I really need you to leave now. I have to finish making dinner." She reached for the door handle.

I reached through the portal again and felt terror rolling off of her in waves. I had to do something before she kicked me out. I blurted, "Elana, are you afraid of Don?"

"Afraid? Of Don?" She looked genuinely surprised and gave a derisive snort.

My eyes widened. Don being who he was, I hadn't expected my question to be met with such nonchalance. "I only ask because you seem a little nervous tonight."

"Oh, don't worry," she said, her smile touched with a hint of mania. "If anybody should be afraid of anybody, Don should be afraid of me."

"Why should Don be afraid of you?"

"Look, Cate." She dropped her voice to a conspiratorial whisper. "I don't mean to be rude, but you really need to get out of here. Some of Don's...*friends* are on their way over. The police picked Don up for something last week, but they let him out so quickly that his friends think he must have snitched in jail. They called and asked me to help them find him, so I said I would. I mean, after all, he cheated on me. Can you believe that? That's why I ended up in the hospital," she said through gritted teeth. "I told his friends that I'd have Don over for dinner tonight so they could come over and set him straight."

"Set him *straight?*" God knew she had every right to be angry with Don. But I also knew that if anything happened to him because of her, she would never forgive herself, and that would probably send her on another downward spiral. Not to mention the fact that she could be putting herself in harm's way.

She flipped her hair back and planted a hand on her hip. "That's right. I mean, knowing Don, he probably *did* snitch, and since he hasn't been treating me right, his boss said they'd teach him a lesson. I know *you* probably don't approve of that kind of thing, but like his boss said, somebody like Don only understands one language."

I searched for something I could say to make her change her course of action. "I know Don has treated you badly, but I also know that you care about him. You do know that if these friends of Don's think he talked to the police, they might be planning to kill him?"

She shook her head. "Oh no, it's not like that. He's one of their best dealers. His boss promised me they would just rough him up a little."

"And you trust his boss, why? Do you even know him?"

A cloud of doubt passed over her face. She began to bite one of her fingernails. "Yes. I mean, I've talked to him on the phone. I've never met him in person because Don always kept me away from everybody he works with. He never even wanted them to know who I was or where I lived."

"Why not?"

"*I* think it's because he's so possessive and jealous. But *he* always said he was afraid that if they knew who I was, one day they might use me to get to him, and he didn't want me to get hurt." I stood silently as she considered what she was saying. The terror she'd been broadcasting to me all night crept into her features. "But you don't think that's what they're doing, right? I mean, why would they want to hurt *me*?"

"I'm sure they don't," I said, trying to keep us both calm. "But just think for a minute. Don's not stupid. He probably knows they're looking for him, and I'm sure he'll try to defend himself. What if he's armed? What if his 'friends' are? Once they all get here, you can't control what happens. It could be an explosive situation. You're not safe here, Elana!"

I could see that she was visualizing the scene that might unfold. "Oh my god, oh my god." She clutched at my arm. "You're right; anything could happen. I didn't think…Oh god, Cate! What am I going to do?"

There was a series of sharp knocks at the door. Before I could stop her, Elana ran to the door and peered through the peephole. "I think it's Don's friends!" Her voice squeaked with terror.

"Okay, listen to me. You need to hide!" I grabbed her by the arm and steered her toward the bedroom hallway.

"What? Hide?"

"Yes, hide. I'll stall them." Even as I spoke, I wondered from what place in hell that idea was springing. "I'll tell them they have the wrong apartment. That will get rid of them long enough for us to make a plan."

She looked like a deer in the headlights. "Are you sure?"

"Yes, I'm sure. Go in the other room and close the door. And lock it."

"Okay," she said, stumbling down the hallway. Once I heard her turn the lock, I went to the front door. There was another series of sharp knocks. "Who is it?" I asked.

A gruff voice answered. "Elana, it's us. Open up."

"Nobody by that name lives here."

"What the—" The handle turned and someone pushed against the door. Fortunately, the deadbolt held. "Quit messin' around. We can't stay out here. There's too many people around."

"I'm opening up—with the chain." I secured the chain on the door and unlocked the deadbolt, then opened the door a few inches and peered through the opening. A steely-blue eye stared back at me from an unshaven face marked with scars. A couple of other figures stood behind him in the shadows.

I cleared my throat. "You must have the wrong apartment."

The eye examined me skeptically. "You're not Elana," the gruff voice said.

"That's what I told you." My heart pounded into my throat.

The man at the door turned to consult with his colleagues. They collectively examined a photo and a small piece of paper, upon which I guessed Elana's address was written. Steely Eye came back to the door. "Where does she live?"

A tremor went through me. Was I actually going to get away with this? "I don't know an Elana. She must be in another building."

"Shit," he muttered to himself. He turned to his companions. "Let's go." With that, all of the figures turned away and melted into the darkness.

I closed and dead bolted the door and leaned against it, not trusting my legs to hold me up. I heard the click of Elana's bedroom door unlocking and the creak of floorboards as she crept down the hallway toward me. Her pallid face peeked around the corner of the wall. "Did they go?"

I nodded. She came over to me and embraced me as though she were drowning in the ocean and I was a piece of driftwood. "Oh my god, Cate. Thank you so much!"

"No problem," I said, trying to smile.

She pulled away and began pacing the rug. "I didn't really think about what might go wrong, I just figured—oh my god, what about Don? They might run into him out there. Or one of my neighbors will tell them I *do* live here, and they'll be back, and oh my god, Cate, they'll kill us too!" She ran to me and grabbed my wrists. "And I've got to call Don! Oh god, where's my phone?" She rushed into the kitchen and began searching frantically.

I followed after her. "Calm down," I heard myself saying, although I had absolutely nothing with which to back up that suggestion. "We have to get out of here now. My car's outside."

"But what about Don? I have to tell him not to come…oh, it's in my pocket!" She pulled her phone from her pocket and held it aloft like a victory medal. "Hold on, where did I put my purse—"

"Elana, stop!" I chased her around the kitchen as she searched. "Listen to me. Forget your purse. If they come back here and kill us, it's not going to matter whether you have your purse!"

Before she could answer, we were both startled by three loud pounds on the door. "I know you're in there!" It was Don, and he sounded irate.

We both ran toward the door. I managed to wedge myself between her and the handle. "They could be out there with him!" I whispered desperately. "Go back to the bedroom and let me get the door. If he's alone, I'll call for you to come out."

Her widened eyes darted back and forth. "But—"

"Open up!" This time the voice belonged to Steely Eye. There was another loud pound on the door. I heard the wood crack around the dead bolt. They could easily break the door down.

Elana held her hands up. "Okay, okay," she whispered. "Just

get rid of them. Tell Don I went to stay with my friend Tonya. He'll believe that."

I nodded and steered her back toward the hallway. When she had disappeared, I returned to the front door. "Okay, I'm opening the door, but I'm keeping the chain on," I shouted.

The second I unlatched the dead bolt, the chain broke off and the door flew open, slamming into me with such force that I fell backwards onto the floor.

Don was the first one in. He looked down at me with a face like a thunderstorm. "You!" He spat in disgust. "I told you to stay away from her!"

"Get out of here!" I shouted, tapping into some mysterious well of courage. "She's not even here. She went to stay at Tonya's!"

The shadows of Don's colleagues began to gather around the door. He took a step toward me, fist raised. "I warned you, bitch—"

He turned his head at the sounds of a scuffle outside. Don's colleagues disappeared suddenly. Then I heard a sickening thud, and Don crumpled to the floor like a marionette whose strings had been cut. I made out a tall, thin figure in a black ski mask standing behind him. "You okay?" a muffled voice asked as the masked man tucked a large flashlight into his belt.

Thunderstruck, I nodded. The man turned and walked out the door.

Elana emerged from the bedroom, draping herself over Don's limp body as we heard more sounds of fighting on the walkway outside—muffled yells and what sounded like some punches being thrown. Elana and I sat frozen in place. After a few moments, the noise stopped. We slowly got to our feet.

The silence was broken by the sound of heavy boots approaching the open doorway. I wasn't sure which one of us was more surprised by what we saw. There stood Ben and Pete in full camouflage, their ski masks pushed up so we could see their reddened faces. Elana's mouth and mine dropped open in perfect unison.

"Good evenin', ma'am," Pete said, nodding at Elana.

"Y-y-yes?" Elana replied tremulously.

"We're with the United States Marine Corps. We were out on urban training maneuvers tonight, and we heard a disturbance at your door," he gestured toward the walkway. "Do you know these men?"

I followed behind Elana as she took a step outside. To the left, sitting on the ground, gagged and wearing what looked like plastic handcuffs, were three incredibly confused and angry looking men. One of them was Steely Eye.

"Um," Elana stammered. I could almost see her survival instincts kicking into gear. "No, I don't know them," she said.

Pete walked back into the living room. "How about this one?" he asked, kicking the bottom of Don's shoe. Don moaned softly.

"I used to know him," she answered carefully, "but not anymore."

"Well then," Pete said, "we'll bring him out here with the others and wait 'til the police come to pick 'em up. They were all carryin' what look to be illegal firearms."

"You ladies be safe now," Ben said. The tension in his voice told me that he wouldn't be at ease until Don and the others had been taken away. Still, when our eyes met, it was with a cymbal clash of emotions. Our gazes locked for a moment, but a shuffling sound on the walkway drew Ben's attention. "Hey!" he shouted as he went to deal with their prisoners.

"Elana, why don't you come back inside," I said. My focus had to remain on making sure that she was all right. With a look of utter perplexity, Elana turned and walked back into the living room.

I turned back to Pete. "Thank you, sir," I said, playing along with their story. Then, just to let him know that he was officially forgiven for spying on me earlier, I added, "We certainly feel safer knowing that you're out there protecting us."

"No problem, ma'am," Pete said with a grin. "Have a good night."

Then he, too, disappeared through the doorway. Elana looked as though she were on the edge of tears. I sat down next to her on the sofa. "Are you okay?"

She shook her head in wonder. "I have no idea what just happened, but I'm so glad those soldiers came." Tears started to fall from her eyes. "I didn't *really* want those guys to hurt Don!" I reached out and embraced her as she cried. It felt like holding a small trembling bird. "I was just so angry and fed up…"

"I know. It's okay." We stayed like that for a long while.

After she stopped crying, I fixed her some tea. We talked while we waited for the police to arrive. The events of the night had left Elana feeling very fragile. She decided it would be best to go back into the hospital for a while. I made the call to the staff at Washington Hill. They said they had a bed available and would welcome her back.

When we saw the flashing blue lights outside of her window, I accompanied Elana out to the police cars. Ben and Pete were nowhere to be seen. The police said that they had received an anonymous tip about the men with the illegal firearms. They questioned us briefly. Elana told them that I was her therapist making a house call, that Don was her ex and had broken her door down, and that she'd never seen the other three men before—all of which was true, technically speaking.

The police arrested the men, two of whom were carrying illegal drugs in addition to firearms. As they loaded Don and the others into the backseats of their cruisers, I pulled one of the officers aside and explained Elana's psychiatric situation. He agreed to take her to the hospital and wait with her until she was admitted. I said a silent prayer of gratitude as they pulled away and Elana waved to me through the car window.

Once all of the police cars had gone, Elana's curious neighbors returned to their apartments. *Thank God it's over,* I thought as a wave of exhaustion swept over me. I was too tired even to think. I started walking back to my car.

As I approached the road, a familiar-looking black Land Rover with tinted windows pulled up to the curb. The back door opened, and Pete smiled out at me. He had taken off the ski mask and put on his cowboy hat. "Hop in." I let him give me a hand up into the vehicle.

Ben was driving and Kai was in the front seat on the passenger side. "Hi, honey," Kai called back cheerfully. "Hiya, Cate," I heard behind me. I turned to see Asa grinning and waving from a third row of seats. I caught Ben's eye as he looked at me in the rearview mirror, and suddenly I knew: not only was Elana safe, but I was safe, too.

"Hi, guys." I laid my head back on the headrest and promptly passed out.

CHAPTER TWENTY-SIX

Hell Week, Day Six

When consciousness returned, I was lying on my back in a very comfortable bed, more comfortable than my own. I didn't want to be awake yet. I rolled over onto my stomach and tried to go back to sleep, but my brain bothered me with questions: *Where are you? Whose bed is this?* Finally I gave in and opened my eyes.

I was lying under a canopy in a room decorated with peacock-blue silk fabrics and painted wooden furniture. There were shelves filled with books and knickknacks. On the bedside table was a framed photograph of a child—a miniature version of Ben—sitting in a wheelbarrow and wearing an impish grin.

So I was somewhere in the MacGregors' house. I couldn't remember anything after climbing into the Land Rover. My jeans were folded neatly on a chair with my sneakers tucked beneath. I hoped that I'd undressed myself, at least.

There were two doors in the room. One was ajar and led into a well-appointed guest bathroom stocked with new toothbrushes and other toiletries. As I spotted my purse on the dresser, it occurred to me that I hadn't taken any of the pills Dr. Nelson had given me for more than a twenty-four hours, but I felt fine. Maybe something about being in the program *was* working for me.

I ran my mind over the events of the night before. I still didn't know what Ben and Pete had been doing at Elana's apartment—or how they got there, or why. At least Elana was safe; that was the most important thing. That, and the fact that Don and those other guys were no doubt in jail.

I threw my hair into a braid, took a deep breath, and opened the bedroom door. Voices drifted up the staircase at the end of the hall. I followed them down into a large, open-plan kitchen and living room. The first person I saw was Ben. He was barefoot in jeans and a rugby shirt, leaning back against the kitchen counter and slathering cream cheese on a bagel.

The second my foot hit the bottom stair, he looked up and our eyes met. Both of us froze, and my heart thumped against my chest. I was reminded of the day we met, and that stunned moment when we'd seen each other for the first time.

Ben put down his bagel and straightened up. His features softened with affection. "Good morning, Cate."

"Hi," I said as a shy smile pulled at the corners of my mouth.

Dr. MacGregor turned away from the coffeemaker and looked me up and down. She was wearing a designer suit dress and holding a mug. "Good morning, Cate. Glad to see you're none the worse for wear." She gestured toward the coffeepot. "Any for you?"

"That would be great, thank you!" The smell of whatever she was brewing was intoxicating. "And thank you so much for letting me stay here last night. Your home is lovely."

"Thank you, dear." She poured both of our cups. "Did you find everything you needed?"

"Yes, it was much appreciated."

Dr. MacGregor placed my mug on the kitchen island, and Ben brought over cream and sweetener. "Thanks," I said, trying not to look at him directly for fear of blushing.

"You're welcome," he murmured, lingering for a few seconds longer than necessary before returning to his perch.

"So, Cate," Dr. Macgregor said cheerfully, "Benjamin tells me that he filled you in on our desire to have you come work for us—both the conventional reasons, and the strange ones."

I bit my lip and looked from Ben to Dr. MacGregor. They both appeared perfectly relaxed, so I guessed it was a safe topic for discussion. "Yes, he did."

"Hmm." Dr. MacGregor glanced sideways at Ben. "You know, my son thinks that the Bronze Age origins myth is nonsense—"

"Not nonsense," he said brusquely, "just irrelevant to our work."

Dr. MacGregor breezed past his objection. "And Benjamin didn't listen to his father when he was alive, so he's certainly not going to listen to him now that he's dead."

Ben scowled in silence.

"You have a scientific mind, Cate, so I'm sure that having heard all of this, you must think I'm an eccentric old lady." She smiled as though the title pleased her.

"No, of course not," I insisted, but the truth was I didn't know *what* to make of her. She was clearly a complex person. It would take time to figure her out.

"Well, regardless," she said, "we would like nothing more than for you to be a member of our team. I hope you'll take our offer under serious consideration, if only for the conventional reasons. As for the strange ones, what you've learned this week is just the tip of the proverbial iceberg. I hope that won't scare you off, though. As Shakespeare wrote in *Hamlet*: 'There are more things in heaven and earth, Horatio, than are dreamt of in your philosophy.' If all of my years in psychiatry and paranormal research have taught me nothing else, they've taught me the truth of that quote."

The MacGregors sure loved their quotes. So she wanted me to keep an open mind. Well, I was working on it. "I'm very grateful for your offer, and I promise to give it serious thought."

"Good." She put her coffee cup in the sink. "Unfortunately, I can't stay and chat. I have some patients this morning." She blew Ben a kiss. "Glad you're all right, Cate. I'll see you soon."

As she headed out the door, the rest of the MacGregor group arrived. They barreled into the kitchen, offering us boisterous greetings and foraging for bagels and coffee.

"Good morning, everybody," Ben said. "Get whatever you want to eat or drink, and let's get this meeting started."

He offered me a seat on the couch in the living room area.

Then he sat at the other end, about two feet away. It was though an energy field filled the space between us, buzzing with unresolved emotions. I felt the urge to move closer to him and further away at the same time. I kept avoiding Ben's eyes, unsure what would happen if I looked into them.

Vani settled into a rocking chair by the fireplace. Kai and Pete took the loveseat opposite the couch, and Eve and Asa sat at the kitchen table, forming a circle of sorts. As the room began to quiet down, Ben spoke. "So Cate, I'm sure you have a few questions for us."

"You could say that!" I shook my head as I looked around the room. "My question is: what the heck happened last night?"

"We saved your ass, that's what happened," Pete said, grinning. Kai smacked him on the arm.

Ben said, "Maybe we should let Vani start since it all began with her."

"That's true," Vani acknowledged, "but only because when I was working at my desk yesterday afternoon, I saw a bright yellow flash coming from Asa's cubicle, like a silent flare. I went over to check it out and the first thing I saw was that piece of paper on the floor, the one with Elana's name written on it. It was as though it had called me over."

I shuddered as I remembered that paper—and the outcome of my Distance Healing experiment.

"Elana's energy was all over it," Vani said. "As soon as I picked up the paper, I could see her aura. It was almost completely yellow—that means fear. And while I could feel your energy, I couldn't see your aura at all, which was highly unusual. It was almost as though her aura had swallowed yours. In any case, it was clear that you two were closely connected, and given how scared she was, I got pretty worried. I tried to call you, but you weren't picking up your phone."

I remembered with a pang of guilt that I'd turned off my phone after getting rid of Pete. I hadn't wanted Sid and me to be disturbed. In fact, it was probably still turned off. I wondered how many frantic messages from Vani and Ben I had to look forward to.

Vani nodded toward Eve. "That's when I called Ben and told him I thought something might be going on, and that I could use Eve's help figuring out if there was in fact anything to worry about. Fortunately, they were almost back from Rockville."

"I was so glad to have an excuse to practice, Cate!" Eve exclaimed. "The future only comes in flashes, but when I held onto the paper, I saw you with Elana, and I saw men with guns. I probably could have seen more, but Boss Man heard 'men with guns,' and that was the end of that."

"You did great, Eve," Ben said firmly. "You were pretty deep in trance, and we didn't want you to stay in there too long. But we couldn't have done it without you."

"Whatever," Eve said, but she was smiling proudly.

"By the time I picked Kai up from his studio and got back to the church," Pete said, "I could tell Ben here was about to go off all half-cocked, and judgin' from your mood earlier in the day, Cate, I knew that wasn't gonna go over too well. So I said we should ask Kai to check in with the Other Side and see if they had any advice for us." He beamed at Kai, who basked in the glow.

Kai said, "That's when your mother came through and told us that you were already on your way to Elana's apartment."

My eyes widened. Could it be that my mother really *was* watching over me? I pushed myself to focus on the conversation.

"So," Pete said, "we tagged Asa to come with us and tell us what was goin' on in these guys' heads so we could tackle them before anything serious went down."

Asa spoke in the rapid-fire manner of a sports commentator. "Okay! When we got there, the three guys were already standing at the door, so Pete and Ben were loading up their guns. But then the guys walked away, which bought us some time. So I hid behind the storage shed and focused in on them and the fourth guy once he got there. I got to wear one of those earpieces with the little microphone on the end of a wire, and I told Pete and Ben when those guys were coming and from where. Once that one guy broke the door down it was like, whammo! It was just like in the movies!

They totally nailed 'em! I had a bad headache afterwards, though. I had to give myself Reiki for like an hour."

"I got to stick needles in his head too," Eve added with enthusiasm.

"Oh my god, that's incredible." I started to pull all of the pieces together. "Was that you, Pete, who knocked Don on the head?"

"You know it." He winked. "Don't worry, though, no permanent damage done."

"And you did all of the talking."

Pete sucked in his cheeks and rubbed his chin. "Well, Big Ben and I had a little talk about that and decided my cowboy drawl might put your friend more at ease. Plus, Ben was more in a mood to deal with bad guys than to talk. We pretended we didn't know you cuz we figured the more distance we put between you and us and the fewer questions asked, the better."

"That was probably wise," I agreed. "By the way, which one of you figured out where Elana lived?"

Ben slowly raised his hand. "That was me."

I looked at him in shock. Had he been concealing some secret paranormal ability the whole time? "Really? How did you do that?"

Ben gazed at me affectionately, as though I had been put on earth specifically for his amusement. "There was only one Elana Bruter in the phone book."

"Oh right." I blushed as I recalled furtively logging onto the clinic's computer to get the same information myself. I cleared my throat. "So you guys do this kind of stuff a lot?"

"No, actually," Ben said. "Most of the time we do individual healings. We occasionally work as a group when a client has a particularly complex problem, but this was our first 'mission,' so to speak. Having to protect one of our own was pretty motivating."

One of their own? I looked around the room; all eyes were on me. I felt completely embraced by their warmth, their acceptance. Gratitude welled up inside of me.

"So, Cate," Ben asked softly, "do you have any other questions?"

"No, just…thank you. Thank you all. I don't know what else

to say. I'm just amazed by what you did." I stood up and went to each of them, embracing them and thanking them individually. They responded with various versions of "No problem, our pleasure, anytime."

I reached Kai last. He pulled me into a tight hug and murmured in my ear, "We all care about you, you know. Everyone here would love it if you joined us."

So everybody knew I was being recruited. "Thanks, Kai," I said with a smile, "that means a lot. And I *am* thinking about it."

"Good," he said and patted me on the arm. "Keep thinking. Just be sure you decide 'yes.'"

Ben stood and clapped his hands. "Okay, everybody, I'm sorry I have to kick you out, but we have to get ready for lunch. We're having a special guest—not that all of you aren't special."

"What special guest?" I asked Ben as the others started to gather their things.

"Oh, don't worry," he said lightly, as though he weren't about to drop a bomb on my head. "It's just Dr. Nelson."

• • •

Ben and his mother had invited Dr. Nelson to lunch, thinking that it would be good for us to talk everything over in a relaxed setting. Although I was initially resistant to the idea, it turned out to be a good call on the part of the MacGregors. I'd feared that Dr. Nelson would be angry with me for acting on my own to help Elana. But the first thing he did upon arriving was to apologize to me for the deception he and the MacGregors had wrought.

Ben eased the mood by telling his mother and Dr. Nelson about the successful work we had done on his eating issue. After we all promised not to die during or immediately following lunch, Ben managed to eat with us, instead of just sitting idly through the meal like he usually did. I sensed that he had pushed through his fears just because he knew I needed a boost. I became aware that in the face of Ben's heroic acts, both large and small, the anger

I'd felt toward him after our huge argument the day before was steadily receding.

As it turned out, Ben had told me the truth. Dr. Nelson's decision to terminate my employment had nothing to do with my failures as a clinician. Instead, it had everything to do with his desire to protect me from the deterioration he had seen other empaths suffer. He made it clear that his decision that I should resign was final, and that although he sympathized with my reluctance, nothing I could say would change his mind.

I felt a heavy ache in my chest when I thought about leaving my clients. I had no idea how I would find the courage to say all of those goodbyes. Ben and Dr. MacGregor reassured me that they would help me cope with whatever emotions came up, and Dr. Nelson promised that he and Simone would fully support all of us in making the transition as smooth and positive as possible.

As I suspected, Dr. Nelson was none too pleased with my multiple violations of clinic policy the day before. But he seemed to feel so badly about lying to me and making me leave his clinic that as a goodwill gesture, he decided to overlook everything I'd done. By the end of the afternoon, the mood was warm again, and a small seed of optimism for the future was sprouting inside of me.

The MacGregors left me to accompany Dr. Nelson to the front door. As we reached the threshold, he embraced me.

"Cate," he said, "your departure will represent a great loss for our clinic and for your clients. But it will represent a great gain for the work the MacGregors are doing and for all of your future clients there. They've been looking for an empath for a long time, one who would be a perfect fit for their needs, and it appears that they've finally found her. Believe me, joining the MacGregors is the best thing you can do for yourself and for your future."

"That's nice to hear, Dr. Nelson, but the truth is that I haven't decided whether to join their group. I haven't had a spare moment to think about it yet."

His voice grew gentle. "I don't have a daughter, Cate, but if I did, do you know what I would tell her?"

"What?" I asked, touched by the implication.

"I'd tell her to listen to her father. Oh and by the way, I think that MacGregor boy has his eye on you." With a mischievous wink, he turned and walked away.

CHAPTER TWENTY-SEVEN

Dr. MacGregor offered to make dinner, but the strain of the previous twenty-four hours was starting to wear on me. All I wanted was to be back in the comfort zone of my own home. Someone had retrieved Calamity Jane and parked her at the MacGregors'. Ben followed me home in the Land Rover, "in case that rattletrap of yours finally breaks down." But I knew he was really thinking the same thing I was—we had some things to discuss, and we needed to do it in private.

It wasn't long before we were both settled on either end of my couch with fresh cups of coffee. There was an awkward silence. I didn't know where to begin, and I suspected that Ben didn't either. Finally, I ventured, "So you're really good at fixing things up, aren't you?"

Ben looked wary. "You don't mean classic cars."

"No." I shook my head slowly. "What I *mean* is that I was so mad when I left the church yesterday that I never wanted to see you again. But since then," I said as I began counting on my fingers, "you rescued Elana and me. Then your mother took responsibility for the weird stuff around my recruitment. And Dr. Nelson pretty much took the rap for the whole lying and conspiracy thing, leaving you almost completely off the hook." I wiggled my three fingers. "Did you orchestrate all of that?"

Ben appeared to be weighing possible responses, but ultimately said nothing. Instead he took a sip of his coffee.

I tossed my hands up. "No answer? Nothing?"

"You said I was *almost* off the hook," Ben said carefully. "I'm trying not to say anything that might slide me back on."

I managed to keep from smiling, but barely. “So you just plan to just dangle there indefinitely?”

He appeared to be considering the question as he stretched his arm out along the back of the couch. “Only until you tell me what I’m still on the hook for so I can take care of it.”

“Making me spell it out for you will not improve your situation,” I said, chagrined.

“Well, I don’t want to put words in your mouth.” Ben put his mug down on the table. “But if I had to guess, I’d say it has something to do with the handcuffs thing.”

I glowered at him. “Good guess. That, and the threat of involuntary commitment.”

“Right, involuntary commitment,” he said with a nod.

“*Any* threats to my liberty are completely and utterly unacceptable, actually,” I added, just to make sure the point was well and truly made.

“Got it.” Ben rubbed his jaw. “Well in that case, I believe have a solution.”

As though there were more than one. I gave him a warning stare. “Really.”

He held one hand out, palm up. “I promise not to bring up handcuffs or hospitals,” he said, then held out the other hand, “as long as you promise not to hurt yourself.” He then pressed his hands together. “That serves both of our needs, don’t you think?”

“Oh for God’s sake!” I covered my face with my hands. When was he going to get that it was *not okay* for him to threaten me handcuffs, hospitals, or anything else for that matter—ever, under any circumstances? Who did he think he was? But as I dropped my hands and prepared to tell him exactly what I thought of his “solution,” the look on his face stunned me into silence. His eyes were raw with pain, his expression grief-stricken.

“Cate, if anything ever happened to you…”

The agony in his voice blew my anger out like a candle. For him, the agreement he’d proposed was deadly serious. “Ben,” I reminded him quietly, “I told you yesterday that I would never…you know.”

He closed his eyes and rubbed the deepening lines in his forehead. "Yes, I know. And I knew you'd be true to your word, even though you spoke in anger. Of all of your outstanding qualities, I trust your stubbornness the most." He looked up at me and tried to smile. "But now I'm asking for something more robust—something permanent, not said in the heat of the moment. Please indulge me in this, Cate. Please promise me."

I looked down at my fingers as they twisted around each other in my lap. I knew how Ben felt about me. I couldn't imagine what it must have been like for him to read my suicide note. If our roles had been reversed...well, I couldn't be sure *what* I would have said or done.

Was what he was asking really that unreasonable? Yes, I would have preferred an abject apology without any conditions. But all he wanted was for me to promise not to hurt myself—and that was a promise I finally felt confident making. The crisis with Elana the night before, the dramatic rescue, everything that had transpired since... Somewhere in there, my tenacious infatuation with suicide had evaporated. Maybe helping Elana had given me faith that my life was still worthwhile. Maybe it was finally sinking in that I could use my gifts without destroying myself. Or maybe it was the fact that I felt a new sort of family forming around me. All I knew was that thoughts of suicide suddenly seemed like the twisted artifacts of a distant mindset. Those thoughts were fading from view, as though I'd tossed them out the car window onto the highway and kept on driving.

I wanted to share that with Ben, but I had seen the fear and agony in his eyes every time he thought about something bad happening to me. I wanted to do something to comfort him, to give him a more solid reassurance than mere words. "Hang on," I said as I stood and went upstairs. I reached into the back of my closet and retrieved the envelope that held the remaining suicide notes. I hesitated for a moment, wondering if I should give him the pill bottles as well, but then I thought better of it. After all, my goal was to make him worry less, not more. I would throw the pills out myself.

Ben was waiting for me at the bottom of the stairs. I handed him the envelope. "Will you please get rid of these for me?" I held his gaze, trying to press home the meaning of my words. "I won't be needing them anymore. I *promise*."

Upon hearing that final word, the tension in Ben's shoulders relaxed a bit. He opened the envelope just enough to see the familiar marbled blue stationery. Then he froze for a moment, and I wondered if I'd made a mistake. There were a *lot* of notes in there. I had never revealed something quite so dark about myself to another human being. Hope mixed with trepidation as I wondered what the consequences would be.

Ben carefully folded the envelope closed as if it contained some state secret. "I'll take care of it." He walked over to his overnight bag on the floor near the front door and zipped the envelope inside. Then he came back and gently took my hand. When we returned to the sofa, he sat close to me so he wouldn't have to let go. In a voice filled with gratitude and intense relief, he said, "Thank you."

Swallowing the tears that threatened to rise, I managed to whisper, "You're welcome."

We sat there for a while in a peaceful silence, taking in the sensation that something was deepening between us. After some time, Ben looked down and cleared his throat. He took hold of my other hand as well. "There's one more promise I'd like you to make."

Something *else*? "What is it?"

"Please tell me that you won't put yourself in harm's way again like you did last night."

Slowly, I pulled my hands away from his. Promising not to hurt myself was one thing, but *that*…I started out speaking softly. "I'm sorry, Ben, I can't promise that. And it's not your place to ask me to. If someone I care about is in danger, I'll do whatever it takes to help them. And if that means putting myself in harm's way, then that's what I'll do," I said, my voice gaining volume. "And I know you'd do the same. Don't even try to tell me otherwise!"

Ben's eyebrows rose as I spoke. When I finished, he sat quietly for a few moments, hands flexed on his knees, considering. "You know," he said finally, "one of the things that impresses me the most about you is the amount of heart you have for the people you love. I haven't seen that level of courage very often outside of the Corps."

Another blush feathered across my cheeks. "Thank you," I said, waiting for the other shoe to drop.

"And you're right," he said. "Maybe it's not my place to ask you to change that about yourself. But I think I might have a solution to this problem, as well."

Cautiously intrigued, I folded my arms. "I really can't imagine what that might be."

"Well, no, you wouldn't. It has to do with my mother."

I scooted closer to be sure I'd heard him properly. "Did you just say your *mother*?"

He nodded. "I talked to her about us, and she said that in her professional opinion, given our unique personality traits, the unconventional nature of our program, and our probable future together as colleagues, she believes a relationship between us wouldn't breach any ethical boundaries—provided that you initiate things, of course."

Dr. MacGregor had said that? "She *did*?"

"Mm-hmm." He spread his hands out with a flourish, as though revealing a hand of cards. "So, problem solved."

He looked so satisfied with himself that I figured I must have missed something. "Problem solved *how*?"

Ben reached out and took my hands in his again. This time, he stroked my palms lightly with his thumbs to hypnotic effect. "If we're dating, hopefully you'll feel comfortable asking for my help if someone you care about is in danger. Then I'll handle the situation and you won't have to put yourself in harm's way. No more problem. What do you say?"

As he spoke, Ben's touch kindled its usual process in my body. Tendrils of warmth wended their way from my hands up my arms, then slowly spread from head to toe. I wasn't sure if *that* was causing my confusion, or if he was just being cryptic. "Wait, what do I say to what? Promising not to put myself in harm's way, or dating you?"

Ben tilted his head slightly, as though the answer should be obvious. "Both. Like I said, they go together nicely."

I was so disoriented by the twists and turns our conversation had taken—especially the involvement of his *mother*—that I had no idea where to go from there. I decided to tap into the portal; at least then I'd know where Ben was coming from. I willed the door to open, and all at once, his emotions crashed into me like a waterfall. Ben's determination to keep me safe was eclipsed only by the sheer force of his caring and passion for me. I inhaled sharply, flooded by his feelings.

As our eyes locked, a latch inside of me that I kept tightly fastened suddenly came undone. An exquisite need pulled my heart painfully toward his. Trembling, I tugged one of my hands out of his grasp and laid it against his cheek. "You mean it, don't you?" I whispered, stunned. "You really want to be with me."

"More than I've ever wanted anything," he murmured, the truth of his words surging through the portal. "All I need to know is, do you want the same thing?"

So this was the moment of truth. Ben wanted an answer. My mind froze. Anxious thoughts churned. *Did* I want the same thing? Was it possible that we were moving too fast, too soon? If I started something with Ben, how could I be sure I wouldn't screw it up like I had with everyone else I'd ever dated?

At the same time, though, a calm certainty emerged from deep within me: *Yes, this is right. This is what you want. Ben is where you belong.* As that quiet knowing filled my heart, it seemed as though we'd been dropped underwater. Everything in the room disappeared, leaving only Ben and me.

The heat Ben's touch had ignited in my body kept building until my attraction transformed into craving. He inhaled sharply as my eyes fell on his lips. I slid as close to him as I could and tilted my head up. Pushed forward by a tide of longing, I placed one soft kiss on his lower lip and another on his upper one. Ben's mouth opened slightly as his breathing grew fast and hard. Then I shifted to the side, my lips nearly touching his earlobe. "In case you were wondering," I whispered, "that was me initiating."

Ben turned his head and in an instant, his mouth was on mine—softly inquisitive at first, then frankly passionate. My body began to respond of its own accord. I pressed myself against him, my arm sliding around his waist. He wrapped his arms around me and pulled me even closer. As though in answer to a question his lips were asking, I felt my own lips part.

As his tongue pushed gently inward, though, a bolt of panic shot through me. This was the point at which every previous kiss with anyone other than Sid had turned into a disaster, ending with me stammering excuses and running from the room. I turned my head to the side and broke the kiss.

Still holding me close, Ben asked, "What is it? Are you okay?"

The blood in my face pounded. "I'm just scared, you know, that I might have trouble tolerating..." Too humiliated to say more, I shrugged.

"Cate, I'm sorry." His arms tightened around me. "Of course you're scared. I should have thought of that before. But you have nothing to worry about. As long as you're wearing your pendant, you won't absorb my emotions or anyone else's. You're protected."

"Oh, of course. That's right." How could I have forgotten? I reached up and touched the pendant. Could it really be that simple? But the fearful part of me—the part that remembered past failures and didn't want a repeat with Ben—couldn't quite believe it. My pulse skipped and stumbled.

Ben brought his hand up to my chin as his eyes searched mine. "I'll tell you what. You've been through a lot this week. We have plenty of time to explore the limits of your pendant," he said, the gold flecks in his iris flickering. He glanced around the room and nodded toward Sid's racy card deck. "Maybe this would be a good time to play a few hands."

I swallowed hard. My whole body protested the end of the kiss and clamored to have his lips on mine again. But as he spoke, I could feel my heartbeat growing steadier and the flush of panic ebbing away. Maybe he was right; there was no need to rush things. I slid my arms around him and squeezed, burying my face in his chest. "Thank you," I whispered.

Ben wrapped his arms around me. "Anything for you, Cate." He stroked my hair, kissed the top of my head, and murmured, "Anything but let you win at cards, that is."

Chapter Twenty-Eight

Hell Week, Day Seven: Graduation Day

The next morning, we reached the church before the others. Ben said he had some things he wanted to discuss with me before everyone else arrived. He had spent the night on my couch—"just in case you need me," he'd said. Ben had also awakened before me and made us both coffee and scrambled eggs. Then we stopped by his mother's house so he could get a change of clothes.

Ben opted for his usual business attire, while I wore jeans and a peasant blouse. Although our uniforms hadn't changed, given the shift in our relationship, it felt a little strange to be back in his office again, sitting on opposite sides of his desk.

Thankfully Ben took the lead. "So, you survived Hell Week. As of today, you've officially graduated to the internship portion of your training. Congratulations."

He made it sound so formal that I couldn't help smiling. "Thank you."

"Before we talk about whether you've decided to join us for good, though..." His voice became soft and intimate. "There's... something I want to ask you."

I'd never seen Ben look so unsure of himself. I figured that could only mean one thing. *Goddamned Pete,* I thought. "Pete told you, didn't he?"

Ben appeared puzzled at first, but then said, "Everything that has to do with you, yes."

I knew it! I thought with an exasperated sigh. "Well, it's not actually any of your business."

Ben raised an inquisitive eyebrow. "It isn't?"

"No," I said, "but if it helps you to know this, I'll satisfy your curiosity: I did *not* sleep with Sid the other day, okay?"

Ben leaned back in his chair and clasped his hands behind his neck. "You didn't?"

Suddenly feeling restless, I stood up and walked over to the window, looking up at the white autumn sky. "After Pete left, we just talked. And we decided not to see each other anymore—not like *that*, anyway. From now on, we're just going to be friends."

"I see." Ben walked over, stood behind me, and wrapped his arms around my waist. "I'll admit that it's nice to hear the competition has officially dropped out."

I was reminded once again of how easy it was for Ben to flip my switch to the "on" position. It was a bit exasperating—especially when I was trying to do something. Like think. Or speak. With no small effort, I pulled myself out of his embrace and returned to my chair. "Are you satisfied now?"

Ben went back and sat behind the desk. "While I appreciate your openness, the truth is, I already knew that nothing happened with Sid."

I gaped at him. "What do you mean you knew? Did Pete secretly stick around with binoculars or something?"

"Oh no, he wouldn't have dared—not after what you did with that umbrella," Ben said, visibly amused. "Although he did keep driving a two-block radius around your house until he saw the living room light go out and the bedroom light go on. Then he assumed Sid was spending the night."

"Argh!" A hot flush exploded across my face. "I *knew* it! Pete and his lies." I pointed an accusing finger at Ben. "And *you*!"

Ben held his hands up as though my finger were a gun. "Okay, yes, I told him to keep an eye on you—*from a distance*—but as you recall, I had legitimate reasons to be worried. After you chased him off, though, Pete decided to stick around all on his own. He couldn't reach me to discuss it, remember? I was in the hospital. My phone was turned off."

"And if he *had* been able to call you, what would you have told him to do?"

A deep indentation formed between Ben's eyebrows. "We'll never know, will we?"

"Very funny." I rolled my eyes—still seething, but slightly less.

Ben slowly lowered his hands. "If it helps, Pete was really kicking himself when he found out later that Sid had left and you'd gone to Elana's."

Imagining Pete's face when he realized I'd given him the slip did help a little. "That still doesn't explain how you knew nothing happened with Sid."

"I knew because I know you. You have a loyal, honest heart. Now that you understand how catalysts work, I figured you'd be too worried that you might be using Sid, even unintentionally." He held his hands up again. "Not that it would have been any of my business if you had."

I squeezed my eyes shut. "So Sid wasn't what you were going to ask me about."

"No, but you clearly wanted to get something off of your chest. I didn't want to interrupt." Ben leaned forward and folded his hands on the desk. "Anyway, to go back to what I was saying..."

Out of sheer annoyance, I decided to steal his thunder. "You want to know if I'll join your group. Yes, I'll join your group. Okay?"

I'd been thinking that one over. Even though Ben could be obstinate as hell, Dr. Nelson had been right. As much as I hated to admit it, I'd come to realize that my old job had been getting the better of me. And as painful as it was going to be to leave my clients, the MacGregor Group might be a better place for me long-term. While I would've much preferred to have a choice in the matter, the truth was that the church was already starting to feel like home. I figured it was worth a try at least. "*Now* are you satisfied?"

"That makes me very happy, yes." He came over and sat in the chair next to mine. Then he took my right hand and held it between his. "I couldn't be happier, in fact. Welcome."

The combination of his touch and the sincerity in his eyes warmed me. "Thank you," I said tentatively as the magnitude of what I'd just agreed to struck me.

"And that *was* one of the questions I had for you, so I'm glad we got that settled." He slid one of his hands out from under mine and reached into his pocket. "But there is one more thing."

He lifted my right hand. Something hard and cool slid onto my ring finger. I looked down. There sat a stunning gold ring set with a flat, round stone. The band consisted of two delicately carved birds, curving around each other and holding the stone in place with their beaks and the tips of their wings. The stone itself was highly polished and looked as though it had been colored with luminous brushstrokes of orange, red, and gold.

I whispered, "What is it?"

"Scottish agate. Do you like it?"

"It's the most beautiful thing I've ever seen." I felt the blood pounding in every part of my body. "But I mean…why are you giving it to me?"

Ben lifted my hand and placed a kiss on my finger just above the ring. I shivered. "I know that you're prone to anxieties and doubts," he said softly. "I want you to have something solid to remind you of me when I can't be with you, to remind you how I feel about you."

"Oh." I'd never told him how alone I felt, and how often. His sentiment touched me deeply. "So it's a gift."

"Yes." His eyes shone. "Will you wear it?"

I looked down at the ring. Exquisite and unusual, it appeared to be handcrafted, as though it might be one of a kind. I figured it must be worth a lot of money. And we'd only been dating for one day… It felt like a wild bird was trying to beat its way out of my ribcage. "I don't know, Ben. I mean, it's quite a gift." I bit my lip. "What will other people think?"

"Come over here." Ben helped me up and pulled me onto his lap. He drew me close and stretched my arm out, holding up my hand so that both of us could admire the ring. I felt the vibrations in his chest against my body as he murmured in my ear, "This is a gift from me to you. No one else has to know about this if you don't want them to. The goal is to make you feel less anxious, not more. It can be our secret if you like."

"Oh." The wild bird was somewhat soothed.

Ben ran his finger along my jaw line. "I know we just started dating yesterday, but there has always been something between us—or was I the only one who felt it?"

That day in the parking lot, in the rain, when he scared the living daylights out of me. "No, you weren't the only one. I felt it, too. I just didn't think that *you* did."

"Well, I tried not to," he quipped, "but we both see how that worked out."

A smile played on my lips. I dropped my hands into my lap as I leaned back against him, letting my head fall onto his shoulder.

Ben tilted my head, swept the tail of my braid aside, and placed a kiss just beneath my earlobe. I barely suppressed a moan as my fingers twisted around the hem of my blouse. "Also," he said, "since it's been such an intense week, we've gotten to know each other pretty well in a short period of time. And there's another thing."

Ben kissed my neck again, a little bit lower. I sucked in a sharp breath. "What?"

"You're very easy to fall for." With his hand on my cheek, he turned my face toward his. His eyes were dark with desire. "May I?"

I froze in place, bracing myself for the coming panic attack. Ben had said he was falling for me. That sounded serious, and whenever past relationships had approached "serious," I had promptly freaked out. I sat in trepidation, waiting for the heart palpitations, the shallow breathing, the sweaty palms, and worst of all, the feeling of dread.

But by some miracle, none of those things came. Instead, in that moment with Ben, I fell into a great calm. I felt comforted and warmed, like I was sitting by a campfire on a cold night. Ben's words called to my heart, and instead of responding with terror, it opened up like a fist uncurling, as though it had been waiting twenty-six years just to hear his voice. Somewhere in the core of me, a strong emotion swelled, filling my chest to the point of bursting.

And on top of that, Ben wanted to kiss me. My body began to tremble. I was halfway through a whispered "yes" when Ben's mouth found mine. In an instant, we were right back where we'd been when I'd stopped him the night before.

A powerful rush of attraction started in my belly and spread throughout my body as my mouth worked urgently to drink him in. His mouth responded with the hunger of the reunited. I reached up and tangled my fingers in his hair, and I felt his hands sliding into my braid.

The longer we kissed, the more Ben's energy encircled me—warm, golden, and electric. But as he'd promised, the pendant was working. Although his energy was all around me, I wasn't absorbing it. And I was feeling no emotions but my own—which was a relief, because mine were powerful enough.

As though he'd read my mind, Ben pulled away. My lips keened silently as he whispered, "How's your pendant holding up?"

"Fine," I whispered. I tried to pull him toward me, but he resisted.

"Of course, you can't wear the pendant every minute of every day," he whispered low. "Eventually we'll have to find a more permanent solution. But I'm glad to hear that it's working for now."

A more permanent solution? That made it sound very much like he intended to kiss me again, at some future point in time—and again, and again…

Before I knew it, Ben's mouth was again covering mine, his insistent tongue finding its way inside. We lost ourselves completely, no thought of anything but devouring each another and becoming one, body and soul. My muscles went weak and my breathing became fast and ragged. All of the places inside of me that had been empty were being filled by him.

I was overwhelmed by emotions I still couldn't identify, let alone express. But the weight of the ring on my hand gave me courage. I poured everything I was feeling into our kiss, like Prometheus releasing fire into the world. The volcanic heat between us kept building until I was certain that I would burn up from the inside out—and in that moment, there was nothing I wanted more.

Eventually, we both seemed to sense that we were approaching a tipping point—if we didn't put the flames out soon, they would consume us completely. Although a whimper of protest escaped my swollen lips, I drew my arms up between us, resting my hands on his chest. With his fingers still twisted in my hair, Ben gently tilted my head back and pulled his mouth away from mine. We sat there for several moments, perfectly still, eyes closed, gasping. Slowly, so slowly, the lava that had filled my body began to cool, and Ben's breathing evened out.

I opened my eyes first. It gave me a surge of satisfaction to see the heavy effort Ben was making to pull himself together. At least we'd both experienced the same intensity. When Ben's eyes finally opened, he looked at me with the same wonder I was feeling. We just sat there, staring, giving ourselves time to absorb, to witness, to recover.

Finally, I couldn't hold myself upright any longer. The adrenaline rush had gone, leaving my muscles quivering and useless. I leaned against Ben and rested my head on his shoulder as he drew his arms around me. I held up my hand, once again admiring the ring.

"So this can be our secret," I whispered. The prospect touched me deeply. Ben had no ulterior motive in giving me the ring. He just wanted me to feel reassured by his constant presence. For some reason, keeping something so intimate a private matter between us struck me as incredibly sexy.

"If that's what makes you feel comfortable." He softly kissed the top of my head. "You'll wear it, then?"

A calm like I'd never experienced came over me, and I knew with a certainty that this was what I wanted—*Ben* was what I wanted. My heart swept in and took over; my head and all of its bothersome anxieties would just have to catch up later. "Yes, I will. Thank you."

As my words sank in, a parade of emotions marched across Ben's face. Finally he smiled back, and with impossible tenderness said, "I'm glad."

For many moments, we sat like that, locked in each other's eyes. I swam with abandon through the portal, learning everything I needed to know: that he cared deeply for me, he wanted to be with me, and no matter how often I gave up on myself, Ben would never give up on me. For the first time, I understood what it meant to never want a moment to end.

• • •

When the others arrived at the church, they were carrying balloons and a cake that read, "Welcome to Team MacGregor, Cate!" Apparently, I had been the last one to know that I would be joining their group.

Vani and Kai quickly noticed my ring and were duly admiring. But when I deflected their questions with vague answers, they didn't push, only exchanged knowing looks. True to his word, Ben did an impressive job of pretending that he had no idea what we were talking about.

After cutting the cake, we moved on to a lively discussion about whether I should be put through some kind of welcoming ritual to mark my joining the staff. Eve suggested that we all get matching tattoos or piercings of some kind, but Ben quickly shot down that idea. Asa suggested an inaugural online multiplayer game tournament. Kai wrinkled his nose and proposed instead that Ben, Asa, and Pete could set aside a day to play the latest release of *Apocalypse Slaughter Death House* while Kai, Vani, Eve, and I took a spa day.

I had to admit that I liked that idea, but Eve said she'd rather play *Death House* than go to a spa. Then Vani insisted that there were no decent spas stateside, anyway, so the only way for us to celebrate properly would be to go to London. When the conversation turned to how we could arrange a stopover in Iceland to enjoy the hot springs, Ben objected that we were getting carried away and reminded everyone that they had a busy week ahead.

His pragmatism did nothing to dampen the jovial mood,

however. As the party carried on, I looked around at the incredible group of people embracing me—my new friends and colleagues—and finally felt reassured that by joining their group, I'd made the right decision.

After the festivities at the church wound down, Ben and I returned to my house. He collapsed onto the couch and I settled down in front of him. I held my right hand out and stared at my ring. Although I'd been stealing glances at it ever since Ben put it on my finger, that was the first opportunity I'd had to really examine it closely. It was beautifully crafted, and the way the birds intertwined was so romantic. I knew that when I told Simone about Ben and me, she was going to freak out. I smiled as I imagined her reaction not only to the ring, but also to the fact that I was finally dating someone.

Ben brushed the hair away from my temple and kissed it tenderly, lighting a flicker of attraction in my belly. I was reminded of his promise that we would soon be "testing the limits of my pendant," as he'd so creatively described it. As we lay there spooning, two weeks suddenly seemed like an interminably long period of time.

"Ben?"

"Hmm?"

I rolled over just enough so that I could look at him. His eyes were closed. "The no sex during training thing—that doesn't really apply anymore, does it?"

"Those are the rules, Cate."

"I know," I said softly, "but things have changed between us. I mean, I'm wearing your ring..."

"And I couldn't be happier about that. But you're still an intern."

I gritted my teeth. No one could have *that* much self-discipline. I closed my eyes and focused on the portal between us, searching for a weak spot. I had to know what was going on underneath that cool exterior of his.

To my delight, I felt clearly the strong note of his desire—and then, to my annoyance, the even stronger note of his conviction. Obviously, feminine wiles were going to be required.

I shifted back into our spooning position. "Still, you know I'm not big on rules, right?"

"I'm not a huge fan of this one myself at the moment," Ben said, "but it's important, Cate. You know it's there for a reason." He slid his arm around my waist and pulled me closer to him. "Don't worry, though. Once these two weeks are up, I'll see to it personally that you're well taken care of."

He placed a kiss on the back of my head and my whole body sighed with pleasure. But I was determined not to be diverted. I slowly pulled myself into a sitting position on the edge of the couch and stretched provocatively. Ben's hand fell onto the small of my back. "I see. Well, if that's how things are," I said with a casual glance back, "I think I'll go give Sid a call and see what he's up to."

I yelped in surprise as Ben swiftly hauled me backward onto the couch and maneuvered me into our spooning position once again—but this time, his arms and legs were locked around me. I tried to wriggle free, only to find that I had been totally immobilized.

"If you think *that's* going to happen," he growled playfully into my ear, "then you're about to find out what it's like to match wills with a big tough Marine."

If you or someone you know needs help, you may find information and resources, including links to immediate help, on the following website from the U.S. Department of Health and Human Services:
www.mentalhealth.gov

The National Suicide Prevention Lifeline has trained crisis workers available to talk 24 hours a day, 7 days a week:
1-800-273-TALK (8255)
www.suicidepreventionlifeline.org

If you are outside of the U.S., a database of international resources can be found on the website of the International Association for Suicide Prevention:
www.iasp.info

Connect with Anise Eden at her website:
www.AniseEden.com

Thank you for reading *All the Broken Places*. Our sincere thanks to all of the bloggers and reviewers who take the time to get the word out about books they love!

Look for *All the Wounds in Shadow*,
coming August 2016 from Diversion Books!